# WATCH ME

## Dangerously Intertwined, #2

K. Knight
xo

# WATCH ME

## ME

**Dangerously Intertwined, #2**

Kimberly Knight

# COPYRIGHT

# NOTE FROM THE AUTHOR

Dear Reader,

If you read the short story version that was featured in the *Cop Tales Anthology for a Cause* or the one given to new newsletter subscribers, please know that I had to change a few things to make this a full-length novel.

Please also keep in mind that I am not a cop. My background is in law, but working for attorneys and not law enforcement. I was a paralegal before I began my writing career, but I'm also a true crime addict. I've tried my best, done my research, and asked wives of police officers for help, but there's a chance we got something wrong. Each city, state, and district seems to do something slightly different from the others. But remember this is *fiction* and from the voices in my head.

Hope you enjoy *Watch Me*.

Happy reading!

XOXO,
*Kimberly*

# CHAPTER ONE

I never thought I would be forty-two and divorced with two kids. But I was.

My father was a retired Chicago police chief, and one day, I hoped to follow in his footsteps and become chief before I retire. I was quickly working my way up in the ranks, and in the last two years, I had gone from detective to sergeant. One of the reasons for my promotion was my involvement in a situation that involved my sister.

Three years ago, I'd walked into her condo and found her drugged unconscious by a stalker trying to kidnap her. The fucker had a gun pointed at her boyfriend—who was trying to stop him—and before the perp could fire, I did. I shot the asshole square in the forehead and killed him.

It was the job.

It was in my blood to protect.

It was *my sister.*

Needing a place to live, I moved into the condo where I'd killed him. To some, it might be creepy, but it made me smile every time I walked over the spot where he died because it was a reminder that I had saved my sister and my future brother-in-law's lives.

And I'd do it again.

Since my divorce a year ago, I worked as much as possible unless it was my night or weekend with my sons. Those times were for them and only them. The case I'd been working on was closed, and I had no kids waiting for me. In fact, I had no one waiting for me. So, I did what my sister and her husband used to do when they were single.

I walked down the street to Judy's, the neighborhood bar.

# CHAPTER TWO

*Reagan*

*S**tart living your life fearlessly. This is the beginning of anything you want.*

Two months ago, I'd read those words on a sticky note next to my laptop over and over before hitting the submit button on my school application. Class started last week, and it would take me ten short weeks to get my crime scene investigation certification.

I'd always been interested in solving crimes. When I went off to college after high school, I obtained my bachelor's degree in criminal justice. I never worked in the field because I got married right after college, and then about a year later, I had my daughter. But, when I hit the submit button, it felt good to make a decision to do what I wanted to do after so many years of putting others before me.

Two years after the divorce, I was still living in Denver and my daughter was starting her freshman year at the University of Michigan. Since I was born and raised in the Windy City, and Chicago was a lot closer to her school than Denver, I made the move back a few months ago. That way I could help her if she needed it but still be far enough away that she was on her own doing her thing, which meant I needed to do my own thing, too.

For the last twenty or so years, I worked as a wife and mother, but had a come-to-Jesus moment after a bottle of wine by myself and decided to take back my life, find out who I was at age forty-one, and get certified in a field I'd always had an interest in. I needed excitement in my life, and what better way than to help put criminals behind bars? Even though the certification was the bare minimum in the CSI field, I was okay with that. It was like dipping my toe in the pool to test the waters. If, after getting a job in the field, I loved it, then I would look into becoming an analyst or senior analyst. Plus, since I'd never actually worked in criminal justice since I earned my degree, I needed a refresher on current techniques and procedures.

With the wine still coursing through my veins, I'd had another *a-ha* moment. I'd tended bar when I was in college and knew it was a great way to make extra money, so I decided to become a bartender again while pursuing my CSI certification. I needed to make a little bit of an income while in school despite getting spousal support from my ex. By taking a forty-hour online course, I freshened up my bartending skills and found a job at the local bar.

Because of my school schedule, I worked the mid-shift at Judy's Thursday through Sunday from four to midnight. It was good hours, and I would still be able to get my classwork done during the week.

"Hey, Tommy," I greeted as I stepped behind the bar. "Busy afternoon?"

"No more than usual. After work crowd should be here soon." He filled a pint glass with beer as he spoke.

"Perfect," I replied and grabbed a towel to wipe the bartop.

"Oh, and a new barback should be here soon too," Tommy advised.

"Okay. Sounds good."

A few minutes later, Judy came from the back with a guy in tow. "Tommy, Reagan, this is Derrick, your new barback." We all shook hands, and then Judy left to work in her office while Derrick shadowed Levi, the other barback.

People started to trickle in, and the bar was humming with laughter and conversations. I tried to keep up with all the orders, and I was proud of myself for doing so well after only a week. It felt good to be back behind the bar—despite my aching feet—and I knew I'd made the right decision to do something for me even if it was working behind a bar. It was fun.

Throughout the next few hours, Tommy would ask if I needed help, but I didn't. I was in the zone. Whiskey sours, margaritas, Negronis—they weren't a challenge for me. At seven, our closing bartender, Frank, and his barback arrived.

The crowd was steady, and the drinks were flowing. The atmosphere of Judy's was amazing because this was just what I'd wanted when I came back to bartending—working with people again, feeling useful and making money. What I hadn't expected was being hit on by patrons. It used to happen when I tended bar in college, but I'd assumed it wouldn't happen to me this time since I was over forty.

I was wrong.

"What's your name, sweetheart?" a guy with slicked-back gray hair and a mustache asked. He was dressed in a suit, which gave me the impression he'd come straight from work.

I leaned on the bar, already knowing where this was going, and decided to play into it because I knew I could get more tips if I flirted. "Reagan."

"That's a pretty name for a pretty girl."

I chuckled. "I'm not a girl."

His gray eyes moved to my breasts, and I instantly felt as though he could see them through my black T-shirt. "No, you're not. I bet you could teach me a few things."

I stood quickly so he could no longer look down my shirt. Before I could respond, Derrick poured ice into the ice bin next to me. I jumped slightly at the noise. His brown eyes flicked up at me, and he smiled. "Did I scare you?"

I held my hand over my chest. "Just a little."

"Sorry about that," he replied.

"No worries." I was actually grateful for the commotion. It had been years since a man had flirted with me, and I wasn't sure how to go about it, even if it was harmless.

I turned back to the gray-haired man. "Can I get you another whiskey sour?"

"You can get me your phone number," he countered.

My gaze flicked to Derrick, who was still standing next to me. He looked at me, silently asking if I needed him to step in, but I smiled warmly to let him know I was okay. We were in a packed bar, and this guy was only flirting.

My attention moved back to the customer. "Sorry, but that's not going to happen."

"Why's that? Do you have a boyfriend?"

I noticed that Derrick was pretending to wash glasses in the sink under the bar—glasses I'd already washed. "Doesn't matter if I do or not. I'm here to make you drinks, so if you'd like another one, let me know."

I turned and walked to a new customer, not letting the guy respond. By the time I went on my dinner break, the guy had left, settling his tab with Frank.

"How's your first night going?" I asked Derrick. He had walked into the break room just as I was clocking back in.

He sat down at the small, round wooden table and opened his sack lunch, taking out a sandwich. "Good."

"Is this your first job in a bar?"

He took a bite of what looked like a PB & J. "Yeah."

"It's exhausting, but you meet interesting people."

He nodded and bit into his sandwich again. "Yeah, my friends are going to want to come in for free drinks."

I chuckled. "Lucky for Judy, you aren't a bartender then."

He took another bite of his sandwich. "True, but we'll make good tips once I tell my friends from school how hot the bartender is."

I snorted and ignored the part about my looks. "You're in school?"

"Yep."

"What's your major?"

"Undecided."

Of course, it was. Even though I was starting school again, I didn't bother to tell him that I was in college too. "Well, I'll see you back out there." I turned to leave.

"Hey, Reagan?"

I stopped and turned back to him. "Yeah?"

"*Do* you have a boyfriend?"

I chuckled, remembering he was there when the customer had asked. "No."

He bobbed his head again and smirked. "Good to know."

I balked because he looked young enough that I probably could have been the kid's mother. "Not looking for one either."

"Good to know that, too."

Before the conversation turned any more awkward, I turned and left. What I had told Derrick was true. I wasn't looking for a boyfriend. I needed to find out who I was before I tied myself to a man again. Though, when I came around the corner and saw the man sitting at the bar, I wanted to change my mind.

He still had the short, dirty blond hair I remembered from many moons ago, but flecks of gray dotted the sides now. I couldn't see most of his body because he was seated behind the wooden bartop, but I figured he was still in great shape given his shoulders were broader than I remembered, and his arms pulled against the fabric of his long-sleeved, black shirt as he rested his hand against the glass of his beer.

With a smile plastered across my face, I stepped behind the bar and moved in front of the blast from my past. "Well, as I live and breathe, Ethan Valor."

Ethan's deep blue eyes looked up from his amber-colored beer and met my green stare. A smile curved his lips, one I hadn't seen in over two decades. "Reagan Hunter, is that you?"

I ran around to where he was sitting and threw my arms around his neck as he stood to greet me. "How are you?" I asked. My last name changed when I got married, but I didn't bother correcting him because I never changed it back after my divorce.

"Better now." He squeezed me one more time before we broke apart.

"What are you drinking? Let me get you a refill." I went back around to the other side of the bar.

"Just what's on draft. Doesn't matter," Ethan replied as he slid back onto the barstool. "If I'd known you were a bartender here, I'd have come in sooner."

I grinned and grabbed a clean pint glass to fill for him. This was my high school boyfriend in front of me, and even though I had only worked at Judy's for a week and had never given free alcohol away before, I wanted to give the man I'd first loved a beer on the house.

Plus, I'd noticed he wasn't wearing a wedding ring either.

# CHAPTER THREE

### Nineteen Years Old

I didn't want to let her go.

For the past two years, we had been inseparable. It didn't matter that I was a year older and had already graduated. I didn't go away to college after my graduation, opting instead to attend a local school to obtain my bachelor's degree in law enforcement. I'd always wanted to be a police officer like my father, so I knew what my future held.

I was destined to be Chicago PD.

Reagan, on the other hand, was leaving to go across the country because she'd gotten into Stanford. Summer was over, and the day we'd dreaded had arrived. We'd known it was coming for a long time, but neither of us had wanted to admit it would *actually* happen. She was leaving. As the girl I loved stood in my arms, crying because in five minutes her family would drive her to the airport so she could catch her flight to California, time seemed to speed up when all we wanted was for it to stop.

"We'll talk on the phone every night," I reminded her.

"It's not the same," she sobbed into my chest, her tears soaking through my T-shirt as we stood in her driveway.

I knew talking on the phone wasn't the same, but we had no choice. "Winter break will be here before we know it, and then we'll spend every day together once you're back home."

"But I'm going to miss you."

"I'm going to miss you too, Buttercup." I squeezed her tighter.

"Reagan, get in the car. You have a flight to catch," her father ordered.

Reagan looked up at me. Her emerald eyes were rimmed red with tears running down her cheeks, and it was killing me.

"One second," I called back, held up a finger, and took Reagan's hand, leading her around to the back of her house and away from her parents' eyes.

"What if I don't go?" she questioned.

"You have to. You got into Stanford." I knew Reagan was smart—getting into one of the most prestigious colleges in America proved it. She *had* to go.

"I know." She sighed. "But I don't want to be apart."

I lifted her chin with my fingers, making her look into my eyes again. "I'll save up and come visit you before winter break."

Reagan sucked in a quick breath. "Really?"

"I'd do anything for you, Buttercup, and the time apart is going to kill me too." I leaned down and captured her lips with mine. It would be months before I could taste her again. Months before I could hold her, touch her, see her.

"Reagan!" her father shouted. "Let's go!"

We broke apart, and I laced her fingers with mine. Without another word, we walked back to the driveway. I nodded to her father, and he stepped into the car where Reagan's mother was already waiting.

"I love you," I admitted and brought her against my body again.

"I love you too."

We let go of each other a final time, and Reagan slipped into the car. I watched her tear-stained face as she waved goodbye from the backseat, not knowing that twenty-three years would pass before I'd see her again.

## Present Day

I watched Reagan move behind the bar, talking to customers and making drinks. She wasn't the eighteen-year-old I'd last seen. No, she was a woman. A fucking beautiful woman. Her hair was still long, dark, and luscious, and her eyes were still the familiar deep emerald color I'd stared into so many nights when we were younger. But her body ...

*Fuck.*

She was curvier in all the right places. Her breasts were larger than I remembered, and so was her ass, but not in a bad way. She'd filled out nicely.

She was stunning, and I wasn't the only one who noticed. While I sipped my beer, I noted that her barback had his eye on her too. He would smile when they bumped into each other, making sure to accidentally brush her arm every time he was near her, and he watched her when he didn't think anyone was looking.

*But I was looking.*

It was hard not to focus all my attention on how beautiful she was, but being a police officer, I always tried to be aware of everything around me. A part of me was jealous that he got to work with her, but my cop senses told me something was off with this guy. I couldn't put my finger on it just yet, but I knew I needed to watch him.

So, I did.

"Want another?" Reagan asked, coming over to me a few minutes later.

I looked down at the half-finished warm beer. "No, I'm good."

"All right. Just let me know if you do."

"Hey." I reached out my hand and grabbed her wrist, stopping her from walking away. "What time do you get off?"

She smiled warmly at me and then cocked a hip. "Are you flirting with me, Mr. Valor?"

I smiled back, leaving my hand on her warm skin. "What if I were?"

Before she could respond, her barback bumped into her, causing my grasp to break free. "Sorry," he muttered.

"Are you okay?" I asked her.

"Yeah."

"Clumsy, ain't he?"

Reagan chuckled. "Yeah, first night working with him too."

*Interesting.*

She stepped back in front of me. "I get off in an hour. Are you sticking around?"

*Hell yeah, I was.* I looked at my watch and noted it was just after eleven. "Yeah, I don't live far."

"Oh, really?"

"Just down the block actually," I replied.

"Then you'll need to visit more often."

I grinned, and my gaze moved to her left hand, which didn't have a ring. "Already planning on it."

I noticed the barback stopped putting glasses away for a split second as though he were listening to us. He clearly had a thing for her, and honestly, I did too. The years had treated Reagan nicely, and my body still reacted to her as though I was a horny teenager.

Judy's was still humming with people, but as soon as twelve o'clock hit, Reagan came out from the back and walked straight to me. "Want to go somewhere quieter?"

My face widened with a smile. "Are you flirting with me, Ms. Hunter?"

She chuckled. "What if I were?"

I slid off the stool. "Then I'd say we should get out of here."

A glass shattered behind the bar, and I glanced up to see that the barback had caused the noise. The closing bartender walked over and said to him, "Clean this up, and then you're good to go home." The barback nodded, glanced at us, and then walked to the back.

"Ready?" I asked.

Reagan turned to me. "Yeah. Where are we going?"

"Well, I do live right down the street," I reminded her.

"Moving a little fast, don't you think?" she teased. At least I presumed she was teasing. Even if we did have sex tonight, it wouldn't be our first time together. Was that moving too fast? I wouldn't turn her down, but I also wanted to go somewhere quiet and have her all to myself for a while so I could find out what had been going on in her life since we were teenagers.

I moved a step closer to her and whispered into her ear, "Or we can go to your car and pretend it's like old times."

# CHAPTER FOUR

*Reagan*

From the first time Ethan *literally* ran into me in the halls at school, he'd always made my belly feel as though it was swarming with butterflies. No man, not even my ex-husband, had ever had that effect on me.

"How far away do you live?" I asked. While making out with Ethan in the back of my car made my belly dip, I didn't think we needed to be confined to a tin box. We weren't kids anymore.

"Just another block."

When we were younger, the man walking next to me would always grab my hand when we'd walk side by side. But now, as we walked down the street, we were at least three feet apart.

Those three feet felt like three miles.

We hadn't seen each other in many years, but I wanted him to touch me. I wanted to remember what it felt like to be in his arms because, when I had been there before, I'd felt safe. And even though I had no reason to feel unsafe, I wanted to remember what it felt like to know that no matter what, he'd protect me. Something about Ethan instantly put me at ease.

I hated how our relationship had ended because it was all my fault.

*The phone rang in my ear as I held the receiver and waited for Ethan to answer. I didn't want him to pick up the phone, didn't want to hear his voice, but I had to break up with him because I'd cheated on him. I'd drunk one too many beers and kissed another guy. A guy who wasn't my boyfriend. A guy who wasn't my first love. A guy who wasn't Ethan.*

*"Hello?" Ethan answered.*

*I took a deep breath before I replied, "Hi."*

*"Hey, Buttercup."*

*A tear ran down my cheek when I heard the term of endearment leave his lips. He always called me Buttercup because my favorite flower was buttercups, specifically the Persian ones that resembled roses.*

*"We need to break up," I blurted.*

*"What?" he questioned.*

*"It's—It's just not working out."*

*"Bullshit," Ethan snapped.*

*"Please," I begged.*

*"Is there someone else?"*

*"No." There really wasn't. I didn't even remember the name of the guy I'd kissed. "It's hard to keep up our relationship and school. It's just not working out." Part of that statement was true, but if I hadn't kissed whatever-his-name-was, we wouldn't have needed to have this conversation, and my heart wouldn't have been ripping out of my chest and breaking in two.*

*"We can make it work."*

*More tears ran down my face as I tried to hide the sorrow in my voice. "We can't."*

*He paused for a moment before replying, "I don't know why the fuck you're doing this, but one day, Reagan Hunter, you'll regret it."*

*I already did.*

The closer we got to his apartment, the more I wanted to tell him what really happened to make me break up with him all those years ago, how my stupid teenage heart thought a kiss was the end of the world, but I didn't. I didn't want to taint the moment by bringing up the past. A past that was over two decades old.

"I'm all out of beer," he stated as we walked through the doors of his building. Ethan nodded to the doorman, and we walked toward the elevators. "That's actually why I went to Judy's tonight. But I have apple juice if you'd like."

I laughed. "Apple juice?"

He grinned and pressed the button to call the elevator. "My sons both love apple juice."

"You have kids?"

"Two boys. You?"

"I have a daughter."

The elevator dinged, and then the doors opened. We stepped inside, and Ethan pressed the button for his floor. "Just the one?"

I sighed and leaned against the railing as the lift ascended. "We tried for more, but it never happened." His gaze dropped to my left hand, but before he could ask, I added, "I'm divorced now."

"Me too."

"Is this a normal thing for you then?"

"What's that?" he asked as the doors opened, and we stepped out onto his floor.

"Taking a woman home from a bar." I smiled, trying to make a joke because the situation felt weird. A part of me felt comfortable with him, but another part was nervous as though I didn't know him at all. Even though we knew each other intimately, we really didn't know each other anymore.

Ethan grinned. "No, it's not a normal thing for me. I've dated a few women since my divorce, but work takes up a lot of my time."

"Did you end up becoming a cop?" I already knew the answer, but I asked anyway, trying to make it seem as though I hadn't tried to find out about him. I figured every woman had that moment, the one where curiosity took over and they typed their ex's name in the search field on Facebook. I never found him on Facebook, but on Google I discovered he was a Chicago police officer. I'd also learned that Ethan had been involved in a shooting that killed a man who was trying to hurt his sister.

He nodded and fished his keys out of his pocket. "Yeah, I'm a sergeant now."

"That's amazing," I gushed as Ethan opened the door.

"Yeah, I love it. What made you decide to be a bartender?"

I chuckled slightly. Did he think I went to Stanford only to be a mixologist? Granted, I wasn't using my bachelor's degree. "Actually"—I stepped inside his condo and into the living room area—"I just started at Judy's last week. My daughter recently started college, and I needed something to do with my time. I have my BA in biology, but now I'm taking classes to become a crime scene investigator."

"No shit?" He closed the door behind him and tossed his keys and phone on the table near the door.

I watched him walk to the open kitchen. "I've always wanted to work crime scenes, but I got married and had Maddie right after college. Never pursued law enforcement like I'd wanted to."

"I remember when we were dating before, you wanted to work crime scenes, but are you okay seeing dead bodies?"

It was my turn to balk. Ethan had shocked me with his question because I'd never thought about the dead bodies. It had been years since I thought I'd go down the crime scene investigating path, and sure, I knew there would be dead bodies, but I hadn't considered the fact that in the near future I was going to *see* dead people.

I shrugged. "I guess so."

Ethan pulled a jug of apple juice out of the fridge and then turned to a cabinet for glasses. He chuckled. "You better know so."

"What is it like?" I asked, moving to a barstool at the kitchen island.

He paused with his hand on the cap of the bottle. "I think it depends on the person. For some, it's gross. For others—like me—it is what it is. But the smell is disgusting. It's the foulest thing in the world. I can't even describe it."

"Oh."

"Each one gets easier to deal with, but killing someone and watching them take their last breath is the real deal."

"That happened to you? You've killed someone?" Again, I was playing dumb. There was no way I was going to tell him that I'd looked him up because a part of me had always longed for him. My heart still ached as I thought about how we'd ended.

Ethan sighed and then opened the juice before pouring us each a glass. "Actually, it happened right behind you."

Time stood still as I processed his words. I blinked. "What?"

He slid a glass to me and then leaned forward, resting his elbows on the gray granite. "My sister was almost kidnapped. I happened to come over just in time to see the guy pointing a gun at her boyfriend. Before he could shoot, I did."

"Wow," I breathed, still processing the fact that the man he'd killed had died not ten feet from where I sat. I knew he had killed a person; I just hadn't realized I was in the room where it had happened.

"Yeah, but you won't be shooting people, so you don't need to worry about those nightmares. Which part of investigating are you going to get your certification in?"

I took a sip of the sweet juice. "Forensics." There were several types of investigators: forensics, photography, ballistics, DNA and blood analysis, and crime scene reconstruction. I wanted to gather and preserve physical evidence at crime scenes and then go back to the lab and analyze it, run tests on fibers and hairs, and help solve the cases.

He grinned. "Then maybe we'll work crime scenes together."

"Maybe, but I need to find a job first."

"I might be able to help with that."

I smiled. "Really?"

"I'm sure I can. I know people in this town." He winked.

# CHAPTER FIVE

*Ethan*

The very first person I gave my heart to was sitting across from me.

The same person who first broke my heart, and the person who still carried a piece of it after all these years. When I'd thought about seeing Reagan again, I always thought I would turn the other way. After all, she'd ripped out my heart and never looked back. But when I saw her at Judy's, all those thoughts went out the window, and then she was in my condo, drinking my apple juice as if nothing had ever happened.

I didn't hate her. It was the complete opposite. I …

I still loved her.

A part of me always had. They say you never forget your first love, and that was definitely true. Just the thought of Reagan walking out my door and never coming back again was messing with my head. I needed to prolong the reunion even though it was getting close to one in the morning, and I had to be at work in less than eight hours. I wasn't ready to let her leave my sight.

"I'm sure I can. I know people in this town." I winked.

"A job at your precinct?" she asked.

"Maybe. I'll see what I can find out."

"I just have to get through nine more weeks of school."

"Maybe I can be your study buddy?" I proposed. "I do know all about crime scenes."

Reagan smiled. "You'd do that for me?"

I shrugged and picked up my glass of juice before walking to the other side of the island to sit next to her. "Sure, why not? It'll be like old times." I smirked.

She bobbed her head and chuckled slightly. "Old times that used to lead to not studying or doing homework."

That was true. After school and before our parents arrived home from work, we'd hang out and *study*. We were each other's firsts—in more than one way.

"You never complained," I reminded her.

She threw her head back, laughing. "No. No, I didn't."

Her laughter made my palms itch to touch her, to pull her into my arms and feel her lips on mine again as I kissed her. Instead, I said, "So, tell me what Reagan Hunter has been up to the last twenty-some-odd years."

She took a deep breath. "Well, I graduated from Stanford, moved to Denver, got married, had Maddison about a year later, and have just been doing the mother thing since then. She kept me busy."

"And now you live here?"

"Yeah. Moved far away from my ex and closer to Maddie."

"And me," I stated.

"And you, but I didn't know you still lived here. What have you been up to?" Reagan took a sip of her juice.

"As I mentioned earlier, I became a cop, then got married, had my two boys, dedicated most of my time to the job so I could one day be chief like my father was, got divorced, and then went to a bar that has a reputation for people finding their soulmates."

"What?" she asked, dragging out the word and scrunching her eyebrows.

I chuckled. "My sister met her husband at Judy's."

"She did?"

I nodded and then took a sip of juice. "About three years ago. Didn't realize that the one time I go there, I would run into the only woman I still dream about."

She didn't speak.

I didn't speak.

The clock on the wall ticked …

Tock …

Tick …

Tock …

Tick…

Tock.

I cleared my throat. "Let me give you my number, and you can call me if you need help with anything."

Reagan stood to grab her purse from the table by the front door. After fishing out her cell phone, she said, "Okay, give me your number."

I took her phone, and after I typed my number into her contacts, I sent myself a text so that I had her number as well. "I feel like we're back in high school, exchanging numbers and shit to *help* with homework."

She grinned. "Yeah, it's like we're starting over."

It was on the tip of my tongue to ask if she wanted to try, but I thought better of it. Instead, I handed her back her phone and said, "Would you like to go on a ride-along with me sometime?"

Her emerald eyes brightened. "Really?"

I smiled and went to sit on my couch as she placed her purse on the table. "Yeah. Then we can see how you do with dead bodies."

Reagan sat next to me, but not close enough to touch. "Do you get them every day or something?"

Chuckling, I said, "No, but we do live in one of the thirty cities with the highest murder rates."

"No wonder you're used to it."

"Yeah, and like I said, it gets easier."

"A ride-along sounds fun. I'd love that."

"Great, I'll set it up." Being a gentleman, I should have offered to take her home—or drive her to her car at Judy's—but I didn't want her to leave. "Want to watch a movie or something?"

She paused, and I knew she wanted to do the right thing—the right thing being head home since it was late. Instead, she said, "Yeah. Let me use the bathroom first."

I grinned because her answer gave me hope that we were both feeling something. "Just down the hall. First door on the left."

Reagan returned not long after, and we selected a movie while she got comfortable on one side of the couch, and I got comfortable on the other side. I had to admit that we'd never watched a movie together this way. Even when we first started dating, I'd wrap my arm around her shoulders. Now, she was a mile away, and I felt the distance between us.

While we watched the TV, I made it my new mission to win her back.

Reagan Hunter was going to be mine again.

# CHAPTER SIX

I woke in a bed.

A bed that didn't feel like *my* bed.

After slowly opening my eyes, I looked over and noticed I was alone. I couldn't remember falling asleep or getting into a bed—Ethan's bed. I didn't feel hungover, drugged, or anything like that, so I didn't understand how I didn't remember anything except watching a movie on Ethan's couch.

I lifted the covers, looking down to see that I was still in my clothes except for my shoes. Turning my head, I noticed a piece of paper on the pillow next to me, so I sat up and grabbed it.

> Buttercup,
> You're still cute when you snore.
> Key is by your purse. Lock up when you leave, and I'll
> stop by Judy's tonight to get it.
> -E

I did *not* snore. Okay, I did, but only when I was really tired.

It finally made sense why I couldn't remember falling asleep in Ethan's bed. Usually, after work, I'd go home, take a shower, and be in bed by one, not reminiscing with my high school boyfriend until whatever hour it was that I'd finally fell asleep. I must have fallen asleep during the movie and didn't wake when he—*did he carry me to bed?*

I didn't regret staying.

Ethan's bed was fucking comfortable.

Every time the front door of Judy's opened, I looked for Ethan. I really wanted to see him again. He was currently my only friend in Chicago, and honestly, I was okay with that.

The night before had been nice. He hadn't grilled me about why I'd broken up with him all those years ago, and I didn't pry and ask how long he'd been divorced. I wanted it to be a long time so I wasn't his rebound—*if* anything happened. It was as if we were starting over in a sense, putting our childhood in the past and moving forward as adults.

And that excited me.

The door opened again, and I glanced up. Two women entered, and I turned my attention back to the beer I was pouring from the tap. The door opened once more, but again, it wasn't the person who I wanted to see.

"Waiting for someone?"

I looked over at Derrick, who was standing next to me, refilling the limes and lemons. We were the only ones on the floor because Frank was on break and the other barback had left for the night.

"Yeah, my friend's stopping by to grab something from me."

"The guy from last night?"

I wrinkled my eyebrows, confused, but then realized he must have noticed I left with Ethan. "Yeah, him." I slid the beer in front of the customer and grabbed his money to ring him up.

"Thought you didn't have a boyfriend?" Derrick asked, moving to stack empty glasses under the bar top.

I huffed. "I don't."

"But you left with him last night." It wasn't a question.

"Why do you care who I left with?"

"Just making small talk."

I stopped pressing the buttons on the POS system and turned to face him. "We just met last night"—I waved my hand between him and me—"and I get that we're going to work together, but I don't need you questioning my personal life."

He held up his hands. "Whoa, I'm just trying to make conversation and get to know you."

"Getting to know me is asking me what my favorite color is. Or my favorite flower. Not grilling me about a guy I left with last night." I wasn't sure why I was so put off by his questioning, but I was a forty-one-year-old woman, and if I wanted to go home with a man, that was my decision. Granted, nothing had happened with Ethan.

Derrick leaned a hip on the cabinets that held extra bottles of alcohol behind the bar and faced me. "Okay, what's your favorite color?"

I snorted and rolled my eyes. "Purple."

"And your favorite flower?"

I paused. Not because I didn't know, but because I remembered the note Ethan had left me in the morning, and it gave me hope that he and I could become a 'we' again. A part of me felt as though we weren't done. My teenage heart had thought I would hurt him more if I told him the truth all those years ago, so I'd set him free.

"Buttercups."

Derrick balked as though he wasn't expecting that answer. "Buttercups? That's a thing?"

I laughed and returned to the POS system, finishing the transaction and grabbing the customer's change. "Yes, and specifically the Parisian ones."

He lifted off the counter and turned to grab the overflowing garbage bag. "I'm going to have to Google them and see what they look like."

"You do that."

I hadn't had time to check my phone after my dinner break for any missed calls from Ethan because it was Friday night and we were slammed.

Walking to my locker before I called it a night, I fished my phone from my back pocket and hoped he had sent a text.

He had: *Caught a case. I'll try to stop by before you get off at 12, but if not, keep the key.*

I texted him back as I leaned on the lockers with a grin on my face: *Just getting off now. Should I wait?*

I removed my purse from my locker as I waited for his reply.

Ethan: *Sorry, Buttercup. I'm at the station. Meet for lunch?*

As I walked out the back door toward my parked car, I replied: *Sure. Just tell me the place, and I'll meet you there.*

"Have a good night, Reagan."

I started slightly and turned to see Derrick leaning against the brick wall, smoking a cigarette. "Thanks, you too."

"Oh, I will."

I didn't know what that meant exactly, and I wasn't going to ask and encourage whatever game he was playing. I got the feeling he had a crush on me or something, and if anything, I wanted to be with a man like Ethan and not a boy like Derrick.

# CHAPTER SEVEN

"**V**ic is female. Appears to be in her twenties and has multiple stab wounds," Officer Moore, the responding officer, stated as we walked up to the apartment on the second story.

My partner Shawn Jones and I nodded. After putting shoe protectors on, we entered the home. In all my years on the force, I'd never seen a stabbing like this one, and I'd seen some fucked up shit.

The flashing red and blue lights came in through the front windows as we looked down at the naked body on the couch. Her brown hair was darkened with blood, her brown eyes stuck open and lifeless, and I was certain the couch cushions were soaked with more of the crimson fluid. I looked around the small living room, which had already been cordoned off as evidence was gathered, pictures taken, and prints dusted for.

"Did you find the murder weapon?" I asked.

Officer Moore shook his head. "Haven't found it yet."

I stepped closer to the victim, crouching down to be eye level with her body, and noticed her skin was already turning gray. "Who called it in?"

"Neighbor. The roommate ran next door after finding the body when she got home tonight. Said she usually stays at her boyfriend's Thursday through Saturday, but she forgot her makeup bag or something."

I wasn't sure if she was gray because of how long she'd been dead or because she was lying in a pool of what appeared to be *all* of her blood. There was no way to know until we talked to the medical examiner.

"Where's the roommate now?" Shawn asked.

"The bus took her to med," Moore stated, referring to an ambulance. "She was hyperventilating after finding the body."

I nodded as I shared a look with my partner. We weren't ruling out the roommate yet.

Shawn and I walked around the apartment, looking for anything and everything while we waited for the medical examiner to arrive and give us an estimated time of death. There were no signs of a struggle, and nothing appeared to be missing or stolen.

The victim's purse was in her bedroom. I took out her wallet and got her name: Amy Kenny. I noted everything about the young woman. She seemed happy and had a promising future. The pictures on the wall showed how much fun she had in her life. There were photos of her and her friends at clubs, bars, and concerts, and she even had one of those heart-shaped wood plaques, likely from a fair, with her name carved in it.

At least this young lady had lived a good life before she was brutally murdered in her own home.

# Unknown

My smile hadn't faltered as I watched the cops coming and going through the webcam of the computer I'd purposely left open on the dining room table. It also gave me a view of Amy's lifeless body, where I'd left her on her couch. I hadn't expected anyone to find her so soon, but then again, I didn't expect the roommate to come home early because she usually spent the weekend away. I thought I had another day to watch Amy's lifeless body on her couch. But I had to admit that seeing Chicago PD move around the small living room, not knowing that I was watching them, was giving me another high, a high that was similar to the one I got when I'd watched the bitch take her last gasp of air.

I'd never felt more *alive* than I had at that moment. Especially when my rage took over and I got the redemption I was after.

Watching Amy had been a sport at first. She was only supposed to be a player in my little game that no one knew about. That was how they all were as I watched the female students of Lakeshore University through their webcams.

But Amy was different.

I'd first come across her at the end of the last year school year, I'd kept tabs on her, watching her every chance I got into the summer break. I knew her favorite song, her favorite drink of choice, what she liked to eat when she thought she was alone and no one could see the Snickers she had to have at least one night a week. I also knew what kind of porn she liked, how long it took her to come, and how many times she could get herself off with her pink vibrator. *Three, if you'd like to know.*

God, she *was* beautiful.

I'd wanted to touch her, smell her, taste her. I'd wanted to look into her eyes and tell her I knew all of her secrets. Knew what got her off. I'd wanted to bury my face between her legs and have her ride my face for hours. Be the one who fucked her hard. Make her come over and over and over.

That was until she came back to school and I asked her on a date. She'd laughed and told me, "I don't think so."

Those four words had fueled my fire.

I'd continued to watch her through her webcam because, like most stupid girls, she left the laptop open in her room. I kept tabs on her so my new plan could come to fruition. If Amy didn't want me, no one could have her. I would be the last one to speak to her, to hear her voice, to taste her.

When I knew she was alone, I entered her apartment with the key I'd made with my 3D printer. A picture of her house key and a high-tech printer was all it took to create a copy. Since she left her computer open 24/7, I was able to zoom in on the keys she'd left near her purse. After I'd created the 3D CAD file, I pressed the start button and watched the plastic key form right before my eyes.

While Amy was in the shower, I knew I had just enough time to drive to her apartment and let myself in with my key. When I got to her room, I slipped a pill into her red wine next to hear laptop, knowing she'd drink the rest of her glass before pouring another one. The drug was my first gift to her. I didn't want her to put up a fight, and having her high and out of it would be easier for both of us. My other gift was a wood plaque with her name on it. I was leaving my mark—my signature. Sadly, she'd never know about that gift.

After she drank the wine, I waited for the drug to kick in.

And then I made my move.

*Ethan*

I yawned, leaning back in my desk chair. Catching a new case was what I lived for, but the first forty-eight hours were brutal.

We'd just gotten an update from the ME that the victim had been stabbed sixty-eight times. I'd never seen such hatred in all my life, and that was saying something considering I lived in Chicago where there were, on average, around seven hundred murders a year.

This murder screamed hate, passion, and rage, and I wanted to solve the case as soon as possible, but I also wanted to see Reagan again. There was no way I'd be able to meet her before midnight, so I'd texted her to meet for lunch at a restaurant near my place. I would have said breakfast, but I also knew that she needed sleep—and so did I.

*Fuck, what I would do to have her in my bed again.*

The night before, I'd heard her quiet snores over the movie. After making sure she was in a deep sleep, I carried her to my bed. If she and I were an *us*, I wouldn't have hesitated to crawl in beside her, pull her close, and sleep with my arms around her until I had to go into work. Instead, I took a quick shower and slept on my couch. I left before she woke, hoping I could put in my ten hours and then meet her at Judy's. Instead, some asshole had brutally murdered a woman in the dead of night.

The ME told us the estimated time of death was around three the previous morning. Since it was now after midnight, we were coming up on the twenty-four-hour mark since the time of death, and we had no leads except the roommate, who we hadn't interviewed yet because she was at the hospital. The neighbor had heard nothing unusual, either. Our cybercrime unit was looking into Amy's computer, and Shawn and I had already sent in a subpoena for her cell phone and credit card records.

"I'm going to head home. Want to talk to the roommate first thing?" I asked Shawn. We'd gotten word that the roommate would be released from the hospital after a few hours, and her boyfriend was taking her back to his place.

"Yeah, sounds good."

We both left, and I went directly home. I crawled into my bed, which still smelled like Reagan, like marshmallows by a campfire, and quickly fell asleep, dreaming about her like I usually did.

The next morning, as planned, I met Shawn at the roommate's boyfriend's apartment where she'd gone after she was released from the hospital. Usually, I'd meet him at the station, and we'd drive over together, but because I had a lunch date, we had to take two cars.

We walked to the door and knocked. After a moment, it opened. Shawn and I held up our badges. "I'm Sergeant Valor, and this is Detective Jones. Is Heather Northland here?"

The guy who opened the door nodded and motioned for us to enter. A young lady was sitting on the couch. Her blue eyes were bloodshot, probably from lack of sleep or crying all night, and her blonde hair was pulled into a messy ponytail.

"Mind if we ask you a few questions about last night?" I asked. We already knew some of the answers to our questions because Officer Moore had briefed us the night before, but we'd ask her the same questions again to make sure her story stayed the same.

"Sure," she replied.

Shawn sat next to her on the only couch, and I took a seat in the chair across from them. The man who we confirmed was the boyfriend went to the kitchen to get us water.

"How long were you and Amy roommates?" I asked.

Heather took a deep breath, tears starting to form in her swollen eyes. "About eight or nine months. I moved in at the start of the school year."

"Did you know her prior to moving in with her?"

She shook her head. "No. She had an ad on Craigslist, and I'd answered it."

The guy came back and handed me a glass. Shawn stood and walked with him out the front door, leaving me to finish and for him to get some info from the boyfriend.

"Was Amy dating anyone?" I questioned.

"Not that I know of."

"Amy didn't date?"

"She did, but I don't think she had a serious boyfriend."

"When was the last time you saw her alive?"

Heather sniffed. "Friday."

"What time was that?"

She shrugged. "Around five."

"Did you notice anything missing?" I asked.

She shook her head. "No, but I wasn't in there long. I walked in and saw …" She took a deep breath, tears streaming down her face. "I saw her lying on the couch covered in blood and then I ran next door. I was scared to death."

"Did you see anyone else in the apartment?"

Her eyes widened. "No. Do you think the killer was still there?"

I didn't, given that Amy was already turning gray by the time we'd arrived, but I'd asked Heather to gauge her reaction. "It's possible."

"Oh my god." She covered her mouth and started to cry harder.

I asked Heather more questions about her alibi and how close she was to Amy, but nothing gave me any indication she had killed Amy and no insight into who might have done it. There was no murder weapon found at the scene, there was no forced entry, and it was noted Heather didn't have blood on her when she was transported to the hospital.

Nothing was found in the apartment except Amy in a pool of her blood.

After we finished, I drove to meet Reagan at Big Jones, a rustic restaurant that served southern food. I needed something that was going to keep me full longer than a measly sandwich would, so I could focus on the case. Plus, their fried chicken was award-winning.

When I rounded the corner toward the front door of the restaurant, I saw Reagan waiting outside. She was in jeans, knee-high boots, and a blouse that showed off her assets. Fuck, I wanted her. I wanted her so bad I was salivating. I remembered what it was like to be inside of her, and I wanted to have that again. Have *her* again.

Our gazes met as I walked closer, and she smiled. "I don't think I've ever seen you in a suit."

I chuckled and leaned in, kissing her cheek. "You've seen me in a tux at prom."

Her grin widened. "True, but not grown-up Ethan."

"No, and a lot has changed since I wore that tux to prom." I winked. I was referring to her body as well, but I didn't elaborate. Instead, I opened the door of the restaurant and guided her inside.

# CHAPTER EIGHT

*Reagan*

S eeing Ethan in a suit was doing things to my belly and between my legs. He was gorgeous with the scruff around his face from not shaving for a few days, his piercing blue eyes that reminded me of the sea, and those muscles that I wanted to feel wrapped around me as our bodies slid skin on skin.

"Have you been here before?" Ethan asked after we were seated.

I shook my head. "No. I've only been back a few months and haven't had a chance to explore it all."

"I can show you some time," he offered.

I grinned. "I'd like that."

Ethan paused, reading the menu briefly. "I'm getting the chicken," he said, setting the menu down. "That and the shrimp and grits are amazing."

I bobbed my head, still scanning the menu. In the end, I decided to take him up on his suggestion of fried chicken. It had been a long time since I'd had good southern fried chicken. I set the menu down and sipped the water on the table. "Did you solve the case?"

He let out a long, deep breath. "No, far from it."

"What's it about?"

He leaned closer and grinned. "Can't tell you that, Buttercup. It's confidential."

"Really?"

Ethan nodded. "Really. But when we go on the ride-along, you'll sign an NDA, and then you can know all about whatever we come across."

"I'm excited."

"If it's anything like what I saw last night, then we'll know for sure if you can be CSI."

"It was bad?"

Ethan leaned back. "Yeah. Worst murder I've ever seen."

"Wow," I breathed and took another sip of water. "Well, I'm excited. Class has been fun so far. It will be good for me."

"Want me to come over when I get off work, and we can study?"

I raised an eyebrow.

"I mean it. I can answer questions if you have them."

The waitress came and took our order. After she left, I said, "I'd rather study like we used to *study*."

He choked on a sip of water. "Really?"

I leaned forward, resting my forearms on the table. "Tell me if I'm reading this wrong. You took me home, let me sleep in *your* bed, gave me a key to *your* place, invited *me* to lunch, and offered to see *me* again tonight when you're working on what I assume is a big case since you said it was the worst murder you've ever seen."

Ethan grinned slowly. "Reagan Hunter, are you telling me that you want to *study*?" He put air quotes around "study," causing me to bite my lip.

"Yeah, Ethan Valor. I want to study. All. Night. Long."

"Check, please!"

When I'd decided to take back my life—to do *me*, as they say—I didn't realize it would mean taking back my sex life too.

"What time do you need to be back at the station?" I asked. Ethan was dragging me down the street, our hands laced together.

"Doesn't matter. I'll work all night if I have to—if this really happens."

"It's not going to happen?"

He stopped and looked straight into my eyes. "Yeah, it's going to happen. When do you need to be at work?"

"Four."

Ethan's gaze roamed up and down my body. "Can you wear that to work?"

"Technically I could, but I also have a spare T-shirt in my car."

He smirked. "Tutoring is about to start early, Buttercup."

He tugged on the hand he was still holding and walked another block until we were at his building. Just like the other night, he nodded to the door guy as we walked to the elevator. It was waiting for us, so we entered, and he stabbed at the button for his floor repeatedly until the doors closed.

Ethan turned, gave me one look, and crashed his lips into mine. His soft lips felt both new and familiar as he pushed me back against the wall of the lift and devoured my mouth. His hips pinned me against the back railing, and I felt how much he wanted me, something I hadn't felt for over half of my life. I'd missed it. I'd missed him, and the sparks we'd once shared lit inside of me again as our mouths worked together.

The elevator dinged, indicating we were on his floor, and he growled into my mouth before pulling away. He laced our fingers again, and then we walked toward his door.

"You know," he started to say as he worked the lock to open his door, "I haven't had a nooner since—well, since we were in high school."

The times when we'd ditch school to *study* flashed through my head briefly. "I'm surprised you graduated." He was a year older than me, so after he graduated, we only hung out after school and on weekends, but it hadn't stopped our teenage hormones.

"We didn't miss that many days. Plus, I had a good study partner." Ethan winked as he slammed the door behind us.

"Right, *studying.*"

His lips found mine again, and we raced to discard our clothes, only breaking the kiss when we needed to. Once we were both naked, we stared at each other briefly, and I admired how the boy I once knew was definitely a man now. Hard, strong, and *big.*

"Are you as sweet as I remember?" he asked.

My body flushed. "There's only one way to find out."

He smirked and then led me to his bedroom. Before I realized what was happening, he picked me up and tossed me playfully onto the bed. The softness cradled me, and I bent my legs as Ethan spread my thighs apart. The moment his wet tongue met my pussy, I shivered.

"Cold?" he asked.

"No," I breathed. "Keep going."

And he did.

The first man to taste me was between my legs again, making me wetter and wetter and hotter and hotter until I was moaning, my body spasming as I came. It didn't take long. This was Ethan, and it had been years since any man had pleasured me. I wanted more.

"You taste even better than I remember."

My body heated more at his words to the point where I couldn't speak. He reached over to the nightstand and grabbed a condom from the drawer. Opening the foil packet, he slid the latex on. I wanted nothing more than for him to crawl between my legs and sink into me, but I also didn't want the same old missionary sex I'd had with my ex-husband. This was Ethan.

I stood before he could move another inch. He raised an eyebrow, questioning me silently. "Sit," I instructed. He sat on the edge of the bed. "Scoot back," I said, moving to place my hands on the side of his hips. He did as I'd asked until he was in the center of the bed.

"This isn't what we used to do. You've learned new tricks."

I laughed as I crawled toward him. "I just know what I want."

"And what's that?"

"You," I said. As I positioned myself on his lap, my gaze downcast, I replied, "I've always wanted you."

Ethan grabbed my chin, making me look directly into his oceanic eyes. "Then why did you break up with me?"

I swallowed, feeling a slight lump form in the back of my throat. A part of me had hoped we'd never bring up the past, but never in my life would I have thought that we'd be having this conversation naked, in his bed, and about to have sex.

"Just tell me," he pleaded. "I won't be mad. I thought you didn't love me any more or something and now … now I don't know what to think."

Taking a deep breath, I looked off to the side, not wanting to meet his stare. "I got drunk at a party and kissed another guy."

The air grew still as I waited for him to say something. "Did you date him after me?"

My gaze moved to his. "No, I don't even know who I kissed. I was too drunk to remember."

"Then how do you know you kissed him?"

I shrugged. "I just remember kissing someone."

We stared at each other for a few moments as my heart beat rapidly inside my chest. "Things happen for a reason, right?" he asked.

I nodded slowly, still not sure what else Ethan was going to say.

"I won't hold some drunken kiss over your head. The past is the past, and it's been two decades since it happened. We're adults now. Let's start over."

I breathed a sigh of relief and smiled. "Okay."

Nothing more was said as he adjusted to sit cross-legged. The movement made me slide closer to his cock, and I wrapped my legs around him too. My arms draped around his neck as he guided himself inside of me. Once he was fully in, we started to kiss, and I tasted myself on his lips, tasted what he'd done for me.

We rocked together as his arms reached around my back, moving as though he wanted me to get closer. We were as close as we had ever been, and having the weight of our break up off my shoulders allowed me to relax.

Our lips broke apart, our lungs searching for air. We weren't only fucking. We were in sync, rocking together, Ethan's shaft going as deep as it could and hitting the spot he'd been the first to find.

"I didn't realize how much I missed this—missed you," he stated.

My gaze locked with his, and I smiled warmly at him. "I know."

What would have happened if I had never got drunk at that party? Would we still be together? Would we have kids together? Married? Divorced? He was right, things did happen for a reason, but that didn't mean I wasn't sad about it. My heart ached for the twenty-some-odd years we'd missed.

I leaned back onto one hand, angling so that I could move faster and my pace quickened as I held onto his neck.

"Fuck," he hissed.

"I'm close," I panted. Ethan groaned and stilled my hips, coming as I climaxed around his cock, pulsing to work every drop from him.

After my body stopped convulsing, I wrapped both arms around his neck again and brought my lips to his. We stayed like that until he was ready for round two, and then round three in the shower before we both had to leave for work.

# CHAPTER NINE

O ver the next few days, Shawn and I retraced every hour
of the day and night Amy was murdered. The downstairs
neighbors heard nothing, and Heather's and her boyfriend's
cell phone records put both of them at his apartment from 5:30 p.m.
until about twenty minutes before the 9-1-1 call was placed by the next
door neighbor. Amy's cell phone put her in her apartment at the same
time. She'd apparently never left, and we had nothing. Abso-fucken-
lutley nothing.

"I don't like this," I sighed, throwing my pen onto my desk and
leaning back in my chair.

Shawn glanced up. "I don't either. It's too clean."

All we had to go on was the number of stab wounds. The ME
would take at least four weeks to get us a tox screen, so we could see
if anything in Amy's system might indicate if she was lucid during
the attack. For it to be such a clean murder scene, so to speak, I was
almost certain she had to be either restrained or unconscious.

Will from our cyber unit walked up to our desks. "I have something."

I perked up. "What is it?"

"Well, a little something," he replied.

"Spit it out, man," Shawn coaxed.

"Amy had a malware program installed on her computer, and
someone was using it to access her webcam."

My eyes widened. "Someone was watching her?"

"I need to dig further, but yes."

"Who?" Shawn questioned.

"That's what I'm trying to find out. It's going to take me some time because it seems like this guy knew what he was doing. The data was being routed and re-routed all over the place."

"Could it be more than one person?" I asked.

Will nodded slightly. "Possibly."

"Where are they logging in from?" Shawn inquired.

"That's the thing," Will replied. "The first IP I ran, traced back to Japan. The second one traced back to the Netherlands."

"We don't think her killer is from overseas, do we?" Shawn asked.

"Or, this guy's a pro and knows how to make the IP addresses ping from those places, but he's really here in Chicago."

"Can you find out?" I asked.

"I'm going to try, but it will take me some time," Will stated.

"Keep us updated," Shawn advised.

"Will do." Will turned and left.

"Well"—I stood—"I need to head out."

"Going to your girlfriend's?" Shawn sang as though to mock me. He knew about Reagan because Shawn and I were close given we'd been partners for seven years.

I chuckled. "No. Got the boys tonight for dinner."

"Oh, right. It's Wednesday."

"But after I take them home, I'll be going to Reagan's." I shrugged on my suit jacket.

He stood. "I should head home too. Julie's making fajitas."

Ever since my divorce from Jess, Shawn had made it a point to be more of a family man. We still had our work to do and thought about cases at home, but he didn't want Julia to feel like Jessica had felt. Jess had said she was leaving me because I was never there. I wasn't the husband *she* needed me to be. I might not have been the husband I should have been for her, but I was a damn good father. I made sure to always go to their sporting events, school functions—whatever—because we were a family, but I hadn't realized *she* needed a part of me too.

With Reagan, I wasn't going to make that mistake. I wanted to spend every waking hour with her. I wanted to make up for all the years we'd lost. I didn't care that we'd only been dating again for a few days. I wanted Reagan to be mine forever.

Pulling into the driveway at my old house, I put my F150 into park. The front door flew open as I got out of the truck, and Tyson, my five-year-old, came running out.

"Hey, buddy." I picked him up, hugging him as tight as I could. "You ready for pizza?" Tyson nodded, and I looked over his shoulder to see Cohen, my eight-year-old, walk out of the door. These boys were almost the spitting image of me with blond hair and blue eyes. Cohen was a little more cautious about things than his daredevil brother, but I assumed it was age. At five, you didn't really understand that riding your scooter down a hill could result in crashing and getting hurt.

I reached out an arm to bring Cohen in for a side hug. "Hungry?"

He nodded and stepped back. "Giovanni's?"

I grinned, still holding Tyson. "Of course."

My gaze flicked to the door again and I saw Jess standing in the threshold, arms crossed. For a split second, I thought I should set Tyson down, tell my kids to get into the truck, and go up to Jessica and tell her I was dating Reagan. I didn't, though. We were divorced, I wasn't planning on Reagan meeting my sons tonight, and honestly, fuck Jess. So instead, I gave her a nod and turned to get my kids into the cab of my truck.

After we ate almost an entire pie, I took my kids back to their place. Then I headed over to Reagan's, and my heart was happy. I'd gotten to spend time with my sons, and I was going to see my woman. It had been a long time since I'd been this excited about my life.

When I got to Reagan's door, I knocked, holding a pizza box with leftover deep dish slices inside. A few moments later, it swung open, and her smiling face greeted me.

"I need my own key," I stated.

She stepped back, letting me enter. "Yeah? Don't you think that's moving kind of fast?"

I cupped her smiling face with my free hand, running my thumb across her cheek and looking into her emerald eyes just as the door closed behind her. "Maybe, but you haven't given me back my key." I pressed my lips to hers, then stepped back.

"Do you want your key back?"

I handed her the leftover pizza. "No, Buttercup. That's the point I'm making. We may have just started over, but we're not at the beginning."

She took the pizza to the kitchen, and I followed as she placed it on the counter, taking a slice to put on a plate. "What point are we at?"

I smirked and wrapped my arm around her waist, pressing her back to my front. Sliding my hand down her belly, I toyed with the band of her jeans. "We can be at *this* point."

Reagan chuckled and turned, pushing me back. "I'm in the middle of my homework."

I cocked a brow. "So? We can *study*."

Her laugh made me grow even harder than I already was. "I'm almost done, and *then* we can *study*." She moved to her desk, where her laptop was already open, with a plate of the pepperoni deep dish I'd given her.

Groaning, I grabbed a beer from the fridge, and then went to the couch. After I settled in, I switched on the television to watch the Cubs game. Two minutes later, I felt her gaze on me. Reagan's desk was against the wall behind the couch, so I turned and looked over my shoulder at her. "What?"

"Remember how I told you I was doing homework?"

"Yeah?"

"You're watching TV."

"Yeah?"

"I can't concentrate with the TV on."

"I thought you were almost done?"

She rolled her beautiful green eyes. "I am."

"Then what's the big deal?"

"Are we about to have our first fight?"

I balked, and turned to face her completely, leaning my elbows on the back of the couch. "What? No!"

"Okay. Can you just give me fifteen-twenty minutes?"

"Why don't you let me help you?"

She smiled, and I was instantly at ease. I didn't want to fight with her. "I want to do this on my own. I'll ask you if I have questions."

"Okay." I shut off the TV and walked to her. I placed a kiss against her lips. "I'll go shower."

# Unknown

I needed a new woman to watch. No, I needed another victim. I had to stop thinking of them as women. They were prey—my reward in my new found game.

God, I loved being able to tap into a computer and see what they were doing through their webcam without their knowledge. It was easy, just like getting a key to Amy's apartment. Each student or staff member had a profile on LU's server. Of course, the access portal was different for each, but *I* still had access to them. Whenever new students or staff members started, they received an email with a link to change their password to something they only knew. Each link was coded and gave me their IP addresses plus their passwords. Most students and staff used their own computer to create the password. Of course, there was the off-chance someone used a library's computer or something, but I had enough female students to watch even if that happened.

Logging into the duplicate database I'd created, I started to scroll the names, filtering it to show me only the females who attended Lakeshore U. Their student body pictures were listed next to their names: Lisa Vitous, Ebonie Hill, Cherica Hasner, Sally Oey, Samantha Burch, Reagan McCormick. The first five were nowhere in sight when I logged into their webcams. But, Ms. McCormick—I got a real treat watching her.

I didn't get a good look at the man who walked up behind the brunette, but I continued to watch as he leaned down and whispered into her ear. I had to strain to hear him.

"Now?" he asked.

She pressed a button on her mouse, waited for a second, and then leaned her head against his chest. "Now."

The man moved fast, picking the pretty brunette up out of the chair and walking to the couch. It was then I realized who I was looking at. They say it's a small world, and as I watched the detective who worked on Amy's murder, I grinned. What were the odds? I never thought I'd have a front row seat for his personal life. The game just got even more exciting.

He pulled her T-shirt off. "You have too many clothes on."

She smiled and reached behind her back to free her breasts. "And now?"

"Still too much."

I had to agree.

Watching them was turning me. I continued to watch like a voyeur. Hell, I was. I'd watched Amy with a few men, knowing I could be better than them, but I didn't want this Reagan woman. That didn't stop me from slipping my hand into my underwear and touching myself slowly as she turned, straddled the detective, and positioned herself on his cock. I couldn't see her slide him inside of her because the back of the couch blocked my view, but the thought alone of her pussy being worked was enough for me.

"Fuck," he groaned.

My eyes stayed glued to her chest, watching her tits bounce up and down as she rode him. My hand moved faster, needing to match her pace. I had to admit that even though I was looking for someone else to watch, I didn't expect to get so lucky—and so fast. They started kissing, obstructing my view of her boobs, but I continued to work myself up as I looked on. This was better than any porn I'd ever watched. Knowing that—*at this exact moment*—*those* two people were fucking was making me hot, and I wasn't going to stop watching until they were done.

Reagan came with a jerk and a loud moan, bringing me back into the present. I wondered how far away from me she was being fucked. Could she be in my building? Down the street? Across town? I made a mental note to check the university's files and find out Reagan's address because I was curious.

As I watched the detective stand and Reagan turn to lean across the back of the couch, I decided I wanted them to know I was watching them. They'd never find me, of course. If they caught on that it had something to do with me watching them through their webcam, my VPN would get traced back to China. Or Japan. Or The Netherlands. Or France. Or …

They'd never find me.

The detective lined himself up and sank into her from behind. Doggie was my favorite. Watching a woman being fucked hard, balls slapping, made me come fast each time I watched it. I was close, my hand coated with my arousal as I moved it faster and faster. Just as I was on the edge, Reagan looked up at the computer as though she knew I was watching her. Our eyes locked …

And then I came.

As I watched them finish, I knew what I needed to do. Reagan McCormick was going to get a wood plaque from me.

# CHAPTER TEN

*Reagan*

Working, going to school, and dating a new guy made me feel as though I was in my twenties again. But juggling it all was exhausting.

Honestly, I loved the fact that Ethan was my boyfriend. I'd always loved him. I *still* did. Every moment we spent together, that love grew stronger. He'd said we weren't at the beginning stages, and I had to agree, but, I wondered if it was too soon to tell him that I still loved him.

I never thought I'd want to get married again, but while Ethan and I had just rekindled our relationship, a part of me always felt as though we would marry one day, though I never thought it would be with us both divorced and in our forties. But what if Ethan never wanted to get married again? What if he didn't want something long term? I'd yet to meet his kids, so maybe that was my answer. Maybe we were just killing time. If Maddie were in town, I would have introduced them. Of course, she was older and could handle her mom having a new boyfriend, while Ethan's boys were little and probably didn't understand why Daddy and Mommy didn't live together anymore.

Until I knew where our relationship was going, I was going to enjoy it. We'd been dating again for almost a month, and the sex was better than it was when we were teenagers. Of course, it was because we knew what we were doing this go around, and what we wanted. I couldn't get enough of him, which was why I made sure to wake up each morning with his alarm even though I didn't have class until ten.

I wanted to see him off, wish him good luck on whatever case he was working, and make sure his day got off to a *good* start.

We fell back against the pillows, both out of breath. "Who needs a gym when we wake up like this?"

I smiled. "Exactly."

Ethan crawled out of bed. "I mean, sex twice a day is great cardio."

"It sure is."

He walked over and kissed my lips softly. "Go back to sleep, baby. I'll see you tonight at Judy's."

"Okay." I smiled and pulled the sheet up, ready to get another hour of sleep because I hadn't gotten *much* the night before.

Judy's was slammed.

It usually was on a Friday night, and I made good money, which made it all worth it. Once I got my certificate, I'd find a job assisting at crime scenes, and I wouldn't need to work at the bar. I was looking forward to only working crime scenes and following my dreams. While I didn't know what hours I'd be working, I pictured having dinners with Ethan every night, and I imagined us having lazy weekends when we caught up on TV or took a weekend trip somewhere—depending on his caseload, of course.

"Need anything?" Derrick questioned after he restocked clean glasses.

"Ice, please." I didn't look over at him as I keyed in the drink I'd just made for a customer.

He stepped closer to me. "Do you like to eat ice?"

I balked at his question and turned my head to look over at him. "Why?"

He shrugged. "I heard once that if you eat ice, you're sex deprived."

I chuckled. "Nope, don't eat ice."

"So, your boyfriend is giving it to you good?"

I stopped and fully turned to face Derrick. He had been flirting with me since day one, and I would always brush it off, but it was getting tiresome. I got within an inch of him and leaned forward to whisper into his ear, "Nightly."

"What can I getcha?" I asked as I turned to face the new customer at the bar. He was about my age with dark brown hair and dark eyes.

"Whiskey, neat."

"Any brand in particular?"

He looked up at the bottles lined up behind me, and I turned to see that Derrick had walked off. "Redbreast."

I reached for the bottle of whiskey and poured a glass for him. "Here alone?"

He smiled. "Is it that obvious?"

I chuckled. "No. Just making small talk."

"Fair enough."

I slid the amber liquor to him, exchanging it for the money he handed me.

"Are you having a nice night?"

"Just a bit busy," I replied as I finished the transaction on the POS system.

"That's good, right?"

"It is. Let me know when you need another." I moved to the next customer. "Refill?"

The blonde looked to her martini glass and then met my gaze. "Sure, why not?"

As I began to make her cosmo, I noticed the man next to her stared at her as though he was waiting for her to look over at him. She was alone, he was alone, and we were in a bar where people seemed to meet their soulmates. At least that was what Ethan had told me about his sister and her husband. In the time Ethan and I had been back together, I hadn't seen Ashtyn. When we were kids, she and I hadn't been friends. She was five years younger than me, and at that age, five years was a huge difference, but I liked her. Ethan also had a younger brother, Carter, who was the middle child and two years younger than me. He was a doctor, and I had yet to see him either. I wondered if they knew Ethan and I were back together. What would they think? What would his parents think?

Before I could try to play matchmaker, the man who consumed my thoughts walked in through the door of Judy's. Our gazes locked and we smiled at each other. My heart beat faster, the blood flowing with excitement.

"Hey," Ethan greeted, leaning against a tiny open space of the bar next to me.

"Hey yourself." I wanted to kiss him, to pull the lapel of his jacket and drag him over the bartop and plant my lips on his, but I didn't think that was appropriate with a bar full of people. So, instead, I poured him a beer from the tap and slid it to him. "How was work?"

He shrugged and took a sip of the dark beer. "If I tell you, I'll have to kill you."

I chuckled. "We wouldn't want that."

"No, we wouldn't." He winked and took another sip.

I blushed like a teenager. As I did, I noticed Whiskey Neat was staring at me and not the blonde anymore. "Need another?" I asked him.

His dark gaze flicked toward Ethan and then back to me. He slid his glass forward. "Sure. One more for the road."

I poured him his whiskey, and was about to play matchmaker when a group of three women swamped the blonde, making my night even busier until it was time to walk to Ethan's for the night.

Ethan and I had breakfast in bed on the weekends he didn't have his boys. Afterward, he'd watch TV or work on the case he was investigating while I did homework or looked over my notes from the week, then we'd have lunch before I had to get ready to head to the bar. Okay, maybe there was sex between breakfast and lunch. We were in the *beginning* stages of our relationship, and we couldn't keep our hands off of each other. I wasn't complaining.

Not one bit.

"Next weekend …" Ethan trailed off.

I raised my head from his bare chest and placed my chin on his sternum to look into his dark blue eyes. "Yeah?"

He took a deep breath. "I have my kids again."

"I know. I'll stay at my place like I did last weekend."

He started to play with my hair absently. "That's …" He paused. "That's not what I'm getting at."

"Okay? Then what are you getting at?"

"I ah …" Ethan paused again. "I've never had to do this before."

I grinned. "Are you saying you want me to meet them?"

He smiled back. "Yeah, that's what I'm trying to ask."

I straddled his hips. "I would love to."

"Of course, I need to tell Jessica first."

"I understand." Having Ethan ask me to meet his kids was huge. That meant we weren't just having fun, we were serious. I kissed him. "Does anyone else know we're back together?"

"You mean my family?"

I nodded. "Yeah. I mean, if I'm meeting your boys, then they should probably know too."

Ethan pulled me down, making me squeal as he rolled us over so he was on top of me. "Don't worry about them, Buttercup. They'll be fine with it."

"Are you sure?"

"Not gonna lie. They know you broke my heart, but they'll get over it."

My heart sank. "I broke my own heart too."

He pressed his lips to mine. "I know. We don't need to rehash it. They'll think it's fate since Ash met Rhys at Judy's."

"Then we should do dinner or something with them. I'd love to see them again."

He grinned. "Yeah?"

I snorted. "We're not kids anymore, honey. I can handle meeting— well, re-meeting—your family." Even if they faulted me for hurting their son, it had all worked out, right? I mean, he'd met Jessica and had kids. It wasn't as though he'd been mourning the loss of me for twenty-three years.

Ethan kissed me again. "Okay. I'll set it up and let you know."

Everything was falling into place. At least, I assumed so. "Then, there's one more thing to do."

"What's that?"

I rolled us so I was straddling him again, and then I reached for my purse on the nightstand. "You should have a key to my place." I pulled out my keys and slipped one off.

He took it from me. "It's about time."

It wasn't that I hadn't wanted him to have a key to my place. I still had his key, and I trusted him with my life. I just hadn't had one to give him because Maddison had my spare, so I had an extra one cut on Wednesday while he was with his boys.

"Yep. Now, shut up and kiss me."

Every morning, before I started my first class, I'd swing by the coffee shop on campus for a latte even though I'd have a cup of coffee as I got ready each morning. I needed extra caffeine to get me through the day. While in some ways I felt as though I was in my twenties, I wasn't, and getting little sleep was starting to get to me. I wasn't going to stop anything, though, because I loved my mornings with Ethan.

"Good morning, Reagan. The usual?" Krystal, the barista, asked.

I smiled. It was clear I came here five mornings a week. "Yes, thank you." I handed her my credit card. When I turned around, I ran into someone. "Sorry," I muttered.

"It's okay," a man replied.

I looked up, meeting the dark gaze of Whiskey Neat, and smiled warmly. "Oh."

There was a slight pause as though he was trying to place me as well. "You're the bartender from Judy's, right?"

I grinned and nodded. "I am."

"I thought you looked familiar when I walked in."

"Do you—go here?" I didn't want to assume he worked at the college since I was a student myself. Maybe he was getting a degree for his dream job too.

"Actually, I work here."

"Of course." I smiled again.

"Do *you* go here?"

"I do." I bobbed my head.

"Oh? What's your major?"

"For now, getting my certificate in crime scene investigation."

He balked as though that wasn't what he expected me to say. "You like murder or something?"

I chuckled. "It's always been something that interested me."

He stepped closer to me and lowered his voice. "So, are you a murderer?"

"What?" I laughed. "No! I want to solve them, not commit them."

"Not to be too forward, but I wouldn't mind you tying me up."

*What?*

"Reagan, your vanilla latte," Krystal called.

I went to the counter, grabbed my drink, and turned back to Whiskey Neat. "Have a good day."

He smiled kindly. "You too."

I left the coffee shop, walking out into the slight wind. It was starting to get colder because autumn was approaching.

The time I would walk to class, I spent it calling Maddison. It had been a few days since I'd last spoken to her because I tried to let her have weekends to just be a teenager in college, so I dialed her cell, knowing that she had a break at this time.

"Hey, Mom," she greeted when she answered the phone.

"Hey, baby. How was your weekend?"

"It was good."

"Go to any good parties?"

I heard her laugh on the other end. "I did."

"Just be careful." I took a sip of my latte.

"I am. Are *you* being careful? You're in college too."

I chuckled. "Don't think these kids want a forty-one-year-old at their parties."

"They'd probably be too drunk to even notice your age."

"Maybe." I smiled and took another sip. "Before I go, there's something I need to tell you."

"Okay?"

I took a deep breath. Not because I didn't want to tell her I was dating Ethan, but because I hadn't seriously dated anyone since her father and I had split. "I'm dating someone."

There was a slight pause. "It's not a student, is it?"

I snorted. "What? No!"

"Is it someone from the bar you work at?"

"Well, kinda. He doesn't work there, though."

"He's a customer?"

"He's … He's more than that."

"What do you mean?"

I took a quick sip of my coffee. "A few weeks ago, my boyfriend from high school walked into the bar, and ever since, we've been dating again."

"What? Mom! That's—that's amazing!"

My shoulders instantly dropped, tension leaving my body, and I grinned, thinking of Ethan. "Yeah, it is."

"Do I get to meet him over Thanksgiving?"

"Hope so."

Maddie was coming to visit me for Thanksgiving. For Christmas break, she was spending the holiday with her father in Denver, and the rest of the time with me until she had to go back to school at the end of January. I'd assumed she would want to spend more time in Colorado with her old friends from high school, but she had decided she wanted to be in Chicago. I wasn't going to tell her no. I was excited for her to meet Ethan, and I was excited to meet his boys.

This wasn't how I pictured life would be when Ethan and I dated before, but now that we were back together, I wouldn't change anything.

# CHAPTER ELEVEN

I wasn't nervous for Reagan to see my family again. They knew she had broken my heart, but I also knew they'd liked her when we were kids. People grow, we change, we move on. That was clear when it came to how I felt about Jessica. Sure, she was my sons' mother, but what I'd felt for Jess was nothing compared to what I'd felt or still feel for Reagan.

Once a month, my family made sure to have dinner together, and because I had the boys on Wednesday nights, we tried to make it that night of the week. Sometimes Rhys missed them if there was a Blackhawks' game, or even Carter if he had a surgery or something, but for the most part, we were able to get together.

I wanted to add one more person to that family dinner.

*"Hey, Mom,"* I'd said when I had called her on Monday morning.

*"Hey, sweetie. Everything okay?"*

*"Yeah. I was calling to—to tell you that I'm bringing more than the boys to dinner on Wednesday."*

*"Oh?"* she'd breathed.

*"Remember Reagan?"*

*"Reagan Hunter?"* She hadn't skipped a beat.

I'd smiled. *"Well, she has a different last name now."*

*"Because she's married?"*

*"Divorced."*

*"Oh?"* she'd said again. This time I'd detected a hint of hope in her voice, and I was put at ease.

*"We're um … dating again."*

She'd inhaled a sharp breath. *"You are?"*

I'd smiled and confirmed. *"We are."*

*"I'm so happy for you,"* she'd gushed. *"I can't wait to see her again."*

*"We'll be there for Wednesday dinner."*

"All right." I stood from my desk and grabbed my suit jacket. "I'll see you in the morning," I stated to Shawn.

He looked at his watch. "Shit. I didn't realize it was already five."

We'd been working every hour on duty trying to solve Amy's case, but we still had nothing. We were hoping a witness would come forward, but nothing had happened yet, and the webcam traces had led to nothing. The person—or people—was just too good at masking their actual location, and none of the IP addresses were linked to any leads.

"When do I get to meet her?"

I had started to head to the door, but Shawn's question stopped me. I turned to face him. "Who? Reagan?"

He nodded. "Yeah."

I smirked. "Monday."

"What's happening Monday?"

Oh, right. With everything going on, I'd apparently forgotten to tell him about the ride-along. Plus, the weeks had flown by. "I'm taking her on a ride-along."

"Oh yeah?"

"Yeah, you want to tag along too?"

"Sure." He grinned. "We can give her the full experience and have her ride in the back of a squad car."

I chuckled. "Yeah, she'd like that."

We said our goodbyes, and I drove to Reagan's, needing to pick her up before I grabbed the boys on the way to my parents'. After I'd hung up the phone with my mom about bringing Reagan to our family dinner, I'd called Jessica. I didn't need her permission to introduce them to Reagan, but I did it out of respect for her. We'd been separated and divorced for long enough. Plus, she was already dating again too.

*"Hello?"* she'd answered.

*"Hey, it's me."*

*"What's up?"*

I'd taken a deep breath and just laid it out there. *"I'm dating someone, and she's coming to Wednesday night dinner at my parents."*

Silence had filled the other end of the line.

*"Jess?"*

*"Sorry."* Another pause. *"Are you asking for my permission?"*

*"No. I'm telling you that the boys are going to meet my new—well, not really new girlfriend."*

*"Then they'll meet my boyfriend."*

*"Okay."* I'd nodded. *"Whatever you want to do."*

As I pulled into the parking garage of Reagan's building, I realized I was early, and she wasn't downstairs waiting for me as per the plan, but that was okay. I had a key.

Letting myself in, I opened the door. Reagan was at her desk on her laptop. "Almost done, Buttercup?"

She glanced at the screen, probably the time and then responded, "Yep. Just need to hit save and then get my shoes on."

I walked up behind her, and she turned her head, looking back at me. I lowered my lips to hers. "I hope you're hungry. Mom likes to go a little overboard."

"Starving, actually."

"Good. Oh, and I got the approval for the ride-along. Monday, after you're done with class, we'll take a few hours and see what happens."

"Yay!" she squealed, standing and wrapping her arms around my neck. "You just made this night even better."

"Good. Now, time to meet and re-meet all the Valors. Plus Rhys."

"And Jessica."

I blinked. "Jessica?"

"Well, I'm assuming she's going to come outside and want to check me out."

I groaned and looked up at the ceiling briefly before responding. "Yeah, I guess she will. You know, to make sure you're not a murderer or anything even though I'm a cop and shit."

Reagan laughed. "Monday, I had a guy ask if I was a murderer."

I balked. "Really? Why?"

She took a step back. "It was a customer of Judy's. He works on campus or something."

I furrowed my brows. "And how did the conversation turn into you being a killer?"

She chuckled again and walked into her bedroom. I followed. "He asked what my major was, and I told him I was doing CSI. He teased me and asked if I was into murder."

I leaned against the doorjamb, watching her as she slid on her boots. "Did you tell him that your *boyfriend is* a cop and he wouldn't like that?"

"Nope, didn't get that far."

"If you see him again, make sure you tell him."

Reagan stood and cupped my cheeks in her warm hands. She smiled. "You have nothing to worry about. You're the only man I want."

"Good." I didn't mean to get all possessive, but I wasn't about to lose Reagan a second time. I never wanted to be without her again.

"Can I act possessively when we pick up the boys?" she teased, moving past me toward the kitchen table where her purse was.

"Only when it comes to Jess and not my boys."

"Trust me, I know your boys are your priority."

"They are," I agreed. I hooked a thumb over my shoulder as I followed her to the front door. "Don't you need to turn off your laptop?"

"No. It's plugged in and will go to sleep on its own."

I grabbed her wrist, stopping her. Rubbing the back of my neck, I said, "I'd feel better if you turned it off."

She blinked. "Why?"

"I'm working on a case now, and it appears someone was watching my vic through her webcam."

Reagan gasped. "Seriously?"

"Yeah. In fact, to put me at ease, we're going to cover up your built-in camera with black tape or something when we get back."

I didn't think anyone was watching Reagan but knowing someone *could* watch anyone through their webcam—and without them knowing—made my skin crawl.

Especially thinking about someone watching Reagan.

We pulled up to my old house, and I took a deep breath after turning off the engine of my F150. "Ready?" I questioned.

"Of course. I'm excited to meet the spawn of Ethan Valor."

I chuckled, and we both got out of the truck. Unlike most weeks, my kids didn't come running out of the house. I knew it was because Jess was being a bitch and keeping them inside to make me bring Reagan up to the door.

I grabbed my girlfriend's hand and knocked. It felt weird knocking on a door I used to have a key to, for a house I used to own, but I wasn't going to show Jessica that her little game got to me.

It didn't.

The door swung open, and Tyson was there, smiling from ear to ear. Dropping Reagan's hand, I knelt and engulfed my youngest in my arms. "Hey, buddy."

"Mommy said you have a girlfriend."

I chuckled and looked up at Reagan. She was looking down, smiling. "Yeah, this is Reagan, my girlfriend."

She knelt, too. "It's nice to finally meet you, Tyson. Your daddy told me you like to go fast on your scooter."

He bobbed his head rapidly with a huge grin across his face.

Cohen stepped outside and gave me a quick hug. "Hey, champ. This is Reagan."

Reagan pointed at Cohen. "And you love to play memory match games and Uno. Your daddy told me there's no way I'd ever beat you at either game. Especially match game."

He smiled slowly. "It's true."

We both stood. Jessica had appeared in the doorway. "Jess." I nodded.

"Hi, I'm Reagan." Reagan stuck out her hand, a huge smile across her face. "It's nice to meet you."

"Right," Jess clipped but stuck out her hand. They shook.

"All right. Time to go to Grandma and Grandpa's," I stated and grabbed Tyson's hand.

"Bye, Mom," they both called over their shoulders.

After I got them buckled in, I slid into the driver's seat and cranked the engine. "That went well."

Reagan chuckled sarcastically. "If looks could kill."

"Right." Women were weird. I still didn't understand them, and I was forty-two. Jessica left *me*. She didn't want me, but I suppose she didn't want me with anyone else either. Women and their games.

The boys were on their iPads the entire time I drove to my parents' house. I was certain Regan's reunion with my folks would go the same way. *Easy.*

"Who wants hot dogs?" I sang, looking in the rearview mirror at my sons.

"I do!" they both called back.

"We're having hot dogs?" Reagan asked.

"What? You don't like mystery meat?" I chuckled.

"I do. Chili dogs are a favorite."

"Then what's the problem?"

"No problem. I was just wondering."

"Hot dogs are for the boys. Dad's grilling tri-tip, and Mom's probably making enough sides to feed an army." Dad's butcher always gave him the California cut of beef known as tri-tip. My dad had it once on a trip to California and introduced us to it. It was fucking delicious and juicy, and I loved when he grilled it for us.

"They still live here?" Reagan asked as I pulled up to the house I grew up in.

"Yep." I cut the engine.

We all got out, Cohen running ahead since he didn't use a car seat he needed help getting out of. Tyson ran past us, and both of my boys entered the house without knocking. I was sure they were making a beeline to Rhys like they always did, wondering if he brought them something with the Blackhawks logo on it.

"Last chance to back out," I teased.

Reagan snorted. "Seriously, what could go wrong?"

Famous last words, right?

# CHAPTER TWELVE

*Reagan*

We walked hand in hand up the walkway to the house I'd lost my virginity in.

The night it had happened, Carter was at a friend's house, and Ethan's parents were at a school play Ashtyn was performing in. It was dark out, and the only light source inside was the TV. Ethan and I had been making out on the couch. We went from kissing in the living room to going up to his room.

He flicked the light on as we'd walked in. *"Are you sure about this?"* he'd asked.

I'd nodded. *"Yes. I want to share all my firsts with you."*

*"But we can wait until you're ready."*

*"I am ready. I promise."*

We'd started kissing again. Ethan laid me down on the bed and turned off his light. When I'd opened my eyes, I saw the glow of plastic stars illuminating the ceiling.

*"You have glow-in-the-dark stars?"* I'd asked, even though I was staring at them.

He'd sighed, and I could briefly make out that he was staring up at the ceiling too. *"Ashtyn gave them to me for my birthday a few years ago. She was eight, and I couldn't tell her that a fourteen-year-old boy didn't want stars on his ceiling. She made me put them up."*

*"And you've kept them?"* I'd grinned, looking back up at the neon green stars because he *had* kept them up. He was a good older brother.

*"She would have whined if I took them down. She got stars for her and Carter too."*

*"I'd always wanted my first time to be under the stars. This is ... perfect."*

We didn't speak much after that, but my first time was amazing, and when I thought about that night, I always remembered the stars that I'd looked at over his shoulder as he'd made love to me the first time. Over the years, when I would stare up at the black night sky with real stars flickering, I would think about Ethan and wonder what he was doing.

Walking into the familiar house, which smelled like home cooking, I felt as though I was walking into my family's home and not the home of strangers. It seemed as though everyone was waiting in the living room when we crossed the threshold. Ethan's mom was the first to stand, a huge smile across her face as she moved toward us.

"Reagan!" She wrapped me in her arms. "It's so good to see you again."

I smiled. "Hi, Mrs. Valor. It's good to see you again too."

She pulled back, keeping her hands on my arms. "We're both adults now. You can call me Shannon."

"Okay." I grinned wider. She gave me another hug before moving to the side. Ethan's father, Glen, was next, and I hugged him hello as well. Then Carter and his wife, Rachel, took turns shaking my hand.

"It's good to see you again," Carter greeted.

"You too."

Ashtyn stepped forward next, a sleeping baby on her shoulder. Ethan had mentioned to me that Ashtyn had given birth to her daughter a month or so before and was still on maternity leave. "I was too young to really remember you, but I do sort of. It's nice to meet you again."

I smiled, and we hugged gently to not disturb the baby. "I remember you, and yes, it's nice to meet you again. Who's this?" I ran my finger along the back of the soft baby hand.

"This is our daughter. And this is my husband, Rhys."

Rhys stood, and I shook his hand. "Nice to meet you."

"You too," he replied.

"Your daughter is beautiful."

"Thank you," Ashtyn replied.

"What's her name?"

"Jeremy," Rhys advised.

I smiled, looking around the room briefly because I wasn't sure if I'd heard the name correctly. Jeremy for a girl? I turned my attention back to Ashtyn and Rhys. "Jeremy?"

"Named her after my idol," Rhys answered. "And we know it's unusual for a girl to be named Jeremy, but we don't care. We named our son after Glen's father—Ashtyn's choice—and it was my turn to pick for our daughter."

"I think it's cute," I stated. I knew there were girls named Spencer, Ryan, Avery, Billie, Blake, and more.

"We think so too." Ashtyn kissed the top of Jeremy's fuzzy head. My heart smiled. I missed having a newborn baby in my life. It had been several years, of course, given that Maddison would be nineteen in a few months, but the woman in me melted at the tender moment.

The kids had run off down a set of stairs to what I assumed was the basement playroom. It was a playroom the last time I'd seen it. You could hear the laughter and giggles coming up the stairs, and my heart warmed further. The Valors seemed to have a close, happy family, and I loved that. My parents only saw Maddie on holidays and a few weeks out of the summer months when she was growing up. They were in Chicago while we lived in Denver, and now they lived in Florida, which was still far away from Michigan and Illinois.

"Now that we've gotten the pleasantries out of the way, is dinner almost ready?" Ethan asked, wrapping an arm around my shoulders.

"Just waiting on the meat," Shannon replied as she looked over at Glen.

Glen looked at his watch. "Fifteen minutes until we can pull it off. Then let it rest for ten minutes more."

"Great. Enough time for a beer or two," Ethan stated. "You want one?"

"Sure," I replied and followed him.

After everyone had drinks, all the guys went into the backyard, leaving me with the ladies and a sleeping Jeremy in a playpen. I was fine staying in the warm house while the guys did whatever they did in the chilly backyard. Plus, it gave me time to get to know Ethan's mother and sister again.

"So," Ashtyn spoke up as she helped Shannon grab ingredients from the fridge to make some of the side dishes. "Did you meet Jess?"

"I did." I watched Ashtyn share *a look* with Rachel. "What?" I asked.

"She was always stuck-up," Rachel replied. Clearly, she didn't care that she was talking crap about a previous family member. "I can only imagine how she treated *the other woman.*"

I looked at Shannon quickly, trying to gauge if she felt the same way. She shrugged, not saying anything as she tossed a salad. I took a sip of my beer. "She said one word to me and shook my hand."

"Was it a curse word?" Ashtyn asked.

I chuckled. "Like *bitch*?"

"That's the one," she replied.

"No. I introduced myself, said it was nice to meet her, and she replied 'right.'"

"That's all she said?" Rachel asked.

I snorted. "That's all she said with her words." I didn't want to talk ill about Ethan's ex-wife—the mother of his children—but she was obviously bitter that Ethan was dating again. From the moment Tyson opened the door, Jessica had glared at me, assessing me the entire time.

"She's totally cursing you," Ashtyn replied.

"She's probably making a voodoo doll of you as we speak," Rachel joked.

"Yeah, but I had him first and will have him last." I didn't know if the latter was the truth. We hadn't uttered the L-word to each other since being back together, but I didn't want to have a life again without him in it. I couldn't imagine what would have happened if he had still been married when we reconnected, but I knew I would fight tooth and nail for him.

Before anything else was said, the guys came in with the tri-tip. The kids were set up at a special table, and the rest of us sat at the dining room table. We ate, we drank a little, and we laughed.

"You two want to go to karaoke?" Rhys asked, motioning to Ethan and me with his fork.

"Yes! It will be so much fun. Come." Ashtyn beamed.

"Some of us have work in the morning," Ethan replied.

"And school," I went on.

"Pa-lease," Rhys tsked and rolled his eyes. "When was the last time you got that stick out of your ass, Eth?"

I swallowed my laugh. Ethan was the oldest out of all of us except his parents, and he was a cop. I could sense he was always aware of his surroundings, and because of his protectiveness that meant he did have a little stick up his ass, so to speak. But I knew him differently. When we were alone, locked in one of our condos, fun Ethan appeared. The *real* Ethan Valor.

"Would you want a hungover cop investigating your murder?" Ethan retorted.

"We said karaoke, not bar hopping," Ashtyn stated. "It's our first night out since we had Jeremy. A night out will be fun."

Ethan leaned forward, resting his elbows on the table. "Okay, but to get me up on a stage to sing, I need to be drunk."

"Do you want to come?" Ashtyn asked me, ignoring her brother.

"I …" I hadn't been out on the town, so to speak, in forever. I'd never sung karaoke either, but I did want to go. I wanted to have fun. But I also knew Ethan needed to be at his precinct at eight a.m. I looked over at Ethan next to me. "I would like to, but I know you need to get up early."

"Just come," Rhys pressed. "The latest we'll be out is eleven— midnight, tops."

"And the kids?" Ethan asked.

"We've offered to watch them while they go out tonight," Shannon chimed in.

"I have to get the boys back by eight," Ethan stated. It was seven.

"Drop them off and then meet us at the bar," Ashtyn suggested. "You live right down the street."

Ethan looked over at me again. I shrugged. "It could be fun."

His gaze moved to Carter. "Don't look at us," Carter protested. "I'm on call, remember?"

"If I'm going, you're going," Ethan stated. "You can come sing and shit."

"We're in!" Rachel exclaimed, not waiting for her husband to answer.

"Then it's settled. We're all going," Rhys declared.


I left with Ethan to drop the boys off. While he went to the door at Jessica's, I waited in the truck. Jessica was at the door again, talking to Ethan with her arms crossed. They talked longer than I would have liked, but they had kids together, and I couldn't let it get to me.

After several minutes, Ethan finally slid back into the cab. "Everything okay?" I asked.

He chuckled and started the engine. "She's jealous."

"Of me?"

"Of us."

"But she divorced you," I reminded him—as though he needed that reminder.

He started to drive down the street. "She doesn't want to see me happy."

I smirked, looking over at him as the streetlights cast an orange glow into the truck, one after the other. "You're happy?"

He grinned, laced our fingers, and then kissed the back of my hand. "More than happy, Buttercup."

"Me, too."

We were silent for a few moments before Ethan let go of my hand and pulled over into another subdivision.

"What—"

"I need ... I need to tell you something." He put the truck into park and cut the engine.

I swallowed. "Okay?"

He turned slightly to face me the best he could, given he was still strapped into his seatbelt. I was instantly nervous. We'd had just had an amazing dinner with his family and were on our way to hang out with his siblings and their spouses. This was what I'd imagined life would be like with Ethan Valor. But then the longer I waited for him to speak, the more I second-guessed everything. He'd just told me that he was happy, but why did he seem nervous? Did he want to break my heart like I had broken his?

Ethan grabbed my hand again. "This isn't where I wanted to do this, but I can't wait any longer."

I swallowed again, looking down at my lap. "Just tell me. We're both adults. I can handle it."

"I'm not breaking up with you."

My gaze darted to his. I could barely see his eyes in the dark of night, but there was enough light that I could see that he was smiling. My heart instantly started to slow as a wave of relief washed over me. "You're not?"

"God, no." He shook his head.

"Then, why are you nervous? Why are we on the side of the road?"

"I just can't hold it in anymore. I need to tell you …" He took a deep breath.

"Yeah?" I prompted.

Ethan cupped my cheek with his warm hand, brushing his thumb across my bottom lip. "I just want you to know that I'm still in love with you, Buttercup. I don't think I ever stopped, and I don't want my ex-wife to get between us. That's over. Been over for years, and I don't want anyone except you. I've always wanted you. Only you."

I melted. Right there in the front seat of his Ford F150, I liquefied. I knew that if I needed to get out of the high cab, I would fall onto the ground because my knees felt so weak. I smiled warmly. "I still love you too."

"Yeah?" He grinned.

"As you've said before, we're not in the beginning stages of our relationship. It's hard to know if we're moving too fast, but what I do know is that I have never stopped loving you."

Without another word, he leaned forward and pressed his lips to mine. Our mouths worked together as though a weight had been lifted, and we were *finally* able to express how we felt about each other. I poured everything into that kiss. Telling him I was sorry for breaking his heart all those years ago. Sharing my jealousy of what he'd had with Jessica: marriage, babies—she had his last name. And me—me just loving him in that kiss.

When we needed to come up for air, we broke apart, but Ethan kept our foreheads touching. "You just made this the best night of my life."

"Even better than when Cohen and Tyson were born?" I teased with a grin.

Ethan smiled, pulling his head back. "Okay, the births of my sons and tonight are all tied."

"What about the first time we had sex? Or the lunch—"

He took my mouth again, silencing me. "Fine. Tonight is *one* of the best nights of my life."

I grinned. "Mine too."

He kissed me again quickly. "We better go before Rhys blows up my phone."

I chuckled. "He does seem like the type to question why we're late."

Ethan started the truck again and pulled away from the curb. "He's a good guy and loves my sister. Treats her well too. That's all that matters."

It didn't take long to get to the karaoke bar where we were meeting everyone. Ashtyn and Rhys had told me they met the owner, Otis, a few years back, and they were able to get free drinks whenever they came in. It was also walking distance to Ethan's condo, which was a bonus.

After we parked in Ethan's building's parking garage, we walked a few blocks to the bar. It felt good, walking hand in hand, knowing that he loved me—still loved me. It gave me hope that everything was how it was meant to be. It sucked that we'd had twenty-three years apart, that we'd started our own families separately, but life didn't always go as planned.

The bar was packed when we walked in. Judy's was rustic, but Otis's karaoke bar was what I would call swanky. It was dimly lit with plush, brown leather, half-moon booths facing a stage. The bar had lighting under the bartop, making it look elegant and sleek. It wasn't what I expected a karaoke bar to look like, but more like a jazz club.

"Next to the stage is Rhys," the DJ stated as we walked farther in, searching for Ethan's family. Cheers erupted, and my gaze immediately flicked to the booth where the four of them were sitting.

"Looks like we're just in time," I observed. Ethan led us to the table as Rhys took the stage.

"You made it!" Ashtyn yelled excitedly. The three of them made room for Ethan and me. "You're next, big brother."

Ethan laughed. "Yeah, fucking right. My ass isn't getting up there."

"We'll see about that." She smirked.

Music started to play, and Rhys began to sing. I didn't know the song, but I looked at the screen as he sang: "Downtown" by Majical Cloudz. The band name and title still didn't ring a bell, but the lyrics sounded good to me, and they were perfect for how I assumed Rhys felt for Ashtyn. While he sang, he looked at his wife, causing her to beam ear to ear as she watched. I envied her. I wanted a husband of three or so years who still looked at me like that.

Carter slid out of the booth. "I'm going to the bar. What can I get you all?"

"I thought you were on call?" Ethan questioned.

"Shh," Ashtyn scolded. "Rhys is singing. Just bring us all back shots or something."

Carter left, and by the time the song was over, he was back with a round of Fireball shots for all of us except himself. Rhys slid into the booth, snatching a shot glass.

Ethan shook his head and pushed the cinnamon whisky away. "I have work in the morning."

"Loosen that stick." Rhys smirked at him.

"We all have work. Just take a shot," Ashtyn coaxed.

I shrugged as Ethan looked over at me. "It's not like we do this every night."

Ethan groaned and grabbed his shot glass. Without another word, we cheered and downed the shots of Fireball. A few songs later, Ashtyn sang. We did more shots, and before we knew it, we were all buzzed. Rhys sang again, Rachel sang, and they kept trying to get me and Ethan to get up there.

"It's your turn, big brother," Ashtyn stated as she slid the sign-up sheet and book of song choices in front of him.

He looked at me as though to ask if he should. "If you do it, I'll do it," I offered.

Rachel and Ashtyn started to chant, "Do it. Do it. Do it."

Ethan sighed. "One song and that's it. I never want to do this again."

I smirked. I'd had a feeling he'd do it, but that also meant I had to sing too. It was later in the night, maybe close to midnight, and I was hopeful that everyone was drunk and wouldn't make fun of me. I didn't have a good singing voice—not like Rhys and Ashtyn who clearly sang karaoke often.

Ethan took some time picking out a song while he sipped a beer. I looked over his shoulder, still not having a clue what I was going to sing. "All right." He chugged the rest of his beer and then kissed my lips. "I'm ready."

I grinned like a fool as I watched him turn and make his way to the DJ. He handed him the sign-up sheet and then walked up onto stage. The moment the guitar started to strum, I knew exactly what song Ethan had chosen. It wasn't a song from our past or the ones we'd danced to at prom. It was a more recent song, and I loved it. The style—the words—everything about the song *was* Ethan. He was forty-two and rustic in his own way. I wouldn't say he was an old soul, but he was country. He drove a truck after all.

Ethan started to sing about love being more precious than gold. That it couldn't be bought or sold. When he sang the next verse, the one about having a woman with eyes that shined, his gaze locked with mine and my heart melted for the second time that night. When Rhys had sung to Ashtyn, I was jealous, wanting to know what it was like to have a man sing to me. I had that now because, at that moment, Ethan was singing to me from his heart. It felt as if the songwriter who wrote the song "Millionaire," sung by Chris Stapleton, was written for us. It was silly, of course, and maybe I could blame it on the alcohol coursing through my veins, but I *felt* every word.

Ashtyn gasped, and I pried my eyes away from Ethan for a second. "What?" I asked.

"My brother's in love with you."

I grinned and said the only thing I could because it was the truth. "Yeah, he is."

# CHAPTER THIRTEEN

*Unknown*

D aisy.
When a parent names their child Daisy, they probably assumed their little girl would grow up to be as pure and innocent as the name suggested.

Daisy Witt was anything but.

Since Amy, I'd still been keeping watch on several of the women who attended Lakeshore University. I wanted to keep my options open, and when I'd watched Daisy for the first time, I knew she needed to be next. She wasn't supposed to be. In fact, she was the ninth person I was using for my entertainment.

Amy Kenny - #1

Reagan McCormick - #2

Michelle Cable - #3

Fiona Jones - #4

Pat Wood - #5

Samantha Pitman - #6

Wendy Ballard - #7

Debbie Taylor - #8

Daisy Witt - #9

But the more I watched Daisy, the more I wanted her to be next. And I wasn't the only one watching her. Daisy Witt did live solo porn for coins. She reminded me of *her*, the one who made me watch her have sex for money because she wanted me to learn *how*. She always thought she was in control. I wasn't sure if she was still living. I didn't care.

I was in control now.

Daisy might not have sex with her watchers, but she was no different from *her*. I'd heard of young girls being strippers to pay for college, but this was more. More than taking off her clothes for money. She was spreading her legs and doing whatever was asked of her if the price was right.

Fuck, she got my blood racing.

At first, it was arousal as I watched her finger herself, use a dildo—or sometimes a *cucumber* before eating it. Men were sick like that. They wanted to see a woman do the dirtiest things imaginable because it turned them on.

At first, I didn't pay for Daisy to do things, I'd only watch. Watching was my thing, but over the weeks, men—or maybe women too—would ask her to fuck her ass with … well, *anything*, but the bitch never accepted any money for anal play. Anal play was off limits to her.

How could Daisy Witt be a porn star and not do anal?

She couldn't, and I was going to prove it to her. Therefore, I moved her up on the list. She still had her #9 on the back of her plaque. Woodworking was a hobby of mine, and when I found a good woman to watch, I immediately made my signature keepsake with her number on the back.

I'd picked Sunday night because her roommate would be out—she was always at her boyfriend's place—and I was hopeful by the time Daisy was discovered, Detective Valor would be assigned to the case.

I liked the little game I had planned for him and Reagan. I had yet to give Reagan the wood plaque I'd made for her, but that would happen soon. They'd put black tape over Reagan's webcam, and I couldn't watch them anymore. I could still hear them through the computer, and I knew that Detective Valor was taking her on a ride-along. That would give me plenty of time to get into her condo and hang up my keepsake for her.

I had no intention of making Reagan a victim. She seemed like a good woman from what I'd seen so far. I just wanted to fuck with

Detective Valor, and what better way than to make them think she was next?

*I* was in control, not Chicago PD.

Daisy had the same routine every time she went live. Beforehand, she'd take a shower, pour herself a vodka and cranberry, and then wait for coins to come in. I assumed the alcohol made her loosen up. Not enough for anal apparently.

That was going to change.

Letting myself in with the key I'd made from my 3D printer—the same way I had with Amy—I slipped inside the dark living room. After closing the door and locking it behind me, I moved inside quietly. Walking past the kitchen, I noticed the bottle of Absolut sitting on the counter, waiting to be mixed with cranberry juice. I knew that Daisy poured herself a drink after her shower because she'd slip out of her bedroom while she was logged into her porn site and would come back with her drink while people logged in and waited for her, so I put the Rohypnol in the vodka bottle and in the cranberry juice. I didn't know how much it would take given she was going to drink from both bottles, but I'd put three pills in both, hoping it would be enough and she wouldn't struggle.

I knew others would be watching, so I brought a black ski mask with me. I didn't want to take the chance of another hacker being able to log into her computer because they wanted to watch for free like me. The problem was, I had to wait until she was done with her show or passed out. I couldn't slip into her room and wait in her closet because I knew that her webcam showed the door, and I didn't want someone to tell her that I was waiting. The thought of giving her ass play while her fans watched, turned me on, and the thought of killing her while they watched made my heart beat fast in excitement.

I just had to wait for the drug to kick in, and then I was going to make my fantasy my reality.

It didn't take long for me to hear her slurring, and I knew it was time. Slipping in, I slid a ball gag over her mouth. I hoped the audience thought this was some sort of fetish and wouldn't tip off the cops about what I was doing. It wouldn't take much time for them to track her

IP address and find out where she lived if someone reported it to the porn site. I wanted Detective Valor on the case—it was his jurisdiction, but from what I'd heard and seen through Reagan's webcam, he didn't usually work weekends.

After I tore Daisy's ass up with the head of the empty vodka bottle, I logged her out of the porn site and moved her passed out body to the couch. Daisy moaned around the ball gag and then tried to scream as I let all of my built-up rage out by stabbing her repeatedly until she was dead.

Daisy Witt - #9

Once my breathing returned to normal, I changed my gloves and stripped out of my clothes and changed into clean ones I had brought with me in a duffle bag. Before I left, I placed Daisy's wood plaque on the fireplace and then slipped out into the dead of night.

Murder was such a rush.

*Ethan*

After Reagan got done with classes for the day, I drove to her place to pick her up for the ride-along. I let myself in with my key and saw her sitting at her desk, laptop open, more than likely finishing her homework before the real excitement began.

"Need help?" I leaned down and pressed my lips to hers.

"Nope. Almost done."

I slid the NDA next to her. "Sign this when you're done and then the fun begins."

"What are we doing tonight for the ride-along?"

"Shawn and I need to follow-up with a few witnesses about a shooting that happened yesterday."

"I get to watch you interrogate people?"

I chuckled slightly and kissed the side of her head. "No. These aren't suspects."

She sighed. "Oh."

"I'm sure we'll have fun, though." I didn't think my job was *fun*, but I knew people who went on ride-alongs loved them because they got a glimpse into our world. I felt that way when I would go with my dad before I became a cop. Given the excitement Reagan was already expressing, I knew she would have fun.

She quickly finished her homework while I snacked on chips and salsa. Then she signed the NDA, and we left to pick up Shawn back at the station.

"So, this is your Reagan?" Shawn asked as he slid into the passenger seat and turned to face her in the back seat of the unmarked car.

I grinned. "Yeah, this is *my* Reagan." She had always been mine. Even when we were living our own lives, she'd held a place in my heart. And now that we were back together, I was never letting her go.

"So, you talk about me?" Reagan teased.

"All the time," Shawn stated.

"Bullshit." I laughed.

"It's okay if you do. You stalk me at my job," Reagan joked.

My gaze met hers through the rearview mirror. "I go to Judy's for a nightcap. It's only a bonus that the hottest bartender there is my girlfriend."

Before she could respond, dispatch radioed a 10-31. They gave the address, and Shawn responded that we were en route. I looked at Reagan again through the rearview mirror.

"It's your lucky night, Buttercup."

Her emerald eyes brightened. "A dead body?"

"A dead body."

We arrived at the location a few minutes later. I got out and opened the back door where Reagan was sitting. Leaning in, I said, "Stay by the car for now while we make sure the scene is secure, and then I'll come and get you."

She bobbed her head excitedly. "Okay. I want to watch CSU work."

"Figured you might." I winked.

The sun was starting to set, and the familiar red and blue lights helped light my path toward Officer Moore, the responding officer who was waiting outside of the duplex.

"What do we have?" Shawn asked.

"Another stabbing," he replied as we started for the front door. Before we entered, we covered our shoes with shoe covers. "Vic appears to be in her early twenties. No signs of a break-in, and no signs of a struggle."

The words echoed our unsolved case, and the moment I saw the body on the couch, I started sensing a pattern. She had been left naked, and had long brown hair that was soaked with blood. The amount of blood, the stab wounds, and the lack of disarray in the room, made me think it was the same perp.

After surveying the scene and making sure it was secure, I went back outside to grab Reagan, who was still in the back seat of the car but with the door open and watching everyone work.

"Ready?"

"I'm so excited," she exclaimed.

"Try to keep the excitement down while you're in front of the neighbors." I nudged my head in the direction of the crowd forming.

"Sorry," she whispered.

I reached out my hand for her to take to slide out of the car. "I get it." She put shoe protectors on, and just before walking over the threshold, I turned to her. "You sure about this?"

She nodded her head. "If I can't handle it, then I know to quit school."

"Or do another form of investigating like crime scene reconstruction or something."

"We'll see."

We walked inside, and Reagan followed me to the body. I looked over at her, gauging her reaction. Her beautiful green eyes were wide, and it seemed as though she wasn't breathing.

"You okay?"

She swallowed. "Yeah. I just can't believe I'm looking at a dead body." She looked up at me. "It doesn't smell *that* bad."

"She hasn't been dead that long then," I informed her. "Wait until you have one that's a week old."

Shawn leaned over. "Don't puke on the body."

Reagan snorted. "Not planning on it."

"Stay close and don't touch anything," I instructed. "After you get a quick look around, you'll need to go back to the car."

"Got it," she replied.

Just like Amy's crime scene, everything seemed in order except for the blood-soaked couch. Reagan went back to the cruiser while I looked for anything out of place. Whoever this guy was, he had serious anger issues.

I moved to look at the pictures on the fireplace when Shawn walked up to me. "Are you thinking what I'm thinking?"

"Same guy as Amy's?"

"Yeah."

I was about to respond when something on the fireplace caught my eye. It was a wood plaque in the shape of a heart with a name on it. "What's the vic's name?" I asked.

"Daisy. Daisy Witt."

I pointed to the wood carving.

"Yeah?" Shawn questioned me. "You can get those made at—"

"I know where you can get them, but Amy had one of these on the wall at her apartment."

"Really?" Shawn questioned. "Maybe they went to the same fair or amusement park?"

"Maybe, but I didn't think anything of it at the time. There was no blood on it or anything, so it wasn't put into evidence." I fished a glove from my pocket and used it loosely to pick up the plaque that was leaning against the back wall of the chimney and turned it over. A #9 was written in black marker on the back. "If this is connected, do you think this means Daisy's the ninth vic and we're dealing with a serial killer?"

"We need to speak with Heather again. Check out the plaque you saw there," he responded. "Maybe she knows where it came from."

This could be the break we needed. If we were dealing with a serial killer, then we'd have more to go on and databases to scour looking for any similar MOs.

"Detectives," a crime tech called.

"Yeah?" I turned.

"You two need to see this."

Shawn and I followed her back and into a bedroom. Every form of sex toy imaginable was on the bed next to an empty vodka bottle that looked to be smudged with blood on the neck of the bottle.

Before Shawn and I left, we interviewed the roommate who had called it in. She had no idea who would have done this to Daisy and wasn't much help except to establish a timeline.

I drove Shawn back to the station and then drove Reagan home to drop her off before heading back to work on the case. "Thank you for taking me tonight," Reagan beamed as we walked inside her apartment.

"So, you think you can handle it?" I asked as I closed the door behind me. It was her first dead body, and I wasn't sure if she'd be able to sleep alone.

She wrapped her arms around my neck and kissed me lightly. "Yes. The dead body was creepy at first, but I think it will get easier as you mentioned before."

"Good. I'm looking forward to working with you."

"I'll be the low man on the totem pole."

"Only for a few years until you can get your degree."

"Tru—" She dropped her hands from my neck as she stared past me.

"What is—" I turned to look at what she'd seen.

I didn't need to finish speaking. A wood plaque in the shape of a heart with Reagan's name carved into it was hanging on her wall.

# CHAPTER FOURTEEN

"**W**here did that come from?" I asked.

Ethan didn't reply. Instead, he pulled his gun, and I went rigid.

"Eth—"

"Get against the wall and don't move," he ordered.

"You're scaring me."

"Get against the wall," he gritted out again. "Now!"

I moved, my back going flush against the wall near the front door. My heart started to race, my palms became sweaty. I had no idea what was going on as I watched Ethan check my condo.

"It's clear," he finally stated and put his gun back into its holster under his suit jacket.

"O—kay?"

He grabbed his phone, pressed something on the screen, and then held it up to his ear as he pulled me against his chest. "You need to get to Reagan's." There was a short pause. "Perp was in her condo." I started to shake. *Did he just say a perp was in here? How?* "I don't know. Just fucking get here. I'm calling it in."

"Ethan?" I whispered nervously as he took the phone away from his ear.

He wrapped his arms tighter around me. "It's going to be okay."

"What's happening?"

Turning us slightly, he pointed at the mysterious plaque. "That has been at my last two murder scenes."

"My—my name?"

"No." He shook his head. "Each victim had her name on a plaque."

"Why is it here?"

"I don't know." He sighed. "But I'm fucking going to find out."

"I don't understand."

"I don't either." He stepped back. "I need to call it in. Shawn's on his way now."

"O—kay," I stuttered again. "How did they get in?" I turned to look at my door. It didn't appear as though someone had broken in.

"I don't know." Ethan held up his finger. "Yeah, Maureen. This is Sergeant Valor."

I tuned him out as I looked around my living room. At school, we were going over details that would be at a crime scene. I never thought my home would be one. I checked the windows. They were locked. Everything was as I'd left it less than two hours before except for the mysterious wood plaque on my wall with my picture collage.

What was happening?

"Okay, CSU is on their way," Ethan advised, coming over to me as I looked around at my condo. I felt like a stranger in my own home.

"CSU? This is a crime scene?"

He wrapped his arms around me again. "Of course it is. Someone fucking broke into your home."

I knew that it was. I was just in shock, and nothing was making sense. "Who would do that?"

"If I knew that, we wouldn't be standing here, Buttercup."

"Am I ... safe?"

"I'll never let anything happen to you." He kissed the top of my head, and then we were silent for a few moments while he continued to hold me in his arms. "I need to ask ... who else knows where you live?"

I pulled my head back, looking into his deep blue eyes. "No one. I haven't met anyone since I've been back."

"What about at school?"

"I mean, I have classmates, but I'm not friends with anyone nor have I told them where I live."

We pulled apart. "Someone knows you live here beside me."

I thought for a moment. "Maddie does. I gave her my address for emergencies and whatnot."

"Maddie? Would she—"

"Would she what? Kill people?"

Before Ethan could respond, there was a knock at the door. My heart began to race again as I watched him move toward it. Once I saw Shawn standing on the other side, I relaxed slightly. How could Ethan think my daughter had something to do with this? How could he think she was a killer? Besides, she was at school in Michigan.

I needed to sit down, so while Ethan talked to his partner, I sat on my couch, thinking about who else knew where I lived. No one came to mind except maybe Judy because she had my info in my employee file. But then …

"Eth," I called. It was barely a whisper as uncertainty still coursed through my body.

He paused his conversation and moved so he was crouched down in front of me. "What is it?"

"It's a long shot, but maybe it's someone from work?"

He stood, anger radiating from him. "That fucking barback?"

"Derrick?" I drew my head back slightly because I wasn't thinking about him at all. I was thinking of one of the other bartenders. I knew Tommy and Frank had a key to Judy's office because they needed to get money at the start of the day or put money in the safe at closing.

"Is that his fucking name?"

I swallowed. "Yeah."

"He knows where you live?"

"No. I mean, I've never told him."

"Then why do you think it's Derrick?"

I sighed. "I don't think it's him exactly."

"Then who?"

I looked over at Shawn and then back at Ethan. "Judy has my address for my W-2 and whatever. Maybe Tommy or Frank grabbed my file and got my address," I suggested.

"I'll go check it out. Check out this Derrick guy too," Shawn said.

"Tommy works the early shift, and I don't think Derrick is working tonight," I stated, turning to face Shawn. "We mostly work the same shift because he's in school too."

"Same college?" Ethan asked.

I shrugged. "I don't know."

"Then we'll go to his house. I've wanted an excuse to rough him up," Ethan admitted.

"Captain isn't going to let you work this, man," Shawn advised.

Ethan turned to face him, pointing a finger as he gritted his teeth, seething instantly. "I don't fucking care. This is Reagan we're dealing with. *My* Reagan."

Shawn held up his hands in surrender. "I know, but—"

"No buts. My priority is keeping her safe. Some perp is out there killing women and now"—Ethan pointed at me again—"some asshole is coming after *my* Reagan."

His words started to slowly sink in. *"That has been at my last two murder scenes."*

A murderer was in my condo?

# CHAPTER FIFTEEN

**M**y heart hadn't slowed since the moment I saw that fucking wood plaque on Reagan's wall. I had no idea what was happening or how she was involved, but I needed to figure out the connection before I lost my fucking mind. If something were to happen to her … If she was to be taken—to leave me again—I would lose my shit.

I wasn't going to let that happen.

"Take her laptop too. Have Will do his thing," I instructed the crime scene tech.

"My laptop?" Reagan asked.

"Remember I told you about the case where someone was watching my murder vic through her webcam?"

"Yeah?"

"She had a wood plaque too, and I'd bet the vic tonight has the same shit on her computer that pings to a shitload of countries." When we pulled the plaque from Reagan's wall, on the back was #2 in black marker. Daisy had #9, and that made me even more confused. I needed to find out what number was on the back of Amy's plaque.

"But … we put black tape over the camera."

I sighed. "I don't know how it works, but I want Will to check out your computer. This could be the link."

Reagan nodded. "Okay. This is crazy."

"Yeah, it is." I sighed.

"Will I have my computer back for class tomorrow?"

I frowned. "You're not going to school tomorrow."

"What? Why not?"

I looked at the crime scene techs and nodded as they bagged Reagan's laptop. After waiting for them to leave, I replied to her, "Do you think you can just go on with your day to day life as usual?"

She drew her head back slightly and furrowed her brows. "I … I can't?"

"Not until we catch this guy. If something were to ever happen to you …" I couldn't finish the thought. It felt as though everything was spinning out of control. First, it was my sister, and now the woman I loved for most of my life was in danger. *Fuck!*

"So I need to go into hiding or something?"

I sighed, running my hands down my face. "Let's see what Shawn finds out at Judy's, and what Will finds on your computer."

"Okay."

"Go pack a bag, and we'll leave."

"How much should I pack?"

*Everything*, I wanted to reply because I never wanted her out of my sight. And it wasn't only because some asshole might be after her. I wanted to move in with her. We were together every night, and paying rent for two places was pointless. I'd assumed I would move into her place since I was living in Ashtyn's condo.

"For a few days at least. We can always come back and get more if Shawn and I don't solve this shit." I had a door guy, and that was better than nothing. Since the incident with Ashtyn, Jose, one of the door guys, had taken it upon himself to make sure that the security for the building was up to par given that a man had slipped past him and tried to kidnap my sister.

*Fuck. I hope we solve this shit tomorrow.*

I didn't sleep a wink.

The entire night I held Reagan as tight as I could, as though I'd wake up and she'd be gone again. I didn't know if there was a connection with her laptop, a connection among all three women other than the wood plaques, or if some perp was randomly targeting victims. Reagan was more or less new in town, and when we went on the ride-along, she didn't seem as though she knew Daisy, and I didn't think she was hiding anything from me.

The look on her face when she realized that a killer had entered her condo made me scared too. It would be different if I knew who this guy was, but I had no idea. Amy's murder was clean, in a manner of speaking. We'd found no leads since the person watching her through her webcam was using shit, so we couldn't trace who it was. Will had said something about a chain connection, but the servers were from different countries. I didn't know how it all worked because I was muscle, so to speak. I knew how to use a computer, but the logistics were beyond what I knew. What I did know was that there was no such a thing as a perfect murder, and eventually, we would find out who the killer was.

I just hoped it was before anything happened to Reagan.

Unlike most mornings, I didn't wake Reagan with my mouth or my hand or any other part of my body because I wanted her to sleep as long as she could, given the emotional circumstances. I kissed her temple and then slid out of bed before getting into the shower. The warm water gave me a little bit of energy, but I also knew I'd need cup after cup of coffee to get me through the day.

After the quickest shower I'd ever taken in my life—I was scared to have Reagan out of my sight—I went back into my bedroom, a towel wrapped around my waist. She was awake. "Morning, Buttercup."

She smiled slightly. "Morning."

I sat on the edge of the bed and brushed her dark hair from her face. "Did you sleep okay?"

She frowned. "I don't think I slept for more than thirty minutes."

"More than me."

Reagan sat up. "You didn't sleep at all?"

"How could I?"

"I don't know." She sighed. "But what are we going to do?"

"I'm going to fucking catch this guy."

"I know," she whispered. "I'm just scared."

So was I, but even if I had to go door to door looking for some fucker watching women, I had no doubt Shawn and I would eventually find this guy. I needed to go into the station and talk to Shawn, Will, and the ME, but I couldn't leave Reagan alone.

"I'll protect you."

"I know."

I sighed deeply. "I need to go get an update from Shawn. Come with me and then I'll go with you to class."

"Go with me to class?"

"For now." I stood and went to my closet for a suit to change into. Even though I had told Reagan the previous night that she wasn't going to class, I also knew she was pursuing her dream job and having me shadow her was a way for her to stay safe without giving that up.

"And then what?"

"Are you really going to question me about this?"

I heard her get out of the bed as I grabbed my slacks. "I don't want to argue, but do you have time to go with me to class?"

"You'd rather die?" I shouted, the thought once again crossing my mind. I wasn't angry at her, but my heart hurt and cracked slightly every time I thought about finding her bloody and dead like the two murder victims. I feared that if I weren't standing next to her 24/7, something *would* happen.

"Of course not. I just don't understand why this is happening. I don't know anyone with a reason to kill me."

I sighed and moved toward her, wrapping her in my arms. "That's what I'm going to find out. This is more than a job now. Don't you understand? I'm going to do everything I can to keep you safe."

She nodded against my bare chest. "Okay."

"Okay," I repeated and pulled back. I slipped on a pair of boxers from my dresser drawer. "Get ready to go. Today might be a long fucking day."

Reagan waited in the waiting room at the station while I went to get an update. She said she was going to call her daughter and let her know she was going to be staying at my place for a few days. I wasn't necessarily suspicious of Maddison, but I wasn't sure she *wasn't* involved either. Reagan was going to try to find out if she'd told anyone where Reagan lived. Maddison knew no one in Chicago that we knew of since her grandparents moved to Florida when they retired, but she was coming to visit for Thanksgiving, and she might have told someone her holiday plans at a bar or something. You never know who to trust.

When I got to my desk, Shawn was already at his. "Hey," I greeted.

"You look like you didn't sleep."

"Can you blame me?" I leaned on the edge of my desk that faced his.

"Nope. I take it Reagan is at your place?"

"She's staying at my place, yeah, but she's in the lobby right now waiting for me so I can take her to class."

Shawn nodded. "I'd do the same thing."

"What'd you find out?"

"Nothing much. Went to Judy's and talked to the bartender Frank. He wouldn't let me into the office without a warrant or Judy's permission even though it was about Reagan."

"You think he's our guy?"

Shawn took a breath and shrugged. "I don't know. He seemed cool and collected but didn't want to get into trouble for anything."

"And Judy? You couldn't call her to come in?"

"Tried. Even went by her house, but she wasn't home or answering her phone."

My brows furrowed. "Do you think it could be her?"

"You know as well as I do that a woman probably wouldn't stab someone that many times."

I did know. Profiling would suggest it was a male perp given the number of stab wounds. Women typically used a gun or poison, though it wasn't necessarily unheard of for a woman to stab someone. Just not that many times.

"Right. Mind going back to Judy's and seeing if she's there?"

"Yeah, I was already planning on it."

"Thanks. Have you heard from Will?"

Shawn shook his head. "No. Let's go see what he has."

"Yeah." We both stood and walked to the cyber unit where we found Will at his computer. "Hey."

Will looked up. "Hey. I was just going to come find you. I ran scans on the vic's computer from last night and your girlfriend's. They both have the same malware program that Amy Kenny's had."

My body went taut. "Were you able to trace it?"

"No." Will shook his head. "The computers have the same backdoor program that allows the routing back to IP addresses to be a chain. It's not even a standard VPN used by a lot of hackers use and people wanting to protect their privacy. Whoever this is knows what he's doing."

"How would someone find out all of their IP addresses?" I asked.

"Honestly, it isn't all that hard. Just think about all the times you've connected to a free Wi-Fi at some hotel, restaurant, or coffee shop. Everyone seems to offer free Wi-Fi, but unfortunately, most of these networks are so unsecure that any hacker with a decent packet-sniffing program can steal information from anyone who connects to them without protection. In fact, that's probably the easiest way, so that could be how our victims are being chosen."

"Hackers aren't usually murderers, are they?" Shawn probed.

Will shrugged. "Usually they do it for financial gain."

"Amy had nothing. She was in college," I stated. *Just like Reagan.*

"Why would a pro hacker come out from his parents' basement to kill?" Shawn asked.

I snorted. I knew Shawn was stereotyping as well as being a little sarcastic. "Enjoyment? Money? Anger? Maybe someone is forcing them?"

"Blackmailing them?" Shawn questioned.

"I don't fucking know, but we need to figure out another link beside someone hacking their computers and those fucking wood plaques. And, of course, Amy and Reagan attending the same school."

We thanked Will, telling him to keep us updated if he found anything else, and then we walked back to our desks. "I need to get Reagan to class. Can you go to Judy's and then, after Reagan is out of class, we can head to Amy's place and see if Heather still has the plaque?"

If I had known that a piece of artwork was going to be the link, I would have had CSU bag the fucking thing when we caught the case over a month ago. It wasn't dusted for prints because it seemed to fit on the wall as though it was a keepsake Amy had gotten made herself. That was why it was left behind with all the other pictures. *Fuck!*

"Yeah. What's your plan for Reagan? Keep her here while we're working and escort her to class and work?"

I sighed and closed my eyes briefly as we stopped next to our desks. I hadn't had long to think about a plan other than attending classes with Reagan. "What if—"

"Valor." I turned to face Captain Rapp as he stood in his office doorway. "A word."

My gaze caught Shawn's. He didn't follow, but we both already knew what was about to happen. Captain would try to take me off the case. I wasn't going to let it happen though.

"Sit." Captain motioned to a chair in front of his desk.

"With all due respect, Cap, you don't need to waste your breath. I'm not backing off this case."

He chuckled slightly. "That's not what I was going to say."

"It wasn't?"

He took a seat, smoothing his tie down as he did, and motioned for me to sit again. I sat. "I heard what happened last night." I nodded. Of course he already knew. He ran the department. "How's your girlfriend holding up?"

"As well as she can be, given the circumstances."

"You know as well as I do that protocol suggests I take you off this case, but I promoted you to sergeant for a reason. If anyone can catch this guy, it's you."

"Thank you. I agree."

"But for you to do your best work, you don't need a distraction like your girlfriend."

"She's not a distract—"

He held up his hand. "Before you fly off the handle, I'm trying to tell you that I've already authorized off-duty details to watch both Reagan and her place."

I blinked. "You … You did?"

"Yes, but only when you can't be with her, of course."

"Right." I paused, still not believing Captain Rapp had done this for me—for us. I'd expected to have to beg and plead to use department resources. "Thank you. I appreciate it."

He smiled warmly. "You're welcome. I'd do the same for all of you."

"You'll need to change the home detail to my place. I can't have her go back to a place some fucker broke in to. Without a trace, no less."

"Okay. Will do."

My phone started to ring in my pocket. I pulled it out and saw Jessica's name on the screen. "I gotta take this. Thank you again." Captain nodded, and I stood, sliding my finger across the answer button as I walked toward my desk. "Yeah?"

"Don't *yeah* me," Jessica clipped.

"It's not a good time."

"I don't fucking care, Ethan. I heard."

"You heard what?" Shawn looked up at me as I stopped next to my desk. I rolled my eyes.

"That your little slut has a serial killer after her."

"Don't you fucking call her that," I growled.

"Whatever. I'm calling to tell you I'm changing the custody order."

"The hell you are!" I roared.

"Don't think for one minute that I'm subjecting my kids to that kind of danger, Ethan."

"They aren't in danger!" We didn't know what was going to happen, but I wasn't going to tell Jessica she was right. I would have arranged for her to keep the boys until there was no threat. I just didn't need Jess telling me what to do or how it was going to be with my kids.

"Yes, they are, Ethan. Alicia told me when I dropped the boys off at school."

"What the fuck did she tell you?"

Shawn mouthed, "What?" I shook my head and held up a finger.

"She told me that Braeden has to work an extra shift to do a detail on your girlfriend."

I didn't know who the off-duty cops would be, and I didn't like that Jessica knew before I did. I didn't get the chance to ask Captain Rapp before she'd called. I sighed. "Look, Jess. I'm busy. Keep the boys tomorrow and this weekend if things aren't settled."

"I'm going to change the order," Jess repeated. "This is the second time something has happened with people you know, and I don't want my kids in danger."

"You can't keep my kids from me."

"We'll see what the judge says. Expect to hear from my attorney." She hung up.

"Fuck," I gritted out with a groan.

"Jess wants to keep your kids from you now?"

I sighed, trying to calm my anger. "Yes, because of this mother-fucker and his goddamn wood plaques. I swear to god when we figure out who this asshole is, I will shoot him in the fucking face just like I did that guy that tried to hurt my sister."

Shawn looked around and lowered his voice. "Calm down before Cap does, in fact, take you off this case. Let's fucking figure out who this asshole is."

# CHAPTER SIXTEEN

*Reagan*

I tried to call Maddie, but she didn't answer her cell. I knew she had a class first thing in the morning, but I still tried to call her just in case. I didn't think she had anything to do with this shit, and I wanted to prove that to Ethan. Show him that she was in Michigan and not in Illinois. It didn't make sense for her to be involved, but it was possible she had told someone my address either by mistake or on purpose. But she didn't answer, and I was left with no further clarity.

Since I had nothing to do while I waited for Ethan, my mind raced. Or more accurately, continued to race. Maybe someone had followed me home after a shift at Judy's, or perhaps someone had followed me home after class. Could someone be watching me through my computer as Ethan had said? How would they hack into my computer?

And why?

I looked around the waiting room, wondering if one day I'd work there. *Or what if I was murdered and never got to follow my dreams?* I tried not to think about the reality that a killer was after me somehow, but I couldn't *not* think about it, so instead, I tried to think of the positive. Could I work in the same precinct as Ethan? I'd enjoyed going to the crime scene with him the night before, but could we work cases together? What if we were to break up again? I didn't think we would. We were older, still in love, and I was never pressing my lips to anyone other than Ethan Valor again.

*Think positive.*

I was engrossed in a game on my phone, trying to forget about what was happening in my life for a minute, when Ethan finally came out. "Ready?"

I stared at him. His forehead was furrowed, and he looked even more stressed than when we first got to the station. "Everything okay?"

He rubbed the back of his neck. "We'll talk in the truck."

I stood. "Okay."

Ethan held the glass door open for me. "Did you talk to Maddison?"

"No." I sighed as we walked toward his truck. "I usually talk to her before my first class."

"Well, if it makes you feel any better, I don't think she's connected."

I stopped walking. "Did you seriously think she was?"

Ethan opened the passenger side door. "No, I didn't, but I have to follow all leads."

"Okay, good." I stepped up into the cab. "Then what changed your mind?"

He shut the door and went over to the driver's side. After buckling his seatbelt and starting the engine, he said, "I can't share anything with you because I don't want to put you in any more danger."

"How would telling me how my daughter *isn't* connected put me in more danger?"

He took a deep breath. "I want to tell you—I really do—but I'm already walking a fine line because I'm still on this case."

"Okay?"

"Just"—Ethan laced our fingers—"trust me. I promise I'll do everything I can to keep you safe."

"I know you will."

He kissed the back of my hand. "And since you still want to go to school and work, off duty cops will be with you when I'm not."

"They will?"

"Yes. They'll be nearby in plain clothes."

"Okay. That's probably for the best."

"Yes, it is." He pulled out of the parking lot and turned toward my school. After a few minutes, he said, "I'm going to ask you questions, and you just need to answer them. Don't ask me something I can't tell you."

I swallowed and looked over at him as he drove. "Okay."

"Besides your home, where have you used your laptop?"

"What do you mean?"

"Have you taken it with you to do homework or anything at a coffee shop, library—anywhere you'd have to use public Wi-Fi?"

I thought for a moment. I hadn't taken my laptop anywhere except for his place, school, and work, but Judy's didn't have Wi-Fi. "I've just used my laptop at your place and school."

I felt his hand tighten slightly in mine. I didn't know why, and I didn't ask. "What about before we got back together?"

"I … I don't remember."

"Okay, that's okay."

"Is it?"

"I think I might know the link."

"What is it?" Ethan cut his gaze to me. "Sorry, I just want to know."

"I know, but I can't tell you. Shawn's going to Judy's now, and afterward, he's meeting me on campus. I'm going to run my theory by him, and after you're done with class, I'll get your detail to go with you back to my place and see if this pans out."

I sighed. "Okay. What will they do? Shadow me?"

Ethan pulled into the parking lot at my school. "Yeah. Or, since you're *my* Reagan, I can introduce you to them, and they can walk with you like they're a friend. They're all my friends. Everyone in the department is."

I loved hearing him call me *his* Reagan. It caused a flutter in my belly and made me warm inside. I had no doubt he'd do anything to protect me. "Okay, so, backing up slightly, you don't think Maddie's involved because I must have used my laptop somewhere and some guy got my info?"

"Unless Maddie used it somewhere."

"No." I shook my head.

"Then, I think so. Just pretend everything's normal." He parked and cut the engine.

"Except I'm about to have babysitters."

Ethan sighed. "Yeah, but I'm going to figure this shit out." He pulled me by my red peacoat and pressed his lips to mine. "I have something else to tell you."

"What is it?" My heart stopped, and I was instantly worried before he yawned, which caused me to yawn and remember that we hadn't had any coffee yet. I needed ten cups. "Can you tell me while we grab coffee before class? It's like a ritual—or an addiction—but I get a cup every day before class."

"Yeah, I need caffeine."

We got out of the truck and headed toward the coffee shop. While we walked, I tried to gauge if Ethan was more at ease and less stressed. He wasn't. Whatever he had to tell me wasn't good.

"The usual?" Krystal, the barista, asked. I nodded. "And for you, sir?"

"The same," Ethan replied.

"Do you even know what it is?" I questioned.

"Vanilla latte, of course." He dug into his pocket and pulled out his credit card.

I smiled. "Okay, you do know me."

Ethan leaned over and whispered into my ear, "I do. Every. Fucking. Inch."

My face heated and probably turned the color of the red peacoat I was wearing. He *did* know every inch. And I knew every inch of him too. I was the first to run my hands, my lips, my tongue over every inch of his skin, and he was the first to do the same to me. It felt good to think of something other than what was happening around me.

We turned, and I came face to face with the man I'd briefly spoken to in the same coffee shop. Whiskey Neat smiled, I smiled, and then Ethan and I walked over to wait for our coffees. Even though I frequented the coffee shop five days a week, I hadn't seen Whiskey Neat since then, not even at Judy's, where I'd first seen him when I wanted to hook him up with the blonde.

As Ethan and I waited for our lattes, I caught Whiskey Neat staring at me. He smiled again, and all I could think about was the last thing he'd said to me: *"Not to be too forward, but I wouldn't mind you tying me up."* Could he be the murderer? I felt as though I was going to look at everyone differently now: my teachers, my classmates, Tommy, Frank, Derrick, and even Judy. The cashier at the grocery store, and the attendant at the gas station—every single person because we didn't know who had violated my space.

"I need to change my lock," I stated, breaking my gaze from Whiskey Neat. I was going to tell Ethan that Whiskey Neat was the guy who had asked if I was a murderer, but I didn't. I didn't know why. I should have, but since the guy had been flirting with me, telling him would only lead to Ethan stressing out more.

"Shit," Ethan muttered. "Let me get my dad to do that."

"I can't let him do that. He might be busy."

"It's fine." Ethan pulled his cell phone out of his pocket. He dialed and held it up to his ear just as Krystal called my name to tell us our coffees were ready. We grabbed them as Ethan started to speak into his phone. "Hey, Dad."

As he spoke, we passed Whiskey Neat. He winked, and my eyes widened. Was I going to suspect everyone forever?

We walked out of the coffee shop. My phone started to buzz in my pocket, and I pulled it out and saw Maddie's name on the screen. *Crap.* "Hey, honey," I answered.

Ethan raised a brow, and I mouthed that it was Maddie.

"You called me?" she asked.

"Yes, how was your weekend?"

"It was good. How was yours?"

I swallowed. How was I supposed to tell her a killer after me? I felt as though I was living in an episode of *Halloween,* and Michael Myers was hunting me. "It was good. Ethan took me on a ride-along yesterday."

"Oh my god, that's awesome. Was it fun? I bet it was fun."

I chuckled slightly. The ride-along was fun. Coming home was when it all went wrong. "It was. I can't wait to get a job and start working crime scenes."

"That's amazing, Mom."

"Thanks, honey." Ethan hung up his phone. "I better go. I'm almost to class."

"Okay. Talk to you tomorrow."

"Yeah," I agreed. "Have a good day. Love you."

"Love you too." I hung up and slipped my phone back into my coat pocket.

"Everything okay?" Ethan asked.

I took a sip of my coffee. "Yep. I didn't ask her anything."

"That's for the best." He took a sip of his latte. "My dad's going to stop by and get the key to your place from me and then go and change the locks."

"Thank you."

"Of course, Buttercup. I told you I'd never let anything happen to you. I just wish I would have thought of it last night."

"It's okay. The last fifteen hours or whatever have been crazy."

"Yeah, they have been."

"Now that we've had a few sips of caffeine, do you want to tell me the other thing?"

Ethan sighed. "Oh, right. How much farther to your class?"

"About three minutes. It's just inside that building." I pointed with my free hand at the two-story building where all of my classes were held.

He stopped walking, causing me to stop as well. "Before we left the station, Jessica called me."

"Okay?" I arched a brow.

"She heard about last night."

I balked. "How?"

"My boys go to the same school as an officer who works at my precinct. He told his wife that he has to work OT because Captain asked everyone who could to work your detail."

"And his wife told Jessica?"

Ethan nodded. "I don't think she did it maliciously or anything, but of course Jessica is taking it to the extreme."

"How so?"

"When she called, she told me she's contacting her attorney to change our custody agreement because our kids are in danger."

"What?" I hissed. "Are you serious?"

He rubbed the back of his neck. "I mean, she may be right. They might be in danger if they're with us."

I stared into his blue eyes. "I'm so sorry. This is all—"

"Hey." He reached for me, pulling me into his arms. "This isn't your fault."

"It is."

"It's not."

I pulled my head back to look up at him. "What if it is? What if I somehow caused all of this?"

"Why would you think that?"

I shrugged. "Because a murderer broke into my condo and gave me a wood plaque."

"You didn't cause this, but I'm going to figure out why they're fucking with us."

"I know." I placed my head on his chest, my arms still around him, and both of us still holding our coffees. "I just hate this."

"Me too, Buttercup. Me. Fucking. Too."

# CHAPTER SEVENTEEN

## Unknown

Everything was going as planned.

I watched Detective Valor and Detective Jones assess my handiwork while Reagan looked around Daisy's townhouse until a tech found Daisy's laptop and closed it, blocking me out. I didn't care. The excitement flowing through my veins was electric because it was time for the second part of my little game.

I'd already accessed the school's database, retrieved Reagan's address, and made a key to her condo with my 3D printer. Getting my hands on her keys had been tricky. She didn't hang them up by the door in her living room, and she didn't leave them sitting around on a table. Plus, Detective Valor had put black tape over the webcam. I'd tried to see if I could get a picture when I went into Judy's, but again, she didn't have her keys laying around, so I had to be even sneakier.

Because I wasn't going to lose this game.

My heart rate sped up when I saw her in the coffee shop on campus because I knew what she looked like under all of her clothing. I tracked her and knew she went there every day before class for her coffee fix. I'd watch her ass as she walked in through the door, and I'd picture her naked as she walked outside, imagining my tongue running along her breasts as she poured her cooling latte down her body for *my* pleasure. I'd watch her as she walked to class, not knowing I was behind her. I'd watch her from the tiny square window of the classroom door as she sat in the same seat every day and sipped her coffee.

I was good.

So good that I was able to get into her classroom and take a picture of her house key while the students were in the lab part of the classroom. Once they were out of sight, I slipped in and went straight for Reagan's purse. I was so good that and I would never be caught.

I took a quick picture and left, smiling the entire time. Everyone let their guard down at some point; all I had to do was wait for my opportunity. Reagan leaving her purse in the lecture hall with her book bag was her downfall.

While Reagan was on her ride-along, I'd slipped into her condo and hung her keepsake from me on her wall. I'd written #2 on the back because, after Amy, Reagan was the second girl I was watching. I had no desire to cross her name off of my list, but I *did* have plans for my favorite couple, especially when I saw them walk into the coffee shop on campus the day after her ride-along.

I'd heard how pissed Detective Valor had been when they saw my woodworking skills on her wall, and I'd heard everything until the crime scene unit took her laptop, so I was surprised to see Reagan was still going to class. Still, she had a police escort, even if he was her boyfriend.

That didn't matter though because Reagan McCormick wasn't my next victim.

*Ethan*

While Reagan went into class, I leaned against the wall near her classroom door, waiting for Shawn. I'd texted him where I was, and thirty minutes later, he showed. My father had already come by and got my key to Reagan's place and was handling that situation. I couldn't believe I hadn't thought to change her locks, though there was no way in hell she'd stay there until this guy was caught—or *ever* again.

I liked having her in my bed every night and day. When we were teenagers, I only got to experience waking up next to her once when we went out of town for a weekend her senior year of high school. I didn't realize then how much the older me would want such a small thing to be a regular occurrence.

"Walk with me to the coffee shop?" I asked Shawn. I needed every cup I could get. Reagan still had at least thirty minutes of class, and I knew she wouldn't leave without me, so I felt comfortable leaving for a few minutes. Plus, the MO of this guy seemed to be killing the women at their homes, and I didn't think Reagan was stupid enough to be alone right now.

"Yeah," he agreed.

"What's the word?"

"Talked to Judy. She showed me where she keeps the employee files. They're locked in a filing cabinet, and no one has the key except her."

"And the lock wasn't broken?"

"No."

"Do you peg her for this?"

He shook his head as I opened the door to the coffee shop. "No. She seemed genuinely devastated when I told her that someone had broken into Reagan's place."

"Okay," I replied as we took our places in the short line.

"Okay? That's all you've got to say?"

I turned and lowered my voice. "I have a hunch."

"What's that?"

I stepped forward and ordered another latte. Shawn ordered a black coffee. While he put cream and sugar into his coffee, and we waited for mine to be made, I asked, "Amy was a student here, right?"

"Right."

The barista called my name, and I grabbed my drink before Shawn and I walked outside and into the chilly air. "And, obviously, Reagan is a student here."

"You think that's the connection?"

I shrugged. "Maybe. We need to find out if Daisy was a student too."

He pulled his cell out. "I'll call Shay and have her run a check."

I nodded, and we walked back to where I was waiting for Reagan to get out of class. Shawn waited on the phone while Shay checked the system. If this was the connection, we might be one step closer to finding this guy.

I wanted Reagan safe behind the locked door at my condo and not walking out in the open while I tried to solve the case. My fucking world was in danger, and I fucking hated it. I would burn this town down to find this fucker. I didn't know what Jessica was going to try and pull. What judge would take a man's kids from him? I was a police officer. I was a sergeant working his way to captain. What I did know was that whatever Jess wanted to do, it would take at least a few days for a hearing to be set. Nothing would be set in stone until I go to voice my argument. Hopefully by then, Shawn and I would have closed the case.

"Thanks," Shawn said before hanging up and putting his phone in his pocket. "Looks like you're on the right track."

"Daisy was a student here too?"

"She was."

I thought for a few moments. "How the fuck are we going to figure out who this guy is?"

Shawn shrugged. "We need to talk to Will. Maybe he knows, or maybe we can get a search warrant to check the servers here."

"Yeah."

Reagan was the first to exit a few moments later. "Hey." She smiled at me and then Shawn.

I draped my arm across her shoulder. "Come on, Buttercup. Time for you to be a kept woman."


After I introduced Reagan to Officer Belt and made sure he was going to stay until I returned home, Shawn and I went back to the station. Since we knew that all the women were connected to Lakeshore University, we had to figure out how this fucker was targeting them, and if there were any other women.

Shawn and I headed straight for the cyber unit. "Hey," I greeted Will.

He looked up from one of the computer screens in front of him. "Hey, what's up?"

"All vics attended Lakeshore U. We need you to check their system. See if we can track this guy," Shawn stated.

"Reagan told me that she's only used her computer at home and at school. The school is the connection, we're guessing," I went on.

Will nodded. "Yeah, I'll get a search warrant and see what I can find out."

We left Will's office and went down to talk to the ME's office to find Daisy's time of death. "Gentleman," Rikki greeted.

"Any update for us?" I asked.

She walked over to her computer and brought up Daisy's file. "She had fifty-nine stab wounds. Time of death was around 1 a.m. on Sunday morning."

My heart sank. I'd never had a strong reaction to hearing how someone died, but all I could think about was walking into my condo and seeing Reagan dead and bloody on my couch. I didn't like where my head was. I wanted to go back to stopping by Judy's after my shift, having a drink while I stared at Reagan's ass, and then going home to devour every inch of her. Then I'd hold her all night and do it all over again the next day.

"Any hairs or fibers?" Shawn inquired.

"Nothing. Just like the other case."

"Do you know the type of knife?" Shawn questioned.

"My guess is it's a chef's knife. Same as the other case."

"So, we definitely have a serial killer on our hands?" I asked, though I already knew we were dealing with the same guy.

"Yes, I'd say so," Rikki answered. "Stab wounds are consistent in depth, even though the number is different."

All the knives were tested at Amy's, and none of them had blood on them. There wasn't a knife missing either, so that meant the killer brought his weapon with him—the crime was premeditated. I'd bet the same would be true for Daisy's knives.

"Fuck," Shawn breathed.

"Did you get the tox report back from Amy's case?" I questioned.

Rikki turned to her computer. "Actually, it just came in." She clicked open an attachment to an email. "It's clean."

"There's nothing?" I asked.

"No."

"But there was a wine glass," Shawn stated.

"After death, bacterial invasion of the body commences almost immediately. The body starts to metabolize numerous sulfur-containing drugs and alcohol."

"So, since it was almost twenty-four hours before we found the body, it is possible the killer slipped her something that metabolized before we could run the tox screen?" I questioned.

"Yes, unfortunately."

We had little to go on, but we needed to search every database we had available for leads on killers who use a chef's knife, go after students, and leave behind wood plaques.

The wood plaques that would haunt me for years to come.

Shawn and I made our way back to our desks. "Valor," I heard Captain Rapp call out. "Another minute."

I looked at Shawn, and he shrugged. Being called to the captain's office was like being called to the principal's office—it wasn't good.

I made my way to his office, and as I got closer, I noticed there was a Cook County Sheriff with him. "Sir?"

The Sheriff handed me a piece of paper. "Sergeant Valor, I'm here to serve you with this emergency order of protection."

I snatched the papers from his grasp and scanned them. "So she went through with it then?"

"Do you blame her?" Captain asked.

"This is to stay away from my kids," I snapped.

"I know that, but given the—"

"They aren't in danger," I countered.

"You don't know that."

I went to open my mouth and argue again, but then everything hit me. We didn't know when or if this asshole would strike, and if Reagan was with my kids, they *would* be in danger. I looked at the papers again and read the hearing date. "Two weeks?" I asked the Sheriff.

"It's standard," he replied. My gaze moved to his name: Pierce.

"This"—I waved the papers in my hand—"is bullshit."

"Not to throw salt into the wound," Captain said, "but you'll need to be on desk duty."

"No!" I shouted and then lowered my voice. "We already went through this."

"That was before you were served with an emergency protection order, Valor."

"If I may," Pierce cut in. "One of the guys at my station had something similar happen to him. He surrendered his off-duty firearm, and he was still able to work as long as he was with his partner. At the end of each shift, he'd surrender his service weapon to our captain." He nodded toward Captain Rapp. "He, his partner, and our captain had to sign off on a form at the end of every shift with the time and date. For added protection—because his ex was a bitch from hell—he did it in front of a surveillance camera for proof."

"I can do that," I stated. "I need to work this case."

Captain Rapp nodded. "I agree. So, surrender all of your weapons from home, and then each night, we'll put your service weapon in a locked box and log it in."

"Okay," I agreed.

"Good luck, Sergeant," Sheriff Pierce said. "I'm off to serve the other emergency order."

"Other order?" I asked.

"Yes."

"Who's it for?" I questioned.

He looked to Captain Rapp, and it was Captain who spoke. "I'm assuming he means your girlfriend."

"There's an order of protection against Reagan?"

Pierce didn't confirm or deny it.

# CHAPTER EIGHTEEN

*Reagan*

Not having my laptop for class sucked. My hand hurt from all the notes I had to take during our lab, and I had no idea when or if I would get my computer back.

While Braeden, whose wife had told Jessica he needed to be my detail, watched TV, I used Ethan's home computer to do my homework. There was no webcam on the monitor, and it put me a little at ease that I was no longer being watched. At least that was what I hoped. Could the person have put hidden cameras in Ethan's house? My purse? My cell phone? I felt like a prisoner—or a kept woman, as Ethan had jokingly called me.

When I was done with my homework, I realized I was starving. With everything going on, I'd only had one cup of coffee since before class. It was after one o'clock, and my stomach wasn't happy.

"I'm going to make a sandwich. Would you like one?" I asked Braeden after walking into the living room.

He looked up at me from where he sat on the couch. "Are you sure?"

"Of course. You're doing Ethan and me a favor."

"It's more than a favor. It's your life."

I smiled tightly and sighed. "I know."

"You have nothing to worry about." He stood and patted my upper arm briefly in a kind gesture. "Everyone at the precinct will help keep you safe when we're your detail."

"Thank you. I really appreciate it." We were silent for a moment, and I stepped back. "Turkey okay?"

"Turkey is fine." He smiled.

I went into the kitchen and grabbed everything I needed to make us the sandwiches. Braeden followed. "Are you married?" I asked as I got out four slices of bread. Of course, I already knew he was, but I needed to fill the awkward silence and wanted to make a good impression. I also knew his wife would ask about me and relay the information back to Jessica.

He sat at the kitchen island as I made our sandwiches. "I am."

"Kids?"

"A daughter and another on the way."

"Aw, congrats."

"Thank you. Do you have children?"

I smiled, thinking of Maddie. "I do, a daughter. She's a freshman at the University of Michigan."

His mouth hung open slightly. "You have a daughter in college?"

"I do."

"Are you sure? You don't look old enough," he teased.

I chuckled. "I am. Had her a year after college."

"Wow. I would have never guessed."

I nodded and put the top slice of bread on each sandwich.

"How long have you and Ethan been together?"

"This time around?" I wasn't sure if Jessica knew that I was Ethan's first—well, first everything—but since Braeden asked, I made sure to tell him. I handed him a plate with his sandwich on it and a small pack of plain potato chips.

"*This* time?" He took the plate and chips from me.

I grinned—a full-on Cheshire Cat grin—and grabbed Coke Zeros from the fridge. "We were high school sweethearts."

"Really?"

I slid onto the barstool next to him and handed him his soda. "Yep." There was a slight pause as we both opened our chips and sodas, and took a few bites of our sandwiches.

"If you don't mind me asking, what happened?" Officer Belt inquired.

*Not at all. Please tell your wife.* "I went off to college in California, and he stayed here. Long distance didn't work out." Of course, I didn't want to tell him the exact truth, but what I'd said was partially true. If Ethan and I had been in the same town, I probably would have never gone to that stupid party, or at least not without him.

"California? When did you move back?"

"You ask a lot of questions," I teased, hoping to pretend I wasn't loving being grilled about my relationship.

He chuckled and took a bite of his sandwich. "Hazard of the job. Sorry."

"I'm kidding." I grinned and took a bite of my own sandwich. "I moved back a couple of months ago, and things rekindled after he came into the bar I work at."

"Which bar?"

"Judy's, just down the street."

"Oh yeah. I know it. Cool place." He took another bite.

"It is. Ethan's sister met her husband there, and now Ethan and I are back together. It's magical or something."

"Ah, yes, I knew about his sister and Rhys Cole."

"Oh yeah?"

"My wife is …" He rubbed the back of his neck. "My wife is friends with Ethan's ex-wife, so I hear all the gossip."

*No shit?* "Really?" I smiled.

"Yeah." He sighed. "I'm sorry for asking all the questions. My wife texted me to find out the dirt so she can tell Jessica."

"Dirt?" I slipped a few chips into my mouth.

"They want to know what you're like."

I took a sip of my drink. "And what am I like?"

"Well"—he grinned—"between you and me, you seem much nicer than Jessica."

I chuckled slightly. "Oh yeah? How so?"

"Jessica is one of those women who thrive on drama. She's always up to something at the school the kids go to, and she reminds me of Christina Applegate's character in *Bad Moms*."

I laughed. "Totally know what you mean."

I *did* know what he meant, and that made me sad because not only did Jessica want dirt on me, but I also knew it was because of Ethan's sons. I just hoped it wasn't going to come down to them or me.

There was a knock on the front door, and my gaze locked with Braeden. He slid off the barstool, reaching for his gun. "Get in the hall," he ordered.

I didn't think killers knocked before entering, but I obeyed Braeden just in case. I couldn't see the door from the hall, but I could hear everything.

"Sheriff?" Braeden questioned in greeting.

*Sheriff?*

"Sergeant Valor told me Reagan McCormick is here."

"She is. What do you need with Reagan?" Braeden asked. The sheriff didn't reply, or at least I didn't hear anything. "You can come out, Reagan."

I did, moving around the corner and coming into view.

The sheriff stepped over to me. "Reagan McCormick, you've been served with an emergency protective order. You're to stay at least five hundred feet away from the parties listed until the hearing."

"An emergency protective order?" I questioned as I took the papers. I glanced at them to see that Jessica was the petitioner. "Of course."

"Make sure you show up to the hearing," the sheriff stated. "And you'll need to surrender all of your firearms."

I snorted and gave a tight smile. "I don't have any guns, but I understand. Thank you, sheriff."

He turned and left. Braeden closed the door behind him.

"Seems Jessica didn't want to wait for the dirt you were going to tell her," I stated, waving the papers in front of me.

He grunted. "I guess not."

After Braeden left at three, April, another officer I'd met after class, arrived to take over the task of keeping me safe. We watched a few episodes of a true crime documentary on Netflix, and before I knew it, Ethan was walking in through the front door.

"Hey," I greeted with a smile.

He looked tired, with dark circles under bloodshot eyes, and I was certain it wasn't only because he didn't sleep the night before. Even though we were both worried about a killer, I couldn't imagine the added stress Ethan was under because of me: keeping me safe, fighting with Jessica because a killer was after me, and working to solve the case before another murder happened.

Possibly my murder.

"Hey." He threw his keys and cell phone onto the table near the door. He loosened his tie as he walked toward where I sat on the couch. "Thank you, April."

"Not a problem." She stood. "Now, I need to go home and find out what happens in the next episode. See ya tomorrow, Reagan."

"Bye. Have a good night."

"You too."

Ethan gave me a quick kiss on the lips before he walked April to the door. "See you tomorrow. Goodnight."

"Night," she called back and left. Ethan shut the door and locked all of the locks.

"What do you want for dinner?" I asked as I stood to go to the kitchen.

He grabbed my waist, bringing me onto his lap as he fell back onto the couch. "Whatever you want. I just want to shower and hold you all night. It's been a long day."

"Tell me about it. I assume you know I got served with a restraining order?" I wrapped my arms around his neck.

"Yeah, I know."

"Well, I read it, and I agree with what she wrote. I don't want anything to happen to your boys because of me."

He took a deep breath and closed his eyes briefly. "It's not just you, Buttercup. I was served with one too."

I furrowed my brows. "What does that mean? You can't see your kids?"

"Nope."

"What?" I shrieked and tried to stand. "She's seriously trying to make it so you can't see your own children?"

He tightened his arms around me. "It won't fucking happen, but unfortunately, because it's an emergency protection order, there's nothing I can do until the hearing."

"You can't be serious."

"Trust me, I'm pissed. I called my attorney, but he confirmed there's nothing I can do except stay away until the hearing."

"That's ridiculous."

"I know. I fucking know."

"This is all my fault."

"What? Of course, it isn't."

I closed my eyes and shook my head slowly. "It is."

"Because a serial killer is after you?"

My eyes sprang open. "Um, yeah."

Ethan didn't say anything as we stared at each other for several moments. "Look, I don't want to argue about this with you. We've had a shitty couple of days, and I feel like everything is one step back instead of forward."

"You know I'm here to help, right?"

He kissed me softly. "I know you are, but I can't tell you anything about the case."

"Because I'll be in even more danger," I said, repeating what he'd told me earlier.

"Yes, but also, I don't want to get thrown off the case because if anyone is going to solve this quickly, it's me."

I smiled warmly at him. "I know you will, but if a killer hadn't entered my condo, you'd still have your boys."

"I still have my boys."

"But the court order—"

"A piece of paper isn't going to keep me from my kids, Reagan."

"What are you going to do?"

He sighed. "Honestly, nothing right now. I hate to say it, but having a few days to focus on the case will be good for all of us. I'm going to spend every waking hour working this."

"I understand."

"Now"—he picked me up—"we're going to shower, eat, fuck, and get some sleep. Maybe not in that order." He grinned.

My legs wrapped around his waist, and I laughed. "I'm finished with all my homework, so we have all night." We were both tired, but sex would be a good way to forget what was happening for the time being and hopefully help Ethan get some much-needed sleep.

He walked us into the bathroom that was connected to the master bedroom. "Or until we pass out." We were on the same page.

"We should order pizza. Then it will be here when we get out of the shower."

"That will put a timeframe on how long I can fuck you, Buttercup."

I grinned. "I'll get naked while you call it in. That's multitasking."

He set me down, pressed his lips to mine. "That's why I love you."

"Love you too." I bit my lip.

"Get undressed and in the shower. I'll be back."

By the time he got back—which was less than four minutes later—I was as he'd ordered: naked and wet. The spray of the shower beat down on my chest as I stood under the warm water. I'd heard Ethan come in, and I was waiting for him. The shower door opened. When I turned, I noticed he was already hard and had put on a condom. We did have a timeline—maybe thirty minutes—before the pizza would arrive and had to hurry some.

Without any words, he swept my hair back with both hands, brought my lips to his and pushed us back against the cold tile, pinning me against the wall and grinding against me. He pulled his lips from mine to make his way down my neck with his mouth and back up again, applying little nibbles to my jaw along the way. I reached down and wrapped my hand around his rock hard cock. He let out a groan and brought his mouth to my ear.

"Turn around, baby. Hands on the wall."

I did, putting both palms against the tile, and then rested the back of my head on his shoulder, giving him open access to my neck. He alternated between nipping and sucking, and I pushed my hips back, rubbing my ass against him. His hand made its way up to one of my boobs, massaging the globe as he plucked my nipples, causing them to stiffen. His other hand moved between my legs.

At the first stroke of his fingers against my clit, I let out a satisfied moan. He pushed his fingers inside of me, going deep, gliding in and out effortlessly. Being with Ethan always made me feel as though we were made for each other, and he knew exactly how to work me to make me a puddle of water. I was able to open myself to him in every way and enjoy the way he worked my body.

Ethan bent his knees, lifting me slightly to slide his shaft inside of me in one thrust. My hands went up and down the wall with each drive. The steam from the shower stuck to my skin and made each push up with his hips glide fluidly.

"Fuck," he groaned. "After the day—"

"Shh," I said and turned my mouth to his, tasting and sucking his tongue as he worked me higher and higher. I didn't want him to think about anything except for the present.

Drive after drive, thrust after trust, and push after push, he worked us both until we both tipped over the edge. I went first, clenching his dick as I spasmed.

"That's it, baby," he gritted out as he increased his pace until he followed, stilling and coming too.

Ethan stayed inside of me as our mouths came together, savoring the moment. After some time, we moved apart, and he pulled out of me and set me down. He removed the condom and threw it into the bin next to the toilet just outside of the shower.

"Do you think our sex life would be this good if we had stayed together and gotten married?" He started to lather his body with body wash that smelled like paradise. "I mean, you have to admit we work well together."

I tilted my head slightly as I moved under the spray of the water to clean off. "We do, and I'd like to think that twenty-three years from now it will be the same."

He grinned, switching places with me to rinse off and shampoo his hair. "I hope I can still get it up in twenty-three years."

"I'm sure there will *still* be a pill for that by then."

"True," he replied, and we heard the door buzzer in the other room. "Pizza's probably here." Ethan rinsed his hair quickly, kissed me one last time, and then left to grab the phone.

After we ate most of the pizza, we crawled into bed and slept well for the first time since we'd discovered the plaque in my apartment.

# CHAPTER NINETEEN

*Ethan*

**"H**ave fun in class, Buttercup." It wasn't the first time I'd uttered those words, but it was the first time I'd watched Reagan walk away with an undercover cop next to her.

"Ready?" Shawn asked.

I nodded.

Will had obtained a warrant, and we were going to the IT department with him. There was nothing Shawn and I could do, but we wanted to go. Or, more specifically, I wanted to go. Since this fucker had violated my girlfriend's space, I wanted to know everything on the tech side. I didn't know what I could do, but if Will traced this asshole, I wanted to be the first to know.

Shawn and I were still waiting for Daisy's phone records. The day before, we'd gone back to Amy's apartment to discover that Heather, the roommate, had moved out. We went to the boyfriend's apartment, but no one answered. So, to kill two birds with one stone, Shawn and I were with Will so we could stop by the admissions office and get Heather's schedule to track her down.

We needed that fucking wood plaque.

The three of us found the admissions building. Shawn stayed on the main floor to get Heather's schedule, and I went with Will down to the basement where the IT department was located. When we first entered, I counted eight doors—some opened, some closed—along a long, wide hall behind a reception desk.

Will stood ahead of me as we approached the reception desk. A woman looked up from her computer. "Can I … Can I help you?" she stammered as though they never got visitors.

Will handed her the warrant. "We're here to scan your servers."

She balked. "Really?"

"Yes."

"Okay. Let me … Let me get my boss." She stood.

"Sure."

A few moments later, a man came up. "Jack Clark." He stuck out his hand. He looked familiar, but in the short exchange, I couldn't place him. "I'm the Director of the IT department."

I took his hand. "Sergeant Valor, and this is Officer Nichols. He's the head of the cybercrime unit at our precinct. We have a warrant to scan your servers and computers."

"Why?" Jack furrowed his brows in confusion.

"There have been two murders associated with Lakeshore University—"

"Yes, I've heard. And you think it's connected to our computers?"

"Unfortunately, we can't disclose that information at this time."

When Shawn walked in, Jack's gaze moved to him and then back to me. "Right this way."

"Actually," I stopped them with my words, "Officer Nichols will take it from here."

Jack nodded, and he and Will turned and headed to the other end of the hall. They turned a corner, and were out of sight. The woman went back to her desk, but I caught her gaze a few times and made a mental note to speak with her.

I turned to Shawn. "Did you get it?"

"Yeah."

I pulled my phone out of my pocket and realized Reagan had fifteen more minutes left of class. "Do you want to go see if she has what we need? I want to walk Reagan to the car."

"Yeah, sure."

I gave a quick nod in agreement and turned to face the assistant. "If they get done before I'm back, can you tell Officer Nichols that I'll be back?"

"Sure … sure thing." She stuttered with a smile.

Shawn and I walked toward the elevator. Once we were inside, I asked, "Was she acting weird?"

He thought for a moment. "I was barely there, so I didn't get a good read on her. Why?"

I shrugged. "She was stammering."

"Maybe she just has a stutter or is nervous around cops?"

"Maybe." I wasn't sure if she was acting weird or not. Being close to the case was fucking with me. That was why police officers didn't work personal cases, but I *had* to work this case.

Shawn and I parted ways when we got outside. He went to find Heather's current class, and I went to walk Reagan to Officer Chase's car. If I could, I would go with her every day.

A few steps from the classroom, I saw April leaning against the wall, waiting. April was dressed to go to class with Reagan and make it look less conspicuous, more like a friend or classmate of Reagan's. She gave a small wave.

"Hey," I greeted.

"Find anything?"

I shrugged slightly. "Will's doing his thing now. Anything here?"

"No. It's been quiet."

"Good."

April turned to me, leaning a shoulder against the wall. "I've been thinking. Do you think this is personal?"

I thought for a moment. "Against Reagan or me?"

"Either."

The problem with her question was that I hadn't technically *known* Reagan long enough to know if she'd done anything to piss someone off. I was a good judge of character, and I didn't think Reagan would have done anything to anyone, but it could be *anyone* who had some sort of jealous vendetta against her.

"It has to be someone who knows her," I replied. "They gave her that fucking plaque with her name on it."

"Could still be a stranger," April stated.

"Why do you think that?"

"Think about all the places you say your name out loud: coffee shops, fast food places, there's a sign-up sheet at a bank if you want to meet with a banker, and even some nail salons make you sign in."

"So, you think they overheard Reagan's name or saw her write it and are just fucking with us since I'm on the cases?"

"Could be." She shrugged slightly. "Someone could know that you'd be the one on the case. This school is in your jurisdiction, is it not?" she asked, waving her arm slightly to indicate the school we were standing in. I nodded, not liking where she was going. "Maybe someone is taunting you because they have something against *you.*"

April's theory slowly sank in. Was Jessica behind this? Was it her way to get full custody of our kids? I would lose everything if she were successful, killing Reagan and getting custody of my boys.

But Amy's murder was the night after Reagan and I reconnected, before we were even a couple again. Jessica didn't know about her at the time. Then again, if she had someone tailing me, trying to come up with some sort of dirt on me, then she would know that Reagan was someone special to me. Even that first night at Judy's, we'd left together, and she'd spent the night at my place. Was killing Amy some sort of way to pin the connection on me? To prove that my job was dangerous to my family? I wasn't sure the timeline added up, but it was a theory.

"I hope you're not right," I finally said.

"Me too, but my aunt used to be a cop in Florida, and she's paranoid as fuck. Now that I'm on the force, I understand where she's coming from."

Except if April was correct, it would be more than a criminal wanting to get back at me for sending them to jail. The boys would lose their mother because she would go to prison.

"You're going to make a good detective one day," I stated.

April grinned. "You think so?"

I smiled back. "Yes. You're thinking outside of the box, and that's good."

"Thanks, Sarge." She was still grinning.

Reagan's class was dismissed. Her gaze met mine, and she smirked when she walked out the door. My heart clenched. Every second for the past three days, I'd been thinking the fucking worst—and now even more so, given my conversation with April. If the killer wasn't connected to Jess, why would he place the plaque in Amy's and Daisy's home *before* killing them as he had with Reagan? Wouldn't that be suspicious? I didn't think that was the case.

Another thought came to me. If he was, in fact, watching Reagan—us—through her webcam, did he know everything I'd done on the case since I'd worked on it a few nights over the last month? *Fuck.* That might be why the killer was always one step ahead of us. But, did it mean that Reagan was or wasn't a target? Was it possible he was only fucking with me, and Jess was behind it? But then, how did he get Reagan's IP address to connect it to me? Was it random and they stumbled upon us? Did they not watch her while I was there?

I had too many fucking questions.

"Buttercup." I kissed her lips softly when she walked up to me. I was trying to act normal—as normal as I could be. "How was class?"

"Good." All three of us started to head out. "How was whatever you were doing?" I gave her a sideways look. "I know," she sighed. "You can't tell me."

We continued walking to the exit. I stopped just outside the doors causing Reagan and April to stop too. "April, can you give us a minute?"

"Sure." She smiled and walked a few feet away out of earshot.

"Everything okay?" Reagan asked.

"I wanted to tell you that I'm not sure what time I'll be home tonight."

"I understand."

"It's not just because of the case. I'm going to stop by Jessica's."

Her emerald eyes widened. "You are?"

"It's Wednesday."

"But the protection order."

I rolled my eyes. "No paper is going to keep me from my boys." Especially now that I had new suspicions that Jessica might be behind everything. I didn't know how she had gained access to Reagan's place, how she knew where she lived, or anything, and that was why I needed to talk to her face to face. I needed to read her. I'd know if she was lying or hiding anything because I had been married to her for almost ten years.

"Can't you go to jail or something?"

"That won't happen."

"Are you sure?"

"Just—trust me."

"Okay." She gave a small smile. "Who's my detail tonight?"

"Braeden."

"Officer Belt's wife isn't going to be happy."

I grinned. I was sure she and Jessica had a great conversation at school drop-off about Braeden's time with Reagan. "No, she probably won't."

Reagan and April left, and I waited for Shawn outside the doors to the administration building again. I didn't have to wait long before he walked around the corner. "Well?"

"Heather said she packed the plaque and Amy's mom took it when they boxed up all of Amy's belongings."

"Did you get an address?"

He nodded. "I did, but she lives in Washington."

"Shit," I groaned. I didn't have the file in front of me, and we were talking about something we'd searched a month beforehand, so I'd forgotten.

"Yeah, and Heather said she never saw the plaque until she was boxing up Amy's stuff."

"So, he leaves the plaque *after* he kills them?"

"He has to be."

"That makes no sense when it comes to Reagan." I wasn't going to tell him about my conversation with April. It wasn't because I wanted to hide anything from my partner; I trusted him with my life. But if Jessica was behind everything, I wanted to know for sure before I did tell Shawn.

"I know. I'm going to call Amy's mom and see if she'll mail it to us. Then we can dust it for prints." The chain of custody had been broken, given that the crime scene had been released, and Heather had gone back home to pack up and move.

"And have her check for a number on the back," I reminded him. Wooden objects weren't the best to get fingerprints from, but at this point, since we had nothing, I wanted to see if we could recover anything that wasn't Heather's or Amy's parents' DNA.

"Yeah, I'll try her now."

I bobbed my head in agreement. "I'm going to go down and see what Will has found."

"I'll meet you down there."

When I got down to the basement, the receptionist looked up from her computer and smiled. "Detective Valor, you're back."

"Sergeant Valor," I corrected.

"Oh, sorry."

I opened my mouth to ask her how long she'd worked in the IT department, but my phone started to ring inside the pocket of my suit jacket. I pulled it out and saw it was my father calling. I turned and walked to stand next to the elevator. "Hey."

"Son."

"What's up?"

"When were you going to tell me that Jessica has a restraining order against you?"

"It's a protective order," I clarified. As though that was better. I'd called my mother to tell her that we weren't coming for our monthly dinner and explained why, so of course, she'd told my father.

I wasn't trying to keep it from him; I just had a lot on my mind given the circumstances.

"Ethan!" he scolded.

"I'm handling it, Dad."

"How?"

I rubbed the back of my neck. "It's connected to the …" I hesitated, then lowered my voice because I wasn't that far away from the receptionist. "Remember how I told you someone broke into Reagan's place, and that was why I asked you to change the locks?"

"Yeah."

"We have evidence that the break-in is connected to the murders I'm investigating."

There was a brief pause. "There's a serial killer in Chicago?"

"Yeah." I sighed. The elevator dinged, and Shawn stepped out. "I can't talk about this right now."

"I don't like this."

"And you think I do?" Shawn furrowed his brows, and I held up a finger.

"I'll go talk to her."

"No!" I shouted and then lowered my voice again. "I plan to talk to her tonight."

"But she has a protective order against you. You can't go talk to her even if you're the cop on the case. You can go to jail for violating the judge's order."

"Yeah, I know, but I have to do something."

"Let me go talk to her. The boys can still come over for dinner. It's not good for them to change their routine."

"I know it's not."

"I'll deal with her."

"No. Just let me handle it." I watched Will walk up to the reception desk. "I have to go."

"I'm dealing with this," he repeated.

"Dad," I groaned.

"Come by my house when you call it a night. I'll tell you what happened."

I felt as though we would go around and around, and I really had no time to try to talk him out of going. He knew the life of a police officer, and when Jessica told him she knew—*that she was behind it*—I hoped my father would have my back. I hoped his police senses would spike and he'd get to the bottom of it.

"Fine. Ask her everything."

"Everything?"

"*Everything*," I said again, hoping he'd get the hint. "I really need to go."

"Okay. Goodbye."

I sighed and stuck my phone back into my pocket as I moved toward Will and Shawn. "Well?"

"Still running a few scans, but so far nothing," Will answered.

"Not even that malware shit?" I asked.

"No. I didn't find it."

Well, fuck.

# CHAPTER TWENTY

*Ethan*

**M**y heart was beating fast as I sat in my truck outside of the house that I'd fucking paid for. My dad was inside, and I was two seconds away from going in too. The plan was to let him go in and talk to her, and I prayed he would find out if Jess was behind this shit without me telling him anything about the case or my suspicions. However, I couldn't sit back and hope Dad got my signals, so I'd stopped him before he could go inside.

*"You shouldn't be here,"* he'd stated as I got out of my truck.

He was on his way to the front door, and I'd made it in time to speak with him before he could talk to Jessica. After Will informed us that he had gotten nothing from the computers, I left, knowing my dad was more than likely on his way to talk to Jess. I was right.

*"I need to tell you something before you go inside."*

*"What is it?"*

*"Get in the truck."* I'd motioned for him to get in on the passenger side. After he got into the cab, I drove away from the house, not wanting Jessica to come outside.

*"What's going on?"*

*"Let me park,"* I'd said. A few moments later, I pulled into the parking lot of the grocery store down the street.

*"I don't care if she's your ex-wife—"*

*"That's not it."* I'd parked and cut the engine and sighed before speaking. *"I told you earlier that the protection order is connected to the cases I'm working, but I also think Jess might be behind the murders."*

*"What?"* Dad had shouted. I'd told him everything. He was no longer on the force, but he was a damn good cop, and if anything, he could help me. I needed his help, given I had to stay five hundred feet away from Jessica, and I didn't want to tell Shawn until I knew for sure.

Dad was silent for a few moments, but then he took a deep breath before responding, *"For the sake of those boys, you better hope she's not behind this."*

We came up with a plan for him to question Jessica without her knowing we had our suspicions.

*"What about my boys? How can I let her keep them if she's behind this?"*

*"That will never happen,"* he'd stated. *"I'll find out, and if I think she's behind it, I will take them to my house, and you can call it in to bring her to the station for further questioning."*

*"Thank you."*

I'd driven Dad back to the house, and while he was inside, I had to restrain myself numerous times so Jess didn't know I was outside and breaking the protection order. I didn't know what would make me feel better: Dad coming out with my sons or coming out without them. Either way wasn't good for me. I already missed my boys. I couldn't imagine not seeing them for two or more weeks, but I also couldn't imagine Jessica going to prison and them only seeing her in shackles.

Finally, after the sun had gone down and an hour or so had passed, Dad walked out of the front door. Alone.

*Fuck.*

Dad got into the passenger seat of my truck, and I turned slightly to face him.

"Well?"

He shut the door. "She knows nothing."

"How can you be sure?"

"I treated it like an interrogation. She didn't crack."

"She's a manipulative bitch, Dad. She could have fooled you."

He shook his head just as the doom light shut off, and we were left in only the glow of the streetlight. "I know she is, but I don't think she's behind the killings."

"How can you be sure?"

Dad thought for a moment. "I can't, but if you want to call Shawn to arrest her, go for it. It's on you."

"I don't want to lose my kids," I admitted.

He grabbed my shoulder and gave it a squeeze. "You won't. You're a decorated officer. Go with your gut."

"I have to wait two weeks to fight this," I reminded him.

"I know it's going to be tough but take those two weeks and solve this shit. No matter who the killer is, you'll get your boys back once the case is over. If you can't solve this before your hearing, a judge will do the right thing."

After thanking my dad—who also said that the boys were spending the night at their place Friday night—I left before Jessica got her panties in a bunch and tried to say I was violating the protective order. I went to the station, surrendered my service weapon, and then drove home.

When I walked in through the door of my condo, Reagan was sitting on one end of the couch and Braeden on the other end. The TV was on, but I paid no attention. I just wanted to be alone with Reagan.

"Valor," Braeden greeted.

"Hey," I replied, throwing my keys onto the table by the door.

"I thought you were going to be late?" Reagan asked.

Braeden stood, and I moved to give Reagan a quick kiss. "Wanted to rush home to you, Buttercup."

"And that's my cue," Braeden stated. "See you tomorrow, Reagan."

"Have a good night," she replied.

After seeing Braeden out and locking the door behind him, I sat on the couch next to Reagan. "Did you go to Jessica's?" she asked.

I sighed and tipped back my head onto the back of the couch and closed my eyes. "Yes, but I didn't speak to her."

"What happened?"

I wanted to tell her my suspicions about Jessica but then thought better of it. My gut was telling me Jess wasn't behind the murders. I trusted my father, and I had to trust his judgment. "My dad talked to her for me. Worked it out so the boys will spend the night at their place on Friday."

"So, you'll get to see them?"

I shook my head, not raising it from the back of the couch. "No. The protective order is for them too. If Jess heard that I showed up, she'd have me arrested."

Reagan moved closer and rested her head on my shoulder. "I'm so sorry."

I took a long, deep breath. "Me too."

"Do you think you'll solve this before Thanksgiving?"

I finally looked at her. "Thanksgiving?"

"Yeah. Thanksgiving is in three weeks."

"I sure fucking hope so."

# Unknown

I wasn't nervous when I saw Detective—*no, Sergeant* Valor and his partner walk into the IT department. I was in my office, with the door open. I knew he and the other detective would be by eventually because my process *wasn't* foolproof. But I knew how to cover my tracks, and it was only a matter of time before they'd find the malware program I'd created and then put onto each computer via the link each student and staff clicked on when they needed to create their Lakeshore U profile. I also knew that they'd realize all three ladies were students too.

I wasn't worried because I was still one step ahead of them. I wasn't stupid. I'd never tie my shit back to my work. What I had done was create a copy of our database and used that along with the pictures of students from their student IDs to find *my* women to watch.

After the cops left, I felt giddy. I was flying high all day and wanted to celebrate my win. I knew Reagan wasn't working since it was Wednesday, and she only worked Thursday through Sunday nights, but I wanted to go to Judy's and have a drink to rub it in their faces.

Three drinks in, Jack walked through the door. I knew he frequented Judy's, and I was secretly hoping I'd run into him, even if he was the director of IT—my boss—and I was more or less a peon who did the grunt work.

His gaze met mine, and we both smiled. I'd always thought he was handsome, especially for an older man. I assumed he was at least fifteen, maybe even twenty years older than myself. "Boss," I greeted.

He slid onto the barstool next to me. "I didn't know you came here too."

I grinned. "There's a lot you don't know about me."

Jack slowly smiled. "Oh yeah? Tell me more."

I leaned my head close to his and whispered, "Then I'd have to kill you."

Another drink for me, and three for Jack, and we were both feeling good. We got closer and closer, our shoulders touching, our hands brushing against each other. Then his mouth met mine, and everything changed.

For the better.

I'd never expected to have sex with my boss, but it was so good. So good that I started to think women were no longer my thing. I needed a man to bend me over and fuck me hard. And that was what Jack did in the bathroom of Judy's.

And many nights after.

# CHAPTER TWENTY-ONE

## Reagan

Ethan didn't go to school with me like he had the last two days. Instead, he went to the precinct. I didn't blame him. I could tell everything was weighing heavily on him. How could it not?

While out in public, I was trying not to show that it was getting to me. If the killer was watching, I wanted him to think I wasn't scared. But sometimes I'd catch myself worrying about everything, and honestly, I didn't like it.

Ethan wasn't sharing any details with me, but given that I was studying CSI, and from what I'd remembered from college, I figured the police probably didn't have DNA or fingerprints or anything that would lead them to the killer.

When I was at the crime scene, I'd expected to see a disaster, but to my untrained eye, it looked almost staged, though the amount of blood on the couch said otherwise. That led me to believe the woman was unconscious when she was brutally stabbed.

Until Ethan and Shawn solved the case, I was never drinking from anything I didn't pour myself. In fact, I hadn't been to the coffee shop except for the day after we found the wood plaque on my wall. It wasn't because I didn't trust them, but at this point, I couldn't trust any stranger.

My phone rang in my purse as April and I walked to class. "I need to get this," I said to her after taking my phone out. It was Maddie. "Hey, honey."

"What's wrong?"

I stopped walking, causing April to stop too. "What do you mean?"

"You usually call me every day while you walk to class, and I haven't heard from you in days."

"Oh," I sighed. Really, I hadn't called her the day prior, not *days* as she put it, but it *was* unusual for me not to call her while I walked to class. "Nothing's wrong."

"Then why haven't you called?"

"I …" I looked at April. She looked concerned, but I smiled, hoping she'd know that my phone call wasn't bad. "I met a new friend, and we've been walking to class together. I'm sorry."

"Oh," Maddie replied. "I thought something was wrong."

I frowned even though she couldn't see me. "No, nothing's wrong," I lied. "Are you doing okay?"

"I'm fine. I just … I just miss you."

My heart sank. "I miss you too. Are you sure you're doing okay?"

"Yeah. I wanted to tell you …" She paused.

"Tell me what?" I asked after a long moment of silence. April tapped at her wrist, indicating that we needed to hurry so I wouldn't be late to class. I nodded and started to walk again in the direction of the building.

"I started dating someone."

I stopped walking again. "Oh yeah?"

"Yeah. I've been waiting to tell you for *days*."

April and I started up the stairs into the building. "I'm sorry, honey. You didn't mention it on Monday or Tuesday."

"Because I didn't know if it was serious or not."

"And now it's serious?"

"Yeah," Maddie sighed as though she was thinking about her new relationship at that very moment.

"I'm happy for you, but I'm just heading into class now. Can I call you tonight on my dinner break? You can tell me more then."

"There's actually a party tonight."

I grinned. "Right. You're a college girl."

"Yeah." I heard her chuckle.

"Listen, honey. We're preparing for our final exam that's next week, and I need to go before I'm late. I can't wait to meet him, and we can chat more about him later."

"Yeah—okay."

"Love you."

"Love you too."

That afternoon, I went to work my shift at Judy's. Neither Braeden nor April were on my detail. This time it was Officer Cash, whom I had met at Ethan's condo before my shift. The plan was for Officer Cash to already be inside the bar before I got there so it wasn't obvious I was walking in with a detail.

April saw me off, and when I pulled into the alley behind Judy's, Ethan was waiting. There was no parking lot for the bar, but given I worked until the early morning, I parked as close to the back door as possible, hoping no one would crash into my car as they drove down the alley. Ethan was leaning against a squad car, ankles crossed. We walked toward each other after I got out of my car.

"I didn't know you were coming by," I stated.

He reached up with one hand and cupped my face, pressing his lips to mine. "Just wanted to make sure you made it here safely."

"Yep. Doors stayed locked, and I came straight here." Of course, I wasn't taking any chances: get in the car, lock all the doors, don't stop anywhere, and go straight to work. *Check.* I only had to drive two blocks given Ethan's condo was just down the street.

"Good. I'll come back in a few hours, and then I'll drive you home."

"Okay."

We started walking toward the back door of the bar. "I was thinking we should hire private security for you. That way, you aren't bouncing you from officer to officer. Eventually, Captain Rapp won't let me keep using department resources."

"You don't think you'll solve this soon?"

Ethan faced me. "Honestly? No."

My heart sank. There was a lot riding on finding the killer, including my safety and Ethan seeing his sons. "Maybe I should go somewhere. That way you can get your boys back and—"

"I'm not letting you leave again," he stated.

As I looked into his deep blue eyes, I understood. Ethan thought that if I drove away, I wouldn't return for twenty-three years. That, of course, wouldn't happen. I wanted to stay and not leave. Forever.

"But, it can just be until this is all over," I suggested. I could leave temporarily—just until they caught the guy, however long that may be—so Ethan could see his kids. They were more important than me.

"No." He shook his head and pulled me to him, wrapping me in his arms. "Don't you get it, Buttercup? Our relationship is only easy when we're together. We spent twenty-three years apart, and we're never going to be apart again."

"But—"

Ethan silenced me by placing his finger over my lips. "No buts. Everything will work out the way it's meant to."

There was no point in arguing with him. "Okay. I should go before I'm late." If the judge decided in Jessica's favor, then I would revisit the suggestion that I should leave.

He kissed me again as though he wanted to remind me that he loved me and couldn't get enough of me. That he was starving for me. We broke apart after several long moments. "Have a good day at work, Buttercup. I love you."

I smiled and sighed, happy. "I love you too."

With lingering hands, we finally broke apart. I walked through the door, and Ethan went toward his car. I still had the feeling of being a teenager when I was with him. Ethan kissing me at the door of my work reminded me of when we were in high school, and I worked at an ice cream shop. He made sure to kiss me before I clocked in, and he always drove me home.

As I walked past Judy's office, I stuck my head in through the open door and said hello.

"Hey, Reagan. You doing okay?"

I smiled at the older blonde who had owned the bar since I was a kid. "Yes, I'm good."

"I mean with the break-in."

I gave another small smile. "I've been staying at my boyfriend's. He's keeping me safe."

"Well, don't walk outside alone. We don't want to take any chances."

"I won't. He's coming back at the end of my shift to drive me home." I blinked at my last word. *Home? Was Ethan's place home?*

"Good."

I turned and made my way down the skinny hall to where the lockers were, stopping just short when I saw what looked like a flower looped through my lock. I moved closer and saw that it was a light purple Persian buttercup. Slipping it out, I ran my fingers along the petals and realized it was fake. They weren't in season, so that made sense.

Taking my phone out of my purse, I sent a text to Ethan: *Thank you for the flower. I love it and I love you. Always.*

I opened my locker and placed my purse and jacket inside. Before closing the door, my phone started to ring, and Ethan's name appearing on the screen.

"Hey—"

"I didn't give you a flower."

I froze, and my heart fell to the pit of my stomach. "What?"

"I didn't give you a flower," he repeated. My mouth opened, but no words came out. "Where was it?"

"On my locker."

The back door flew open, and Ethan stalked through it. It was as though he'd turned his car around when he got my text because he was just down the alley. Or maybe he hadn't had time to pull away yet. "Let me see."

A few long strides put him in front of me. I tried to hand him the flower, but he shook his head.

Judy stuck her head out of her office. "Is everything okay?"

Ethan turned to her while I pressed the disconnect button to end the call. "Yes, Judy." Ethan stuck out his hand. They shook as he continued. "I'm Sergeant Valor and Reagan's boyfriend. Do you know who put this on her locker?"

"No," she replied. "I haven't seen that before."

"Who has access back here?"

Judy blinked. "Mostly employees."

"But I just walked in through that door"—Ethan pointed at the back door—"without a key."

Judy blinked again and opened her mouth. Nothing came out.

Ethan took out a plastic evidence bag that he had in his back pocket that I assumed he'd grabbed out of his squad car. He opened it and, without instruction, I placed the silk flower into the clear bag.

"I'm going to test this for prints," he stated.

The door that led out to the main part of the bar opened, and we all looked in that direction. Derrick walked through, carrying a black trash bag. He looked at me and then over to Ethan as he stood still.

"Do you know about this?" Ethan snapped.

"I …" Derrick tried to reply. He looked back at me and then to Judy before his gaze landed on Ethan's again. "No."

Ethan took a step toward Derrick. "Are you sure? Because I'm going to run prints, and if—"

The bag fell from Derrick's grasp, causing glass bottles to clink against the concrete floor. He held up his hands in surrender. "Fine, I did it."

"You did what?" Ethan asked and took another step forward.

"I put the flower on her locker, man."

"Why?" Ethan seethed.

"Because … Because Reagan told me it was her favorite flower," Derrick stuttered.

Ethan cut his gaze to me, and I shrugged. "It was back when we both first started. He was asking me about you, and I told him it wasn't his business and if he wanted to get to know me since we were working together, then he should ask things like my favorite color, flower, etc. So, he did, and I told him."

Ethan glared back at Derrick. "Let's have a chat, yeah?"

"What? Why?"

"Many reasons," Ethan replied. "Mind if I use your office for a few minutes, Judy?"

"Not at all. Please…."

Ethan walked to the threshold of Judy's office and turned to see that Derrick wasn't following him. "Now," he ordered.

"Go on," Judy coaxed.

Derrick looked at me as he passed, and I gave him a tight smile. I had my suspicions he could be the killer, but I wasn't sure. Before I knew that a serial killer had entered my condo, Derrick and I got along. We both did our jobs, and he had to know that I had a boyfriend even though I told him I wasn't looking for one because Ethan came in frequently.

Was Derrick hiding in plain sight?

# CHAPTER TWENTY-TWO

**M**y blood was on fire.

Since Shawn had spoken to Judy, and she'd advised him that Reagan's address was in a locked drawer and that drawer hadn't been tampered with, I had put Derrick low on the suspect list. I should have trusted my gut. Something was off about this kid.

"Sit," I ordered, pointing at Judy's desk chair. The office wasn't much, but at least it had a chair. It was small, and I planned to stand, to tower over Derrick and intimidate him. I closed the door as he sat.

"Look, man. I'm sorry."

I crossed my arms over my broad chest. "Sorry for what exactly?"

"Trying to close in on your woman."

I chuckled. "Yeah, tell me about that."

"About what?"

"Your plan."

He balked. "I didn't really have a plan."

I leaned down, placing my hands on the arms of the chair, the evidence bag clutched in one, and caged him in. "But you bought her favorite flower." I waved the evidence bag in front of his face then put it back down, still caging him in. "Did you think that would win her over?"

He shook his head and shrugged. "I don't know, man. She's hot."

"She's twice your age." I didn't mean that as an insult toward *my* Reagan, but this kid was barely twenty-one. In fact, when I'd looked into him, I found out that he turned twenty-one in June—only five months prior.

"She … She is?"

"Yes," I confirmed and then asked him where he was the night of Amy's murder, not wanting to beat around the bush any longer.

He furrowed his brows and thought for a minute. "I don't know. That was like months ago."

I stared into his dark eyes as I asked him about the night of Daisy's murder less than a week prior.

"I don't know. Probably at home."

"That's not a good answer," I replied.

"Why do you care? It has nothing to do with the flower or Reagan."

"Doesn't it?"

He balked. "What? No."

I pushed off the chair and crossed my arms again. "Okay. Tell me where you purchased the flower and when."

"The internet, and last week."

"The internet? What site?"

He shrugged. "I don't know. I searched for buttercup flowers and found it. I tried to find them at flower shops and was told they were out of season. Then I tried craft stores for the fake ones, and they didn't have them either, so I did the next best thing."

I stared at him, really looking at his face, and looked for any sign that he was lying.

"Are we done here?" he asked. "Are you going to arrest me for giving a flower to your girlfriend?"

I took a deep breath to calm myself down. I wanted to throw him against the wall and scream in his face that Reagan was mine. But, I also valued the badge and Reagan. I didn't want to cause any more of a rift that this incident would already cause her. "No, but make no mistake that Reagan is mine, and I'm never giving her up. You need to find someone your own age."

He chuckled and started to stand. "Okay, dude."

When I opened the door, I saw Reagan and Judy waiting just outside. "Everything okay?" Reagan asked.

Derrick walked passed me.

"Yeah, everything's fine," I replied.

"I know my shift has started, but do you mind if I talk to Ethan for a moment?" Reagan asked Judy.

"Not a problem. I'll go make sure Tommy's doing okay."

"Thank you."

I started to walk toward the door, but stopped and turned back around. "Hey, Judy."

She turned, and I saw that Derrick had stopped too. "Can we keep this locked?"

Judy's gaze moved to Reagan and then back to me. "Yes. I'll just tell all of the delivery guys that they need to knock."

"Thank you. I appreciate it."

She gave a warm smile and then turned to walk out to the main part of the bar with Derrick.

I grabbed Reagan and brought her in, wrapping my arms around her.

"What happened?" she asked against my chest.

"He just has a crush on you."

"I kinda suspected that."

"I suspected it too since the first night I came in here. I saw the way he watched you."

She pulled her head back and looked up at me. "Do you think it's more?"

I shook my head. "I don't think he's the guy I'm looking for."

"Okay." She sighed. "It's going to be awkward working with him, but I feel better now that I know you don't think he's a killer."

We broke apart, and I held up the evidence bag with the silk flower in it. "I'm still going to run his prints to make sure he's not wanted for something else."

"Okay. I better get out there."

I cupped her face and placed my lips on hers. If I could kiss her every second of every day, I would. I was head over heels for that woman, and I would do anything to keep her safe. That included hiring my own security for her even though she'd had less than a week of police details. Unfortunately, given the lack of evidence, I wasn't hopeful I would solve the murders anytime soon and needed to keep Reagan safe until I could.

"Let's try this again. Have a good day at work, Buttercup. I love you."

She smiled. "I love you too."

### One week later ...

I parked my truck in the underground parking at the courthouse and cut the engine.

"Hey," Reagan stopped me from getting out by grabbing my arm. "If this doesn't go in your favor, remember I said I would leave town until this is all over with."

"I don't want that," I admitted. We had spent every night together for months now, and I couldn't imagine going to bed or waking up without her next to me.

"I can't have you choosing between me and your kids, Eth."

I took a deep breath. Even though I never wanted to spend a day apart from Reagan—*my* Reagan—she was right. These were my kids, my blood, and I'd do anything for them. I'd also do anything for Reagan, which made me feel as though I was wedged between a rock and a hard place. "And I can't do this," I confessed. "This is killing me."

Reagan turned as best she could in her seat and grabbed my hand. "If the judge goes in her favor, it's only temporary. We'll find a place for me to go to until you catch this guy."

"It really fucking sucks that it might come down to that. The killer is a pro. He leaves no evidence."

"You know as well as I do that there's no perfect murder. Eventually, he will screw up, and you'll catch him."

What Reagan said wasn't something new, and I knew she was trying to put me at ease, but I just wanted something to go right.

"Yeah," I agreed because there wasn't more I could say. My future was going to be told to me by a fucking judge.

"We should go before we're late."

"I need another minute," I replied and without another word, leaned over and took her face in my hands.

I needed more than a minute. I needed to get lost in Reagan the only way I could at the moment, so I kissed her as though it would be our last. I kissed her as though my heart was breaking because it was. Some asshole was playing a fucking game with my life and was giving my ex ammunition to take my kids from me.

"Okay," I finally said after I pulled back. "I guess I'm ready."

After we both got out of my truck, I rounded the back and grabbed Reagan's hand. She pulled away from me, and I stopped walking, wondering why the hell she had let go.

"Maybe we shouldn't hold hands?"

"And why the hell not?"

She shrugged and blew out of breath. "I feel like it might fuel Jessica's fire."

"I don't give a shit. She can't dictate who I date," I snapped. I was a ball of emotions. I hadn't seen my kids in over two weeks, and I hadn't solved the fucking murders. But Reagan was still breathing and safe, and if I wanted to hold my girlfriend's hand, I was fucking going to hold my girlfriend's hand.

"I don't want—"

I followed Reagan's line of sight when she stopped talking. Jessica was walking toward the elevator, looking at us. She, of course, didn't have my kids with her, but she wasn't alone either. Her father was with her. They didn't stop, but their steps faltered a bit. While Jessica kept her gaze on Reagan and me, I grabbed Reagan's hand and began walking again. Reagan didn't say anything as we followed behind Jess and her dad, and after a curt nod at Jessica's father, the four of us rode the elevator up to the floor the hearings were on.

"You know you're violating the order, right?" Jessica spat in the awkward silence.

"Then have me arrested."

Technically, Reagan and I *were* violating the temporary order, but I didn't give a shit. Plain and simple. I didn't care anymore because as soon as the hearing started, I was going to get my kids back. I would keep my kids safe, and if Jessica didn't want to be anywhere near Reagan and me, that was on her. *She* divorced me, and she had to have known I'd eventually date again. Granted, no one knew a serial killer would threaten my girlfriend, but that wasn't a good enough reason to keep me from my boys. I couldn't control a criminal.

The elevator dinged, and without a word, I pulled Reagan out of the lift with the hand I was still holding. I saw my attorney sitting on a bench outside a courtroom and walked toward him.

"Randall," I greeted.

He stood and stuck out his hand. "Ethan." Then he turned to Reagan and shook hers as well. "Reagan."

"Morning," she replied.

"Ethan, your case is first on the docket."

"Great, let's get this over with."

We walked into the courtroom and sat on the opposite side of where Jessica and her father were. When the bailiff called my case number, Reagan stayed seated while Randall and I walked up to the wood tables, Jessica and her attorney on one side, Randall and me on the other. I let Randall do the talking—of course—but when it got to the reason behind the request for the protective order, and Randall told him the matter was classified, the judge turned to me.

"Is this true, Sergeant Valor?"

"Yes, it's connected to a few cases I'm working on."

The judge turned his attention to Jessica and her attorney and then back to me. "All parties, let's move this to chambers."

"If I may, Your Honor," I cut in, holding up my file that contained reports and such regarding the murders and Reagan's break-in. "This

is in relation to an ongoing investigation, and anyone but myself—and you, so that you can make your decision—should not be privy to the case. That includes the *former* Mrs. Valor and her counsel, as well as my own."

The judge paused before answering. "Okay. We'll take a five-minute recess while we speak in my chambers."

I followed the judge through a side door and then down a short hall and into his chambers. After he took a seat behind his desk, I told him the bare minimum of how the murders were related Jessica's case against me, and then we went back into the courtroom. I gave Reagan a small smile and returned to my place next to Randall.

The judge returned to his place on the bench a few moments later. "Given the measures Sergeant Valor has taken, and that the initial threat wasn't made against him, I'm denying the restraining order." He turned his full attention to Jessica. "Mrs. Valor, if you wish to seek protection, your fight isn't with Sergeant Valor. You will need to file a protective order against the person involved in Sergeant Valor's case. The children are to return to the previous custody agreement and schedule."

"Thank you," Randall and I said in unison.

One down, one to go.

I shook hands with Randall and then went to sit next to Reagan. She smiled, and I wanted to kiss her. The judge was going to rule in her favor too because Jessica's fight wasn't with Reagan either. We didn't have to wait long. Reagan was called next, and as I'd suspected, the judge ordered in Reagan's favor too.

As Jessica and her dad stepped toward the double doors of the courtroom, I jogged over. "Can we speak for a moment?"

Jessica turned, her brown eyes glaring. "There's nothing to talk about."

"There is," I retorted. "I want to see my kids."

"You heard the judge, you won. Come get them for your weekly dinner tonight."

"Okay, but—" I moved aside to let people exit. "I want to speak to you. Can we go into the hall?"

"What is there to talk about, Ethan?" she clipped.

"Come to the hall and find out." I rolled my eyes.

She huffed. "You have one minute."

I held the door open for her and she stepped out. After giving her father a brisk nod, I walked over the threshold to where Jessica stood next to a window. "Look, I know you're worried about our boys, but you know I would *never* let anything happen to them."

"Is the murder case closed?" She crossed her arms over her chest. Maybe she didn't catch when I'd told the judge that the case was ongoing, or when the judge told her that her fight was with the perp.

"No."

"And why not?"

"I can't give you any information. You know that."

"I also know that you always put your work first, and that's why we got a divorce."

"I never put it before my kids, and you know that."

"But you put it before me." She rolled her eyes and looked off.

"We don't need to rehash that, Jess. It's over and done with."

"I hope you like playing second fiddle," Jessica said, and my gaze followed hers to see that she was talking to Reagan.

I grabbed Jess's elbow and pulled her away from Reagan, Randall, and Jessica's father. "I get it, you're jealous—"

"I am not!" she seethed, making a face of disgust.

I sighed. "Okay, fine, but I just want to reassure you that I will keep our boys safe when they're with me."

"And what about when they're with her?" She waved her arm in the direction of where Reagan was waiting. "She will have them when you're at work, right? She's the one who got a death threat."

"Look"—I rubbed my hands down my face—"I've taken measures to keep Reagan safe, and that will include the boys when they're with me."

"Fine, but know this"—she stepped closer and lowered her voice to a growl—"she will never be my sons' mother."

I blinked and took a step back. "She's not trying to be."

Jessica laughed sarcastically. "Oh, she is. The two of you are playing house and shit."

She could say she wasn't jealous, but I knew better. "You had to know I'd move on, Jess."

She snorted. "And?"

"And I'd remarry, and the boys would have a stepmother," I went on.

"You're going to marry her?"

I looked toward Reagan and saw her speaking softly with Randall. "I've wanted to marry her since I was seventeen."

"Wow," Jess breathed, and I finally looked back at her. "Glad to know the mother of your children was someone you never wanted to marry."

"I didn't say that."

"No, but if she was still in the picture"—she waved her hand in the direction of Reagan—"we"—she motioned to herself and me—"would have never gotten together and those boys wouldn't have been born."

I shrugged. I honestly didn't know what would have happened if Reagan had never dumped me. "I don't know, but it doesn't matter. *We* did get married. *We* did have our boys. And *you* did divorce me. Now I'm moving on, and so should you."

There was a moment of silence as Jessica turned her attention toward Reagan. Without looking back at me, she said, "I am, but so help me that if anything happens to our kids, Ethan—"

"I won't let that happen."

"And if she tries to be their mother—"

"Reagan would never."

Jessica turned and walked away without another word. I didn't know if the conversation was over or on pause until some other time, but it didn't matter because no matter what she said, I *did* want to marry Reagan, and I wanted her to be my boys' stepmother. I wanted all the things with Reagan: the forever home, the blended family, the first kiss each morning and the last kiss each night. I wanted Reagan to be the one next to me on a porch overlooking Lake Michigan where we watched our grandchildren play in the water. I wanted her face to be the last face I saw before I took my last breath, and then I wanted to wait for her until it was her time and we'd spend forever together in the afterlife.

Reagan approached. "Everything okay?"

I drew her to me and kissed the side of her head. "Yeah, Buttercup. Everything is how it's meant to be."

That night, my boys had dinner with my entire family, including Reagan, and I felt as though everything was finally starting to fall into place. My kids were ecstatic, to say the least. I wasn't sure what Jessica had told them about why they hadn't seen me for two weeks, but when Cohen said he'd missed me, I told him I had missed him too and that I'd been busy with work. Which, of course, was true. He understood more than Tyson, but I made sure to spend every minute I had with them by actually *being* with them. I played in the basement at my parents' while we waited for dinner to be ready, I hugged them every chance I got, and at the end of the night, I promised that we'd do something fun over the weekend—just the three of us.

When Reagan and I got back to my condo, I was too hyped up and happy to sleep. "Want to go to karaoke?" I asked as we walked in through the front door.

Reagan turned and looked at me, her brows drawn in. "Do *you?*"

I closed and locked the door. "Well, I don't think I'll be able to fall asleep any time soon."

She smirked. "I can think of something else we can do."

She didn't need to tell me twice.

I picked her up, causing her to squeal, and carried her to our bedroom. "Take your clothes off, baby. I'm going to devour your pussy."

Apparently, I didn't have to tell her twice either because, without hesitation, we were both stripping our clothes off. Once I was naked, I got in the middle of the bed, laid on my back and motioned for her to straddle my face. I wasn't joking when I said I wanted to devour her pussy. I wanted her over my mouth and riding my face as I ate at her like a starved man.

Reagan hovered over my head, and I hooked my arms around her thighs. When she lowered down enough for me to take my first taste, I stuck my tongue out, taking a slow lick over her entire slit.

"Yes," she breathed, throwing her head back.

I groaned my response against her, not stopping as I licked, sucked, and *devoured*. From the first time I'd ever tasted Reagan's pussy, I loved it. It was the sweetest cunt I'd ever tasted, and it would also be the last pussy I'd ever taste. I wanted to eat her every chance I got. I was one lucky man.

She started rocking back and forth, doing the work as I held out my tongue. When I glanced up, all I could see was my beautiful Reagan working her tits as she picked up her speed and fucked my face. I'd wanted to devour her pussy—and I was—but having Reagan take control and ride my tongue as though it was my dick was making my cock ache and leak with pre-cum.

I slurped her arousal as she continued, and I grabbed my dick, needing to relieve some of the ache. This was how I knew Reagan was my soulmate. We didn't need the foreplay if we didn't want it. We were so in sync with each other that, with a few licks, we were able to get in the mood. When I had asked her if she thought that our sex life would have faltered if we had been married for twenty some odd years, I actually thought the answer was no. I would still be eating her pussy twenty-three years in the future. We may be a little less nimble, but I would find a way.

"I'm going to come," Reagan panted.

I groaned, not able to speak, and while she continued to ride my tongue, I reached with my free hand and rubbed her clit until she clenched her legs around my ears and came with jerks, squeezing her thighs against my head.

When she was done, I stopped stroking my dick as well as licking between her legs. "Grab a condom, baby," I instructed.

Reagan rose and reached to my nightstand, grabbing a silver packet while I stayed on my back. She reached out to hand it to me.

"You can do it," I smirked. "You like to take control."

She snorted. "I did take control, huh?"

"I'm not complaining." I grinned.

"In that case …"

Reagan ripped the packet open and straddled my hips again. This time she faced away from me and my dick jerked with approval. Grabbing the base of my shaft, she slid the latex over it and then lifted before sinking down all the way. There were no words spoken as I held her hips, her hands on my shins, and once again Reagan rode me to her liking.

"God, you're beautiful," I gushed as Reagan moved back and forth over my cock. My hand went to her clit, and I rubbed, needing her to be close again because I was. If she hadn't come when she had, I would have erupted after a few more tugs.

"Fuck," she hissed and picked up her pace. "This … is … better … than … karaoke."

I chuckled. "Yeah, baby."

Her pace increased again, and Reagan threw her head back. I grabbed a fistful of her long brown hair, making her back arch. Her rhythm didn't falter, and I didn't let up on her clit. She was slick with her cum and arousal as I used two fingers to work her faster.

"I'm gonna come again," she panted.

"Yeah, baby," I coaxed, trying to hold off from losing myself first. "Me too." I felt her pussy clench and then pulse, making me blow my load as she milked me with her own climax.

I fucking loved that woman.

As we lay in bed, both of us on the brink of sleep, I asked, "Move in with me?"

Reagan lifted her head from my shoulder. "I have."

"No, I mean officially. Even after I catch the killer. I want you here every night."

She stared at me and then slowly smiled. "Okay."

"Okay?" I asked, making sure I'd heard her correctly.

"Yes, I will move in with you."

I rolled us, so I was on top of her. "Best day of my life."

"Even better than—"

I silenced her with my mouth, knowing she was going to ask if it was better than the days my kids were born and whatever else was technically better. I didn't care. This one was in the top ten for sure.

# CHAPTER TWENTY-THREE

*Reagan*

When I graduated college the first time, there were caps and gowns and flowers and speeches and tossing of said caps. That wasn't what happened the last day of class. Instead, I simply got a signed certificate from my teacher saying I passed. Ethan made sure to make dinner plans at a nice steakhouse to celebrate, and I'd switched with the Monday night bartender so I could have the night off.

"Order whatever you want, Buttercup. You've earned it."

I smiled. "Thank you."

"How does it feel being a crime scene investigator?"

"I have to get a job as one first." I chuckled.

Ethan grinned. "We're gonna work on that."

"Yeah?"

He leaned back in his chair and set the menu down. "I told you that first night that I'd help you."

"You also told me that you'd help me study," I reminded him. We'd *studied* together, but not my coursework.

"You never wanted or needed my help."

"I know, and this is going to sound weird, but I'm kinda glad you've been working long hours. I've been able to really focus."

"I hope you still feel that way in five years."

The waiter picked that moment to come and take our order. After we both let him know what we wanted to eat and drink, I replied, "Why do you think it will be any different five years from now?"

Ethan took a sip of water. "You know why I'm divorced."

I nodded slightly. "Yeah, but I'm not *her*."

He chuckled slightly. "No, baby, you're not."

"Plus," I went on, "you're nothing like my ex. He had a thing for his secretary."

"I know that. I was merely referring to my job."

"I know. And who knows, I might be working those long hours too."

"Yep, but first, I need to catch this guy."

I frowned. "Why?"

Ethan grabbed my hand and rubbed my knuckles softly. "Given that we don't know who this guy is, I don't want to chance that you'll be put in a trap."

"How?"

"There's a lot of ways, but if you're the tech on a crime scene, you'll be out in the open."

"So, you want me to stay a kept woman on a leash?"

"That's not what you are—"

"But it is. For the past week and a half, I haven't been alone. Haven't been able to go shopping if I wanted to, or get my hair or nails done. I've only been able to go to school and go to Judy's, and now I don't have school. So what am I going to do while I'm not behind the bar? Cook? Clean? Be *your* housewife?"

I didn't need to get my hair done, and I wasn't one to have my nails done every two weeks either. My point was that I wasn't able to leave the house and do whatever I wanted. I knew we were doing it to keep me safe, but I also wanted to be able to find a job in my new field and not have to tell them that a serial killer might be after me, or that I came with private security.

"You know that if—"

The waiter brought us our drinks, and Ethan paused. When the waiter left, Ethan took a deep breath before continuing.

"You know if there wasn't a threat on your life that things would be different."

I sighed. "I know, and I'm sorry. I've just always wanted this and now …" I swallowed. "Now, it feels as if there's something else preventing it from happening. I made the decision after college to not pursue my dreams, and I don't regret having Maddie, but now—"

"I want you to follow your dreams, but I also don't want to be called to *your* murder scene."

"What if you never catch this guy?"

"I will."

"You don't know that. It's been almost two months since the first murder." I only knew that because Ethan had walked into Judy's the night before the first murder, and that was two weeks after I had started school. Given the program was only ten weeks, we were coming up on two months for the first unsolved murder. Would it take two more months to solve the second? Longer even?

Ethan took another deep breath. With the long hours, the lack of sleep, making sure he drove me home after my late shifts, I knew he was tired. I knew he was trying to solve the case—obviously— but there was still that chance it would never be solved. There were countless murders that took ten, twenty years to be solved—if at all. "You're right."

"I don't mean that you're not—"

"I know. There *is* that possibility we'll never catch him, given the lack of evidence."

"Ethan …" He was still rubbing my hand, so I placed my free one on top of his. "I believe in you. You'll catch this guy."

"Hope so, but you're right: you need to live your life. We've taken measures to protect you, and we have to trust that they will. You'll also be surrounded by cops as an investigator. We'll make it work. I want you to follow your dreams and be happy."

"I *am* happy," I corrected. "I'm happy because I'm with you. I'm happy because *of* you."

Ethan stood, leaned across the table, and in the middle of the packed restaurant, placed his lips against mine. "And I've never been happier," he admitted, returning to his seat. "Now, let's pretend we don't have a care in the world. Tonight's about you."

"Want to go sing karaoke?" I joked.

He chuckled. "If you really want to go, yeah. If not, I'm okay taking you home and having a proper date night that ends with you and me naked."

I pretended to think for a moment. "Yeah, that does sound better."

# Unknown

Fiona Jones was number four on my watch list. Since I was already going out of order and had killed my number nine, I wasn't too worried about it. Plus, Fiona was perfect. She hadn't wronged me as Amy had, and she wasn't too good to stick something up her ass like Daisy.

No, Fiona was the opposite.

She went to class, came home, did her homework, and lived a normal college student's life. She also was attending school on a school visa because she was from England, meaning she didn't celebrate Thanksgiving. That was why she was next. Everyone she knew would either be out of town or with their own family, so I could slip in and not worry about someone catching me.

And I had weeks to watch and learn her schedule and plans.

After Jack and I started our love affair—we were sneaking around the office and hadn't told anyone we were seeing each other—I still caught myself logging in each night to watch the women on my list. I thought I was over pussy and just needed dick—Jack's dick—but I still had the urge to be with a woman.

Jack hadn't answered my text about our nightly rendezvous, so I took the time to scope out Fiona's neighborhood. I needed to know how close the house next to hers was—find out if she had looky-loos who watched the street at all hours—and figure out my escape plan. I didn't stay long because it had started to snow, but I got what I needed to know. Fiona had a back door that I could get in and out of without anyone seeing me. It led to an alley behind her house and would be the perfect getaway. The other two times, I had to go out the front door, and I was lucky I wasn't seen.

I was just that good.

After getting into my car, I made the decision to visit my favorite bartender. I knew her shift was ending soon, and I was hoping Sergeant Valor would be there too. I hadn't crossed her off my watch list even though I was no longer watching her through her webcam or watching her at school. I missed watching them fuck, and I missed seeing Reagan on campus now that her class was over.

I swung the door to Judy's open after I'd parked down the street and hurried to get out of the snow and cold. The moment I stepped foot in the warm bar, I saw Jack. He was at the bar laughing with Reagan. Even though I knew he frequented Judy's, I didn't like him flirting with her. He hadn't answered my text, and watching him flirt with Reagan as I stood not three feet away made me angry. I saw him looking at her the same way he looked at me the night he fucked me in the bathroom.

He wanted her.

And I couldn't let that happen.

I turned and left, needing to come up with a new plan because Reagan was next.

# Reagan

It was early afternoon on the day before Thanksgiving, and I was pacing. Maddie was on her way from Michigan. I hadn't seen my daughter in over three months, and that was the longest I'd ever been apart from her.

She was staying in the boys' room for the four nights she was in town, and I was jumping for joy, to say the least. When I told her I'd moved in with Ethan, she was happy for me. We hadn't had a chance to talk about her dating life, but that was going to change during her stay. I wanted to know everything. I wasn't sure if I was going to tell *her* everything, though.

How do you tell your daughter that a serial killer broke into your condo? I didn't want her to think she was in danger. It was going to be difficult, given I had security with me. Ethan hadn't solved the murders, so I was always looking over my shoulder and making sure one of my private security guys—either Evan or Pablo, depending on whose day it was—wasn't far behind. What if this was my new normal? What if Ethan never found the killer? I'd heard a lot about cold cases and unsolvable murders while in school and from the true crime documentaries and shows I was addicted to. I just wished life would go back to the way it was before that stupid plaque appeared in my home.

Finally, I received a text from Maddison: *Parking in the garage :)*

The excitement coursing through me increased tenfold. I wanted to go down and meet her, but then I'd have to explain to her about the big Latino man named Pablo and why he was following us. I was going to tell her, of course, because there was no way she wouldn't see him or Evan shadowing me, but I didn't want to have to tell her out in the open, and I didn't want to freak her out.

Finally, after what felt like an eternity, I heard a knock on the door. I swung the door open without checking the peephole because I already knew Pablo wouldn't allow anyone to knock on my door except the person I was expecting. And that person was my daughter.

She was standing on the other side, a huge grin on her face. Without a word, I rushed the last few steps and engulfed her in a tight hug.

"Hi," she greeted, her chin on my shoulder.

"I've missed you so much."

"I've missed you too."

After another squeeze, I let go and motioned for her to enter. "Come in. I only have a few hours before I need to be at work."

Every bartender was working tonight. Thanksgiving Eve was known to be one of the busiest nights of the year, and therefore, each of us was working two hours extra. I wasn't complaining. The tips would be worth it, and Christmas was coming.

Since the incident with the flower and Derrick, Judy kept the back door locked. The employees had keys, and the delivery guys had to call to be let in. The first few days, it was awkward working alongside Derrick, but we worked the busiest nights of the week and there wasn't much time to talk about the situation. He also stopped flirting with me, and I assumed that whatever Ethan had said scared him or made him understand that nothing would happen between us.

Maddie hesitated. "You know there's a guy standing next to us, right?"

I smiled at Pablo. "Yeah. There are some things I need to tell you."

"Oh-kay."

I waved her in. "Come in. Come in."

"Where's your boyfriend?" she asked as she finally crossed the threshold.

"He's at work."

"Right. Protecting the city."

"Something like that." I chuckled and motioned for her to follow. I showed her to her room, and while she used the bathroom, I made us a couple of sandwiches. "How was your drive?" I asked as she came into the room and slid onto a barstool.

"It was good. Listened to half an audiobook. I'll finish it on my drive back on Sunday."

"What is it about?" I placed her plate with the ham and cheese sandwich in front of her.

"You know, boy meets girl, they fall in love, they break-up for a stupid reason, and then eventually get back together. He'll probably propose, and they'll have ten kids and live off of welfare."

A slow smile spread across my face at her joke. "I think I've read that one already."

We both laughed. God, I'd missed her. Missed hearing her laugh— *seeing* her laugh. How was I going to make it four years with her only visiting for holidays and summer break? Where would she go after college? What if she moved even farther away?

"So, you gonna tell me about the guy outside?" Maddie took a bit of her sandwich.

"Right." I took my sandwich, placed it in front of the other stool, and then grabbed chips and bottles of water before sitting. "I don't know all the details, but there's a serial killer after me."

She choked on her food. "What?"

"Well"—I shrugged—"I was threatened by one?" I said it as a question because nothing had happened since that night. Even with the undercover cops as my details, nothing had happened. Maybe the guy had moved on.

"You're not sure?"

I told her about the wood plaque and everything that had happened. I also told her that we were covering her webcam with black tape. "And that is why I have my own private security."

Maddie stared at me. And stared. And stared. "Mom! You can't just drop a bombshell on me like that over lunch."

"When else was I supposed to tell you?"

She waved her hands around. "I don't know. Over cheesecake or something."

I cracked a smile at her reference to one of our favorite classic TV shows, *The Golden Girls*. I grabbed her hands and held them in my lap. "If I were in any danger, Ethan would take every precaution, but things have been quiet since that night, and I don't go anywhere without either Pablo"—I motioned with my head toward the door—"or Evan."

"That's—that's crazy."

"I know, but Ethan is working the best he can to solve the murders. And like I said, it's been quiet since the last murder. Plus, I don't think he has any leads or evidence to arrest anyone."

"If the person is never caught, will you always have a bodyguard?"

I shrugged. "I don't know."

She slid off her stool and wrapped her arms around my neck. "I feel like we're living in some sort of murder mystery novel."

I grinned. "Yeah, does feel like that."

"Or a second-chance romantic suspense," Maddie went on.

I chuckled. "That sounds more like it."

We hugged for a few moments and then she returned to her seat. "So …"

"Yes?" I prompted.

She took a deep breath. "Okay, I'm just going to tell you because I think you're cool, and you won't care, and you'll be happy for me."

"Okay …?"

"Just …"

"Just spit it out." I gave her a warm smile. Whatever it was, I would deal with it. Maybe she was dropping out of school, or perhaps she wanted to go to Paris for the summer instead of living with me—and Ethan. We needed to figure out another living situation before then because Maddison needed her own room and couldn't share with the boys over the summer.

"Okay." She took another deep breath. "You know I'm dating someone."

"Yes." I smiled.

"It's … I'm dating a girl."

I blinked slightly. I wasn't expecting that. She had gone with boys to her junior and senior proms. I'd known her to have boyfriends too. But I also knew that I didn't care. I just wanted her to be happy, and if a young woman made her happy, then that was all that mattered. I smiled and pulled her in for another hug. "There's no need to be scared, honey. Who you want to date is your decision. As long as she makes you happy, then I'm happy."

Maddison pulled her head back and looked into my green eyes—the same color as her own. "She does make me happy."

"Good. Tell me everything. What's her name? How did you meet? How long have you been dating? Is it serious?"

We sat in our seats. "It is serious, and her name is Sophie."

"That's a pretty name." I wanted Maddie to know that I was okay with her dating whomever. As long as the person wasn't a criminal and didn't hurt her or cheated on her, then I would be supportive.

Maddie began to tell me that they met in one of her classes, and they were both scared at first, but the more time they spent together, the closer they got. She was still telling me her love story when Ethan walked in through the front door.

I smiled and slid off the barstool. "Maddie, this is *my* Ethan."

He closed the door, set his keys on the table, and started to walk toward Maddie. She was walking to greet him too. "It's good to finally meet you," he said.

She threw herself at him, wrapping her arms around his neck and hugging him. He looked at me over her shoulder, and I shrugged. I wasn't expecting her to greet him that way.

"Thank you for keeping my mom safe."

They pulled apart, and I realized we were all smiling. "I'd never let anything happen to her," he assured her.

"Good. Because if you did, you wouldn't hear the end of it from me," she warned.

He grinned wider. "Noted." Ethan turned to me. "Are you almost ready to go?"

"Oh shit," I gasped. "Time got away from me."

He smiled. "I figured it would."

I turned my attention to Maddie. "I need to get to work, but tomorrow we have all morning to talk. I'll make smothered potatoes and bacon for breakfast." I had a friend in college who would always talk about the southern food she missed while she was in California. She was originally from Texas and said that every Sunday, her mom would make smothered potatoes with fried pork chops. I got the recipe from her, and over the years I'd perfected the potatoes. One morning, we had them for breakfast, and it instantly became Maddie's favorite. They were similar to country potatoes—or fried potatoes—but unlike some recipes, I didn't add flour. I just let them do their thing in the oil while they steamed and then fried.

"Go. I have a phone call to make." She smiled, and I assumed she meant she needed to call her girlfriend. Probably wanted to tell Sophie that she'd made it to Chicago, or maybe seeing if Sophie had made it to Indianapolis where she was from.

"Okay. If you want ..." I hesitated and then looked at Ethan. "We can all have dinner during my dinner break. Maybe you can bring pizza?"

Ethan smiled. "Yeah, Buttercup. That sounds like a plan."

Despite how busy I was expecting Judy's to be, I was happy. I finally had the two most important people under the same roof.

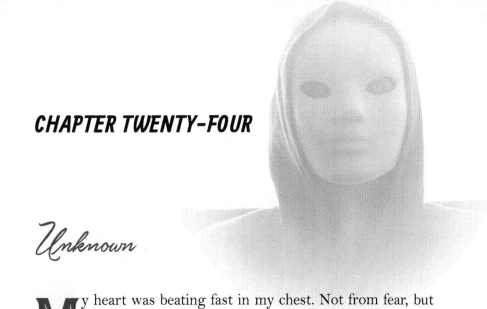

# CHAPTER TWENTY-FOUR

*Unknown*

**M**y heart was beating fast in my chest. Not from fear, but from excitement.

I parked my car down the street from Fiona's, walked through the vacant alley behind her house, and slipped into the backyard. It was quiet, people probably resting before having to cook all day on Thanksgiving. She didn't have plans that I knew of, and the more hours that passed before her body would be discovered, the better.

The key I had made the same way as Amy's and Daisy's slipped right into the lock on Fiona's back door. I eased it open, hoping to make no noise. When it cracked open, I heard the sound of the TV coming from the other room. I stepped through the door into the dark kitchen, and closed the door behind me.

Fiona was different from Amy and Daisy in the sense that she didn't have a nightcap, so I changed it up and got my hands on ether. Everything is available on the internet these days, and I'd purchased the can of diethyl ether when I knew Fiona's death would need to occur differently.

After setting the bag that had my clean clothes in it down quietly on the floor, I grabbed a white rag from my back pocket with my gloved hand. I doused the rag with the ether and placed the can on the counter next to the wood plaque I'd made with Fiona's name engraved on it, so I could grab it on the way out.

I walked slowly to where the TV was on in the living room. Coming up behind the black-haired beauty, I placed the cloth against her face. She struggled, trying to get out of my grasp, but I held her against the back of the couch while she kicked. Her hair caught the light and a blue tint shined in the strands. From the view on my computer monitor, I hadn't realized that her hair was blue. It was pretty and would be the last hair color sweet Fiona would have.

Once she was unconscious, I laid her back on the couch and walked around to stand on the other side of the couch. I brushed her dark blue hair away from her closed eyes and smiled. I wasn't sure how ether would work. Usually, the girls passed out from the pill I slipped into their drinks, but I had to admit that using ether was exciting. It was me who held onto Fiona while she struggled to breathe, restraining her while the ether did its thing, not some drug making her pass out.

It. Was. Me.

My blood started to heat at the thought that, in mere seconds, Fiona would no longer be breathing and that I had caused her to take her last breath. The excitement grew stronger and stronger with each moment that passed.

Then, I heard a noise.

I stopped and listened. Fiona didn't have a roommate—at least I'd never seen one while I watched her through her webcam.

I listened closer.

It was a scratching noise. Not a scratching from a tree limb or an animal on a window or door, or maybe …

"Meow."

I blew out a breath as I saw a calico cat come into the room. It must have been the cat using the litter box.

"Meow," it said again.

"Hey, buddy," I called back.

The black and yellow cat rubbed on my leg, clearly not realizing I was about to kill its owner and make it so it might starve for a few days—or longer. Maybe it would have to eat sweet Fiona.

"Meow," it continued to speak to me.

"What is it?"

"Meow."

"Are you hungry?"

It made a noise just as I smelled the scent of shit in the air. My gaze moved to Fiona, but she was still breathing.

"Did you make room?" I asked the cat. "Are you hungry now that you went potty?"

"Meow." It wiggled its butt and tail weirdly.

"I'll take that as a yes."

I left Fiona passed out on the couch as I went in search for food for the little guy—or girl—I wasn't sure. I didn't want it to starve for too long and figured I'd feed it so its belly was full and it could get a good night's sleep.

Opening cabinet after cabinet, I finally found the cat's canned food. I bent down, running my gloved hand against its fur. "Do you like seafood stew?"

"Meow."

"I'll take that as a yes." I looked around the tiny, dark kitchen and spotted a bowl on the floor at the end of a counter. The moment I popped the top on the can of food, the cat was at *his* bowl, waiting. I put the smelly cat food into the bowl, making sure to get it all, and then filled the water dish with fresh water.

I left the beast to eat and returned to Fiona. She was still unconscious, and she looked peaceful. That wasn't going to last much longer because the moment the first strike of my knife pierced Fiona's chest, I figured she'd wake up.

I went back into the kitchen and grabbed the ether in case I needed it again. I wasn't expecting to have to feed a cat, but I couldn't let the poor thing starve. That would be cruel.

Licking my lips, I withdrew the knife from behind my back, and raised it, stopping for a second and then following through, bringing the blade down toward Fiona's heart. The rush of what I'd done seemed to race through the metal and into my arms just as Fiona gasped, her eyes opening wide and staring back at me.

She started to scream, and I grabbed the ether-soaked rag, placing it over her face and holding her down. Fiona's arms flailed, her feet kicked, but I held her down, her gray eyes staring at me, silently asking me why.

"Because you were on the list," I replied.

Fiona continued to struggle. Blood coated the rag and knife, and once she was no longer moving, I raised the knife again and struck once more, images of another dark-haired beauty flashing in front of my eyes. I wasn't sure if I'd pierced Fiona's heart or not, so I kept stabbing, thoughts of Reagan laughing with Jack clouding my vision as I struck over and over and over.

I brushed loose strands of hair behind my ears as I stood. I hadn't realized that she'd pulled my hair free from its tie at the back of my head during our struggle. Having her fight me wasn't what I was used to, but it also made my blood race faster. The adrenaline, the high, was ecstatic.

I heard a meow, and I looked over to see that the cat had finished eating. I wanted to pet it again, but instead, I stripped off my jeans and long-sleeved black shirt, changed my gloves and clothes, and left Fiona's plaque next to the cat dish on the floor before leaving out the back door.

No one saw me leave out her back gate. No one saw me walk down the dimly lit alley to my car. And no one saw me drive away.

Fiona Jones - #4

# CHAPTER TWENTY-FIVE

*Ethan*

Seeing Reagan laugh and smile while she was with Maddison was heartwarming. I knew that she'd missed her daughter because she had told me on several occasions, and today she looked bright and happy, which was how I assumed I looked the moment I saw my boys after the two-week hiatus.

Reagan cooked us breakfast, and we sat around the table talking about anything and everything until we had to head to my parents for Thanksgiving dinner. Sadly, the boys were with Jessica for the holiday, but I was getting them for Christmas. Reagan and I needed to figure some things out because Maddison was coming to stay with us again the week after Christmas and for New Year's before going back to Michigan, and I had my boys for four days in a row because Christmas was on a Thursday. We needed a bigger place.

We needed a home that was *ours*.

Not a place where I'd once killed a guy and that my sister owned, and not a place that Reagan hadn't even moved all of her belongings into. With everything that was going on, we'd packed up her stuff and put the non-essentials into a storage unit. There was no way in hell she would ever live alone again. I wouldn't let that happen.

Life was good despite the open cases I still had haunting me, but the more time that passed, the more I thought it was connected to me and not Reagan, as April had mentioned weeks prior; I just didn't know how or why. I'd combed through past cases, trying to come up with any sort of connection and had come up with nothing.

After we ate breakfast, the three of us got ready to go to my parents' place. "How good are you at Uno?" I asked Maddie as we rode the elevator down to the garage.

She shrugged. "Probably as good as anyone. It's luck, right?"

I chuckled. "Nope. You have to know when to play a card or hold it for a better time. It's strategy."

"So, you're an Uno pro?"

"I'm not bad," I admitted. "But it is a family tradition to play after dinner."

"Ethan's oldest, Cohen, is apparently a pro," Reagan stated.

I grinned.

"Oh yeah?" Maddie asked. "How old is he?"

"Eight," I replied.

"Oh, I get it. We have to let him win."

"No, he knows how to play," I corrected. "He keeps us on our toes."

The elevator stopped on the garage floor. Maddison looked at Reagan. "Then I'm looking forward to a yearly thing." Reagan pulled her in for a side hug, and we stepped out of the elevator.

I was looking forward to a yearly thing too.

Introductions were made, and Reagan and the girls were doing their thing while me, my dad, my brother, and Rhys watched one of the football games.

"So, Christmas," I said during a commercial. The guys looked at me. "Given my time apart from my boys, I want to make this year a little special."

"What are you thinking?" Rhys asked.

"I don't know yet."

"Is Maddison going to be here for Christmas?" Dad asked.

I shook my head. "She'll be in Colorado with her father for the actual holiday, but then she'll stop here for a week before going back to school."

"Where is she going to sleep?" Dad asked. "You'll have the boys some of those nights, right?"

I shrugged. "The couch?"

"Or, maybe it's time you find a new place?" Rhys suggested.

"Trying to kick me out of your condo?" It was my sister's, but since they were married, it was his too.

He smiled. "Not at all, but your family is growing."

My heart grew at those words. My family *was* growing. "You're right," I replied. "Maybe at the start of the year we'll look for our own place." My gaze met my brother's. He was grinning wide. "What?" I questioned.

He chuckled. "Remember when Jessica wanted to move in with you, and you did everything to prevent it at first?"

"Yeah," I replied, remembering how I'd told her it was against my lease to have her move in when, in fact, she could have been added at any time. I even went so far as to tell her that she'd have to park her car two blocks away every night. I'd told her I needed time to make room for her clothes, which was true, and in the end, after a year of dating, we found a place together that was big enough for her stuff and mine.

"You're barely back together with Reagan and yet you're ready to make things permanent," Carter stated.

"Do you know who you're talking about?" I asked.

"Reagan, of course."

I leaned forward on the couch I was sitting on. "*My* Reagan."

He grinned, and I knew he was fucking with me.

"So, you going to ask her to marry you? You are, aren't you?" Rhys asked.

Smiling, I replied, "Yeah—yeah, I am."

"Want me to set it up for you to do it during intermission at a Hawks game?" Rhys asked. That was how he'd proposed to my sister. And while that would be epic, I didn't want to copy him. I needed my own way. I wanted it to be special—something that was only for Reagan and me.

"No, thanks." I shrugged and leaned back again. "I'll think of something."

"Well, if you need my help, let me know," Rhys said. "I've got ideas."

I glanced at my dad, and he smiled. "It's good to see you getting what makes you happy."

I'd never admit it to anyone, but I had settled for Jessica. Sure, I loved her—especially since she was the mother of my boys—but I never loved her on the level that I loved Reagan.

"You have no idea," I replied.

I stepped away from the table, an exciting game of Uno in full force, and pulled my ringing phone out of my pocket. "Valor."

"We got another murder," Shawn said.

"Same MO?"

"Yeah."

I closed my eyes briefly and took a deep breath. If this was our serial killer, at least the person wasn't Reagan. "Text me the address." I hung up the phone and turned to face the table. "I gotta go."

"Is everything okay?" Dad asked.

"Yeah, duty calls."

"Can you drop us off at home?" Reagan asked.

I didn't want Reagan and Maddison to leave unless they wanted to. Everyone was having a good time. "If you want, or you two can stay."

"How will we get home?" Reagan questioned.

"Actually, yeah, let's get you safe behind a locked door," I replied. My dad, brother, or even Rhys could drive them back to my place, but I would feel better knowing they were home and safe.

"So, it's the same guy?" Dad asked.

"Shawn said it's the same MO, so it appears to be."

We didn't waste any time saying our goodbyes. I apologized to everyone, even Reagan and Maddison, and the only thing my woman said to me was, *"Just catch this guy."*

*"Working on it, Buttercup,"* I'd replied.

I'd called Evan, and he met us at my condo. I felt bad asking him to work on Thanksgiving, but like me, he was the guy on call.

Before leaving, I made sure the girls were safe inside. I didn't want to take a chance that this was some sort of decoy again, and I checked to make sure there were no plaques and no one inside before I left.

At the address Shawn had sent me, the blue and red lights lit up the dark night. I parked and walked to the door where I saw Shawn waiting for me. "What do we have?"

"First responding officer briefed me. We have a twenty-two-year-old female."

"Stabbed?"

"Multiple times."

"Shit," I hissed as I slipped the shoe protectors on.

"Wooden plaque?"

"Yep."

"Fuck," I groaned as I entered the small one-bedroom house. Shawn had said it was the same MO, but it was still horrible that another young woman had lost her life because we couldn't solve the cases fast enough.

Just like the other murders, the vic was laying on a blood-soaked couch. "I called Shay," Shawn stated. "Vic is Fiona Jones, and she was a student at Lakeshore U."

"Of course she was."

"I already sent a patrol cop to take her laptop to Will."

"Good. Listen up," I yelled. "We need to catch this asshole once and for all. I want everything combed over five fucking times, and every piece of lint tested. There has to be—"

"Sergeant," Roberta, with the crime scene unit, interrupted. "We have a strand of hair. It looks like the vic might have fought back."

"Put a rush on both. I want to know tonight."

"You got it."

Everyone continued working as I stared down at Fiona's bloody body. She wasn't naked like the other victims, but given that she had multiple stab wounds and the fucking wood plaque, we were dealing with the same guy. Possibly a guy with red hair. And if Fiona did fight back and we got DNA, this could be the break we were looking for.

*Good job, Fiona.*

# CHAPTER TWENTY-SIX

*Reagan*

The bed dipped, waking me. "Babe?" I mumbled.

"Yeah," Ethan replied, pulling my back against his front.

"What time is it?" I was too tired to look at the clock on his side of the bed. After he dropped Maddie and me off, we'd watched a movie, but the entire time, all I could think about was when this would end. Ethan wasn't home by the time the movie ended, and I'd tried to go to sleep without him, but tossed and turned until slumber finally came.

"Almost four."

I only had one burning question. "Was there a wood plaque?"

Ethan took a long, deep breath. "Yes … There was also a strand of red hair on the body that didn't match the vic's."

I turned to face him, finally opening my eyes to see nothing but darkness. His arm moved to rest on my hip. "Now you have DNA."

He sighed. "But it wasn't enough, and there were no hits in any of the databases."

"Shit." I blew out a breath.

"Yeah, but he fucked up. That means he's slipping, and eventually, we'll catch him."

I paused for a moment. "What number was on the back of the plaque?"

"Four."

I blinked. "But mine had two, so there has to be a three somewhere."

"I'm not sure the numbers are his kill order because the second plaque we found had the number nine on the back."

"That doesn't make sense. Why number them?"

"Could be the order he found his victims and started watching them."

"Do you think he moved past me because he's not able to watch me anymore?"

"Maybe, but we're not taking that chance. You'll have security until we catch this guy."

"That's not what I mean. I just mean that maybe he's not watching number three anymore either."

Ethan sighed. "I hope that's the case and that the third isn't already dead and we just haven't found the body."

"Maybe the third got a new computer or something, and the killer isn't watching her anymore," I suggested.

"Maybe. We're still trying to figure out how the killer is getting the IP addresses. There was nothing on the servers at the school."

Ethan had never told me so much before, and I wanted him to keep talking to me about it. I hated being in the dark, especially when it involved me in some way. "Were the other victims freshmen or new to the school?"

"No, they weren't. They each had been students for at least a year."

I kept thinking. "You know what's weird?"

"What's that?" He yawned.

"I had just started school not a month before. How did he find me?"

Ethan sighed. "I wish I knew. I really fucking wish I knew."

"I mean, I hadn't used my computer except at school and my condo during that time."

"I know."

"It's just weird. Like he got my info from the school."

"That's why we checked the servers. There was nothing."

We lay in bed for a long time while my brain worked. I knew I wouldn't be able to sleep. As dawn crested and the light was slipping in through the gaps in the blinds, a thought occurred to me.

I slipped out of bed, grabbed my laptop from my bag, and powered it on as I sat on the floor, my back against the edge of the mattress. After Ethan's cybercrime unit scanned my computer, they deleted the program the killer was using to spy on me. As the laptop booted, the familiar chimes of its starting sequence pierced the quiet room. I pressed the volume down button repeatedly until it muted, but it was too late.

"Come back to bed, Buttercup. I can't sleep without you."

"One second. I need to check something."

"Is everything okay?"

I didn't reply. Instead, I opened the internet browser, pulled up my email, and searched all the emails from Lakeshore University.

"Reagan?" I heard Ethan sit up, but I didn't turn to look at him.

My eyes widened as I saw that I still had the email I was searching for. I clicked the email open and stood, turning to face Ethan. His gaze moved from the screen and then back up to me as he squinted from the bright glow of the laptop.

I pointed at it, holding the computer in one hand. "See this link?"

"Yeah?" he questioned.

"I'm assuming every student gets it because that's how we create our profiles to log into the school's site for various things like grades, our schedules, whatever."

"Are you saying you think that's how he got your IP address?"

"It has to be. If there's nothing on the servers at school, and that's the Wi-Fi students use while on campus, this has to be the missing link. I don't know how it all works, but maybe the guy is trolling students when they use the university's unsecured Wi-Fi?"

"Holy shit." Ethan grabbed the laptop from me and put it on the bed while he got up and moved to the closet. "You may be onto something."

I grinned. If this was the key and he could trace it, then all of this would be over soon. "Do you think I'm right?"

"I don't know," he replied, slipping into black slacks. "But I'm going to take this into the station." He held up my computer. I didn't protest this time. I wanted him to take it because I was hopeful this would help.

Maddie and I went out for lunch. The entire time, I kept looking at my phone to see if Ethan had texted or called me with an update. I didn't tell Maddison that we might have had a breakthrough in the case because I didn't want her to think about the potential danger I thought about all the time. I just wanted her to have a nice Thanksgiving break with me.

"I'll be home no later than 12:15," I told Maddie as I grabbed my keys from the table by the door. "If you're still awake—"

She chuckled. "I'll be awake."

"Okay." We hugged and then I left, Pablo following behind me. I needed this link with the email to work out because, as it was, my daughter had more freedom than I did. Either Evan or Pablo drove me the two blocks to Judy's, stayed the entire time at a table near the door until Ethan arrived to drive—or walk—me home.

Pablo followed me through the back door after I unlocked it. We weren't hiding the fact that I had a security detail any longer. Ethan told Pablo and Evan to stay near me at all times, and I was okay with that. I didn't *want* to be put in immediate danger; I just wanted it to end.

Hours later, I still hadn't heard from Ethan. I hoped that meant my idea had led to a lead and they were tracking the guy down. I was trying to focus on work, given it was a Friday night and we were busy as hell because of the holiday weekend, but I just wanted to know. I *needed* to know if they had someone in custody so I could stop looking over my shoulder.

Moving to my next customer, I shook my head. "What are you doing here?"

"I came to have dinner with you," Maddie replied, holding up a brown paper bag.

It was on the tip of my tongue to tell her that she wasn't safe, but then I thought better of it. I didn't want her to worry. She wasn't necessarily in danger. She wasn't a student of Lakeshore University, and that seemed to be his MO. The killer might not know who she was or anything about her.

"You made us dinner?" I questioned.

Maddison grinned. "I did, but it's just soup and Cheez-Its."

"Perfect for this cold night." Even though I was sweaty from working, I'd still eat it because I was hungry, and my daughter had cooked for me.

"Am I too early?"

I looked at the clock behind the bar. "Nope, let's go into the back."

After clearing the bar, I stopped. "Let me tell Pablo to take dinner too."

"Okay, I'll go set it up."

Maddie went to the break room, as I turned and headed toward where Pablo was sitting. "Maddison made me dinner. We'll stay in the break room. Why don't you go grab something to eat?"

"Are you sure?" he asked.

"I promise. I won't leave the break room until you come back."

"Okay. I won't be long."

"I have thirty minutes."

He nodded and slid off his stool. I turned and went to the back, where Maddison had bowls set out on the table with steaming chicken soup. It smelled delicious.

"I make this in my dorm."

I furrowed my brows in confusion as I sat at the small table. "I don't remember a stove in your tiny dorm room."

She smiled. "No, but you gave me your Crock-Pot, remember?"

I took a bite and instantly coughed. "Yeah, and this is spicy."

Maddie's grin widened. "Yeah."

"It's good, though. You made this in the Crock-Pot?" Apparently, my little girl had been busy for the past few hours.

"Yeah. It's only four ingredients: chicken, chicken stock, salsa, and cheese."

"It's delicious."

"You have to try it with the Cheez-Its."

I dropped a cracker into my bowl and then grabbed it with a spoonful of soup. It was even better. "Wow. Where did you learn to make this?"

She shrugged. "Pinterest."

We took a few more bites of the soup and crackers. "Thank you for making me dinner."

"Of course. You have to eat."

"And you have to leave me on Sunday." I frowned. I wanted her to stay longer. I missed our mother and daughter time.

"I'll be back in just a few weeks for Christmas break."

"I know, but I'll miss you."

"I'll miss you too." She stood and gave me a hug. "You know that you can visit any time, right?"

"I might take you up on that."

"Bring Ethan."

I grinned. "Do you like him?"

She rolled her green eyes that matched mine. "*Like* is an under-statement. He's perfect for you."

"He is, isn't he?" I sighed dreamily.

"Are you going to get married?"

I blinked. Were we going to get married? That was always the plan when we were younger, but I didn't know if that was still in the cards. "I don't know."

"But you're in love, right?"

"Of course."

"Then you'll get married," Maddie stated. "Can I be your maid of honor?"

I chuckled. "Yeah, honey. Obviously, you can." We finished our soup, and then it was time for me to head back out on the floor. We walked back out to the bar, and I went to make sure Pablo was back. He was. "You're sure you'll be awake when I get home?" I asked Maddison.

"Of course. I'm a college student. I never go to sleep before two."

"Right." I smiled and gave her a hug. She turned and walked out the door, and I went back to work.

Three hours later, it was almost time for me to go home. I still hadn't heard from Ethan despite the few texts I'd sent him, and that wasn't like him at all. But just as I was grabbing my purse from my locker, he called. "Hey, I'm just grabbing my purse," I answered as my greeting.

I heard a sigh on the other end. "I'm not there, Buttercup. I'm still at the station."

"Oh," I breathed.

"Have Pablo take you home, okay?"

"Yeah, of course."

"I love you, and I'm sorry."

"I love you too." I shut my locker. "But this means that things are getting better with the case?"

"Yeah, the email got a hit. We've been trying to track down all employees today."

"It *was* an employee?" I asked and started to walk out to the front to tell Pablo I was ready to leave, and he needed to drive me home.

"Yeah, we're working on a few things, but I finally feel like this was the break we needed. Thank you."

I grinned and stopped in front of Pablo. "Glad I could help."

"Go home and spend time with Maddie. Don't wait up, okay?"

"Okay."

"Love you," Ethan said again.

"Love you too."

We hung up, and I looked up into Pablo's brown eyes. "Ethan is still at the station, so he asked if you can take me home."

"Of course," he replied and motioned for me to lead the way to the back door.

Once outside, we got into a black SUV, and he drove us the two blocks to Ethan's. I suppose it was my place too. I wasn't paying rent because Ethan refused any money from me because his sister was cutting him a deal. It was actually my ex's money, given that I was still getting spousal support, but whatever. If Ethan and I were to get married, that would change too. I didn't need Grant's money, but it was nice to get a monthly check in the mail after he'd cheated on me with various women for the greater part of our marriage. His secretary was the last one before I found out about it at his company's Christmas party when they thought they'd be sneaky and have a quickie in the bathroom.

Pablo parked, and we rode the elevator up to my floor. The higher we rose, the more I sensed something was wrong. I wasn't sure what it was. When the elevator dinged and the doors opened, I got a sinking feeling in my stomach that Maddie wasn't home like she said she would be. *Mother's intuition.*

When I got to the door, I checked to make sure it was locked before slipping in my key. I had a weird beat to my heart like I could sense everything was about to change.

When I swung the door open and found the condo dark, the hairs on the back of my neck stood. I glanced up at Pablo. "Maddie said she was going to wait up for me."

"Let me go in first and check it out."

I swallowed, my mind already going to the darkest place. "Okay," I whispered and stepped aside so he could enter. My heart was beating even faster as I waited and waited and waited for what felt like hours but was only mere seconds. Then dread washed over me when Pablo returned.

"It's clear, but Maddison's not here."

# CHAPTER TWENTY-SEVEN

*Unknown*

It was the night.

The night Jack would know that he couldn't play me for a fool. I'd never killed twice in forty-eight hours, but it was part of my plan. It was how I was going to be able to get Reagan alone. While Sergeant Valor was working Fiona's case, I was getting my revenge on Jack, and Reagan was my pawn.

Since the night I'd seen Reagan and Jack laughing and *flirting* at Judy's, Jack had come to my place almost every night to get laid. That would be no more. I was taking his obsession away from him. I was going to make him beg, to tell me that he was sorry, and then force him to watch as Reagan took her last breath. That would show him what it meant to hurt me, to think I was nothing more than a piece of ass for him. Actions had consequences, and when Jack saw me take Reagan's life, he'd know not to mess with me.

Not to wrong me.

Not to fuck me over.

Reagan's murder was going to be different. I had no key to her place any longer because she'd changed her locks, but I didn't need one. I was going to follow her out the back door after her shift at Judy's, force my way in to her apartment, and use the ether I still had from Fiona's murder. Then I'd take Reagan to my place and wait for Jack to make his nightly visit. That's when the fun would begin.

When I got to Judy's, though, I saw Reagan with a mini Reagan and my plan changed. Mini Reagan would be easier to kill since I wasn't using my usual method of incapacitation. I was still going to make Jack watch me, to show him that if he continued to betray me, I'd take Reagan away too. Show *everyone* that this was my game, my rules, and if they thought they were smarter, everyone had another thing coming.

Since I hadn't been actively watching Reagan, I hadn't known a mini Reagan had shown up. When I saw Reagan on campus, I heard her talking to someone that I'd assumed was her daughter because of words and little phrases I heard her say like *honey, college girl,* and that she was trying to be a *cool mom.* Little did Reagan know that her actions had consequences. If she didn't work at Judy's, she wouldn't have been flirting with my man, and I wouldn't be moments away from taking her daughter away from her.

*Oh well. You win some, you lose some.*

Mini Reagan walked out into the cold Chicago night. Our eyes met briefly, and she smiled politely. I started to follow her as she walked past me. When we walked next to my parked car, I took the ether and rag out of my coat pocket and soaked the rag with the liquid. As I crept in closer, I slipped the bottle back into my pocket and then made my move. My arms went around her face, her long, dark brown hair fell against my chest, and I held her as she tried to break free until she went limp, the bag she was holding falling to the ground. Luckily for me, since it was freezing out, there wasn't anyone nearby. I was able to put Mini Reagan's limp body into the backseat of my car and drive off.

At a red light, she started to stir. I took the damp rag from my pocket and placed it on her face, covering her nose. I needed her to stay knocked out. I'd learned my lesson with Fiona. Ether only worked for about ten or fifteen minutes after being removed from the face, and I needed at last twenty to get back to my house.

After pulling into my driveway, I parked in the garage, got out, and then grabbed the wheelbarrow I had set aside. I dragged Mini Reagan out of the backseat and into it. There was no way that I would be able to carry her all the way down to my basement from my garage. I pushed Mini Reagan out of my garage and into my house, the wheelbarrow barely fitting through the doorway.

Killing my victims in their own homes was *much* easier. I'd slip in, knock them out, drag them to their couches, kill them, and I was done. Since I was at my place and didn't want to ruin my flooring or furniture, I did what I'd seen on TV and covered a portion of my basement in heavy plastic that I'd gotten at the same hardware store where I get my wood for my woodworking. Paid with cash, of course.

When I got to my basement door, I took the rag away from Mini Reagan's face and slid her out of the wheelbarrow. Holding her under her shoulders, I walked down the steps backward as her feet dropped step by step until we were at the bottom. Before tying her to a metal chair covered in plastic, I placed the rag to her nose again for good measure. I wasn't ready for her to wake up yet because Jack was due to come over at any minute.

After I tied the nylon/polyester blend rope tight around her wrists and ankles, I left Mini Reagan tied up in my basement and went to wait for Jack.

The moment my foot hit the top step, my doorbell rang. My heart started to beat faster, knowing Jack was about to learn who I really was. I wasn't worried that he'd tell the police. I was too good to be caught, and there was no evidence linking me to the previous murders. There would be no evidence of Mini Reagan's murder either because when I was done with her, everything would be burned.

Including her.

I locked the door to the basement and hurried to greet Jack. With a huge smile on my face, I opened the front door to see him standing before me. It was always the same: he'd ring the doorbell, I'd open the door, and he'd push me back against the wall as though we hadn't seen each other in months. The door would slam shut, our clothes would come off as we made a trail upstairs to my bedroom, and then we'd fuck.

It *was* fucking. There was no love in what we were doing. That didn't mean I was okay with him flirting with other people. *Okay, fine,* I loved Jack, which was why I was going to show him what I was truly capable of. That was why I was going to show him my other side. The side that got my blood racing. The side that made me feel alive. The side where *I* was in control.

In the bedroom, I let Jack take the lead. He'd take me from the back, the front, every which way until we were both coming. And then he'd leave. At the office we'd grin at each other, wink, have the occasional brush of hands when no one was looking, and then at night, we'd do it all over again.

Except everything was going to be different once he knew the truth.

Jack still pushed me back against the wall when I swung the door open, the door still slammed shut as his mouth met mine, and we still left a trail of clothes up to my bedroom. Jack still fucked me hard, and we both still got off, but before he got out of bed to leave, I stopped him by grabbing his wrist.

"Is it going to be like this every night?" I asked.

He raised a dark brow. "What do you mean?"

"You coming over like a thief in the night to fuck me before leaving me alone, my bed smelling of sex—of you."

Jack grinned. "Is that your way of asking me to stay the night?"

I shrugged. "Yes, I want you to stay."

He lay back down and turned to face me. "I thought you only wanted a fling."

I chuckled. "A fling doesn't last long. We've been doing whatever this is for over a month now."

He brushed a lock of my red hair behind my ear. "I'm your boss. What if someone sees me leaving in the morning?"

"No one from work lives around here."

I'd looked into all the employee files and gotten their addresses not long after I started at the university. No one lived near me. Not even Jack. He lived two blocks from Judy's. I wasn't able to access his webcam because everyone who worked in IT knew to have their Wi-Fi encrypted and use a pin number for their routers. Most of us used hardwires for our internet and didn't have Wi-Fi enabled because of the very reason I was able to access my watch list.

"You know, if I stay, that means we're more than a fling, right?"

"I know, but I also have a proposition for you."

He cocked a brow with a smirk. "What's that?"

"How do you feel about a threesome?"

His eyes widened. "With another man?"

I shook my head. "No. I'm actually bi-sexual, and I was wondering if you'd be up for adding a woman in the bedroom."

Jack threw his head back and chuckled. "No man would ever say no to that."

"Okay." I smiled back.

"We'd have to keep it on the down low. Would you be okay with that?"

"I'm good at keeping secrets." *Was I ever?* "Are you?"

Jack smirked. "I've kept this one for a month now."

I finally looked over at him. "I have something to show you."

"Oh yeah?"

"It's a secret." I grinned. "Promise not to tell?"

"Who would I tell?" He asked and I shrugged my answer. "If I did tell anyone, then that would mean they'd find out about us."

"This is true."

Jack rolled on top of me. "Then I won't tell."

He was hard and obviously ready for another round since he was staying the night, but I figured Mini Reagan was awake and ready to *play* too.

"I'll show you before we go again."

"Is it within arm's reach, because I'm not letting you get up?"

I smiled. "Nope, but it's worth it."

He pressed his lips to mine. "Fine, but let's hurry. We have a *long* night."

"You have no idea." My grin widened. We got out of bed, and I slipped into my jeans.

"We have to get dressed?"

"Yes," I replied. "It's cold down there."

"Down there?"

I threw his jeans at him and started to walk out the door to get the rest of our clothes from the trail. "The basement."

"We're going to the basement?"

I heard the rustling of his jeans and called over my shoulder. "We are."

"What is it?"

"It's a surprise. Put your socks and shoes on too."

"Are you serious?"

"It's worth it." I slipped my black, long-sleeved shirt on over my head.

"I'm so confused."

"Just get dressed, baby."

"Baby? We're on to terms of endearment now?"

I spun around. "Yes, now that we've decided to be official and I lov—"

Jack slipped his shirt over his head. "Okay, *baby*. Lead the way."

We slipped on our shoes, and without any more questions, Jack followed me down the stairs. I unlocked the door to the basement and started to descend those stairs. Moans filled the air, and I wasn't sure if Jack heard.

After I took the final step, I stood to the side and waited for Jack to see what I had in store. Mini Reagan started to thrash in the chair, the legs trying to rip the heavy plastic as it scooted against it.

Jack stopped beside me. "Who the fuck is this, Katrina?"

# CHAPTER TWENTY-EIGHT

*Ethan*

I was running on adrenaline from the lack of sleep I'd had in the last forty-eight hours or so. Reagan's tip had led to a hit, which meant we were more than likely dealing with someone who worked on campus—in the IT department, I assumed. The cybercrimes tech on duty looked into the email Reagan had received, and it had some sort of encryption that collected data, specifically the IP addresses. It was enough to get us a warrant, so I'd been working on the paperwork all day, so that first thing Monday morning, we could get a judge to sign off on them.

Our plan was to collect the DNA and hair follicles from every IT employee to start since the person obviously knew what they were doing with computers. The shitty thing was that it was a holiday weekend, and most employees were out of town. Therefore, we were going to go to the campus on Monday morning to collect everything—after the judge signed off on the warrants. That way, no one could tip off the killer if that were the case.

That was until I got a frantic call from Reagan. "Hey," I greeted. "I'm—"

"Maddie isn't here."

I looked at Shawn, and he raised a brow at me, questioning what was going on. "What do you mean Maddie isn't there?"

"She came to have dinner with me at the bar, told me she was going to wait up for me, but I just got home, and she's not here."

"Did you try calling her?" I glanced at my watch to see that it was a little after midnight.

"Of course, I did. She didn't answer."

"Maybe she's with a friend?" The hairs on the back of my neck stood on end, but I didn't want Reagan to freak out more than she already was. I was trying to think of other possibilities when, in fact, the killer had probably grabbed Maddie thinking she was Reagan. They did look similar, just like mothers and daughters do as they age.

"She doesn't know anyone here, Ethan!" Reagan snapped. "Something is wrong. Do you—"

"Fuck," I clipped. If the killer did take Maddie, we still didn't know who we were dealing with, but I was seconds away from banging on the door of everyone who worked at Lakeshore University. I stood and started to pace as I spoke into the phone. "Do you want me to come home, or do you want me to find this asshole?"

"Both?"

I sighed. "I can't do both. You know that."

"I know. I just want Maddie safe."

"I feel like we're close thanks to you. Have Pablo stay with you, and stay at home in case she comes back. When she does, call me."

"What are you going to do?"

"I'm going to see if I can track her down."

"How?"

I groaned. "By doing my fucking job. Just call me when she gets home." I kept saying *when* on purpose and not *if.* I needed Reagan to stay calm even though I knew she was anything but.

"I'm scared," Reagan admitted.

"I know, baby, but think positive. Call me when she comes home."

"Okay. Please get her back."

I closed my eyes and took a deep breath. "I will." I just hoped I got her back alive. If something were to happen to Maddison, it would kill Reagan. We were already living in fear, and now Maddie was missing, and the weight that had been on my shoulders for the past several months was pressing down.

After Reagan told me what Maddison was wearing and her cell phone number, I promised her again that I'd find her daughter and hung up. One way or another, I *would* find Maddie.

"What's going on?" Shawn asked.

"Reagan's daughter is missing." I proceeded to tell him everything I knew.

Shawn took a deep breath and then breathed, "Fuck."

"My thoughts exactly," I replied as I continued to pace.

"Go home and be with your woman."

"I want to, but if this were Julie, you'd want to find this guy even more."

"Cap wouldn't let me work this just like he won't let you work it."

I stopped walking and faced my partner. "Well, it's good he's out of town, isn't it?"

"You think we can solve this before Monday morning?"

I groaned. "We better. This is Reagan's daughter."

"Right. So let's get the judge to sign off on the warrants and start at daybreak."

I didn't know if we had until daybreak, given what the ME had said about the two previous murders. Amy and Daisy were killed several hours before the bodies were found, in the early morning hours. We were still waiting to have her confirm Fiona's time of death, but she was gray when we'd arrived to investigate.

What we knew about Fiona's timeline was that she had plans to go to a Friendsgiving meal at a college friend's house, the same one who had found her body when she went to check on Fiona because she never showed for the two o'clock dinner and didn't answer her phone.

"Let's see if we can ping Maddison's cell phone."

"That will only triangulate an area," Shawn argued.

"It's better than nothing. Maybe one of the employees will live in that area."

"What if it isn't an employee? What if this isn't connected?"

I ran my hands down my face and took a deep breath. "I don't want to think about that. This needs to be connected."

We stared at each other for a few moments, and then Shawn said, "Okay, let's see what they can find out."

We hurried down to the cybercrimes room. "Maria," I barked as I rusheded in. "I need you to locate a cell phone."

"Sure thing." I handed her the number I'd written down from Reagan. I waited with bated breath for Maria to work her magic. "The phone must be off. It's not pinging."

"Fuck!" I shouted. "The killer must have shut it off."

Shawn clapped me on the back and squeezed. "We don't know if this is the same person—"

"That's not making this any better."

"I know, and I'm sorry. We need to work this like any other case even though it's your girlfriend's daughter."

Reagan was more than my girlfriend, and Maddison was more than her daughter. They were my family, but Shawn was right. We were trained for this, and I needed to work it like any other case because that was how we found people. If I let my emotions cloud my judgment, then it might be too late to save her.

Shawn and I went back up to our desks, and I sent a few cops out to start canvassing the area around Judy's to look for any witnesses or anything that might help us locate Maddison while Shawn and I continued on the paperwork for the warrants. I mindlessly filled out each request and replayed my phone call with Reagan over and over and over in my head until it hit me.

"Oh, shit!" I shouted in the sparse precinct.

Shawn looked up. "What?"

"Reagan said that Maddison had dinner with her."

"Okay?"

"So, that means she walked to Judy's and then was walking back to my place."

"Yeah?"

My eyes widened, and I gestured with my hands. "Cameras. There are bars, restaurants, a bank within walking distance, traffic cams."

"Okay, we'll get subpoenas—"

"No," I stated. "We don't need a subpoena for the *live* traffic cams."

He snapped his fingers and pointed at me. Even though they were live, they were recorded, and we had access to them. "You're right."

We both stood. "So, let's watch from seven o'clock on from the light right outside of Judy's. Maybe we'll see someone following Maddison or something. Maybe get a plate to trace."

"Let's do it."

Shawn and I went down to the cyber unit again, and I had half a mind to call Will to come in, but everyone was with their families for the holiday. Everyone except Shawn and me.

Everyone except Reagan and Maddie.

My stomach knotted at the thought of finding Maddison lifeless and having to tell Reagan that her daughter was dead. I couldn't let that happen. I didn't know how much time we had—if any—but I wasn't going to sleep until we found her.

"Maria, we need to access a traffic cam or two," I stated, walking into the cyber room and stopping at her desk. Again. She was the only one on duty.

"Sure. What street and when?" She started hitting some buttons, and I gave her the information she asked for. "What are we looking for?"

"Who," I corrected and gave her Maddison's description and what she was wearing. When we went down there earlier, I'd only given her Maddie's phone number and not the reason.

Shawn and I stood behind her as she cued up the footage. The black and white recording played a little faster than normal speed. It wasn't fast enough. I needed to find the fucker at that second. My phone dinged in my pocket with a text message. I pulled it out.

Reagan: *Anything?*

Me: *No. I'll let you know. Try to get some sleep.*

Reagan: *I can't fucking sleep, Ethan!*

Me: *I know. I'm trying to hurry.*

Reagan didn't reply, and I went back to looking at the screen. Finally, after what felt like forever, I spotted a white four-door sedan. It parked a little down from Judy's, and a person got out of the car.

It was hard to tell for sure if it was a woman or a small man, but the person was wearing his or her hair back in a ponytail. I sighed. We were looking for a *strong* man. Someone who could overtake a woman without a struggle. My mind quickly changed when I saw the person stand outside of Judy's, waiting, and then when Maddie exited the bar, he followed. My gaze cut to Shawn's briefly. This was it. I swallowed hard as I saw the person take something out of his pocket and then reach out and place it on Maddie's face. The viewpoint was as if we were looking from the back, so I couldn't see what the person looked like.

"We need another view," I stated.

Maria pressed some buttons and then we were looking at the screen from the front view. She sped up the feed until it was at the time we needed, and we watched as Maddison was again grabbed from behind, her body going limp, and the person dragging her a few feet to the sedan.

"I want every person here running a cross-check on the vehicles registered to Lakeshore U's staff," I ordered. "And pause on this bitch's face."

Maria did, and I squinted. It was gray and grainy.

"It's a woman," Shawn said.

I nodded. It definitely looked like a woman. "Yeah," I agreed. "See if you can clean this up," I stated to Maria.

"Will do."

Shawn and I went back upstairs and started to cross reference the employee list with the car records the school had for all of their employees. I didn't want to tell Reagan that we saw Maddie get taken. I wanted to wait until I knew more. Unfortunately, we had fewer people working because it was the dead of night, and a holiday weekend, but every single person was helping us. I thought we finally had the break we needed. I just hoped Maddison's kidnapping was connected to the murders. I hated to wish for that, but I was running on fumes.

"Sergeant," Officer Kendrick called, walking up to my desk.

"Yeah?" I replied and looked up at him.

"I think I have something." My heart started to race as he set the paper down in front of me. "Katrina Carpenter owns a white Toyota Camry. She works in the IT department at Lakeshore U."

"Address?" I questioned.

He flipped the page. "Yes, right here. I also have her facility photo."

"A redhead?" I asked, hoping and praying.

"Yes."

We fucking had her.

"All right. Roll out. This fucking ends now."

# CHAPTER TWENTY-NINE

*Katrina*

**"W**ho the fuck is this, Katrina?" Jack asked.

I stepped toward the still struggling girl and ran my finger along her cheek. "This is Mini Reagan."

"Mini Reagan?" He balked, clearly surprised. I thought the resemblance was uncanny.

"Who are you? What are you doing? Let me go!" Mini Reagan shouted and struggled against the rope.

"What do you mean 'Mini Reagan'?" he questioned again, ignoring the girl as he stared at me.

"Well, I was going to get the actual Reagan, but then I saw the younger version and thought you'd like her more."

"Like her more for what?"

"Let me go!" Mini Reagan shouted.

I grabbed a piece of duct tape and placed it over her mouth. She mumbled against the barrier and still tried to wiggle free from the rope. I ignored her as I turned back to Jack. "You said you wanted to have a threesome."

He drew back his head. "You have a girl tied up in your basement, and you think this is what I want?"

I walked toward him and ran my finger down his hard chest. "Do you know what it's like to take pleasure from someone and then kill them?"

"Do *you?*" he snapped, his gaze moving to Mini Reagan as she continued to fight as though that would do anything.

I grinned and looked back at Mini Reagan too as I spoke. "I do. I'm the Lakeshore Killer."

"You're … what?" Jack stuttered.

I smiled proudly. "The Lakeshore Killer. They haven't named me that, but it's fitting, no?"

"You killed those two girls?"

"Three," I stated. "Killed my third last night."

"Are you fucking serious?" he asked, taking a step back.

"It's so much fun, Jack." I looked at Mini Reagan and smirked.

"Katrina, this is some crazy shit." Jack began to pace.

"Yes." I turned back to face him. "But just imagine what it will be like to taste her, to fuck her, and then kill her. I can't even describe to you the high I'm on when I'm in control."

He stared at me for a beat. "Okay, show me."

I clapped excitedly. Mini Reagan's cries for help were muffled by the tape. "I usually do this with them unconscious." I moved to get the ether I had set on a built-in shelf behind our captive.

"Wait!" Jack shouted, and I turned to face him again. "There's two of us. Can't we just … hold her down and … take what we want?"

I slowly smiled. "You like it when they fight?"

He swallowed. "I like to be in control."

"So do I."

"But," he went on, "I'm willing to let you take the lead on this one."

I moved toward him and placed my lips against his briefly. He still tasted like me, and I couldn't wait to get a mixture of myself and Mini Reagan off of his lips. "I knew we were more than a fling."

"Right. So, how do we do this?"

"Well"—I looked at Mini Reagan—"she's already tied up."

"Yeah, but we need to be more comfortable. Let's go back upstairs."

"Upstairs isn't covered in plastic. The blood will be too hard to clean up and leave traces of our *fun.*"

"No, I'm not saying to—to kill her in your bed, baby. Let's go and play with her up where there's heat, and then we can bring her back down here," he suggested.

"But she might escape," I argued.

"Then we leave her tied up."

I grinned. "I can tie you up too if you want."

Jack chuckled slightly. "I like my hands free. I can tie you up."

I thought for a moment. "Do you think you can handle two women tied up?"

He smirked. "Only one way to find out."

"Maybe another time." I didn't want to take any chances with Mini Reagan. If I was tied up and she tried to get away, I couldn't trust Jack to stop her. I wasn't going to give up my control. This was my game, and Jack was only my teammate.

"Okay, then what's your plan?"

I started to get giddy, and my blood began to pump faster at the thought of my plan coming to fruition. "Usually I give them wood plaques with their names on them. Reagan already has hers and, well, I don't know her name." I pointed to our captive.

He walked up to Mini Reagan and peeled the silver tape off her mouth. "What's your name, sweetheart?"

"Fuck. You," she gritted out with a snarl.

I grinned. "Feisty. I like it."

"Feisty women taste the best," Jack stated and smirked at me.

"Do you mean me?"

"I do. We haven't tried you being tied up. What if we tie you up first and let…" Jack paused and turned to Mini Reagan. "What's your name?"

"Fuck. You," she repeated.

He leaned down and whispered into her ear. I couldn't hear what was said, but then he leaned back up and asked again for a third time, "What's your name?"

She stared up into his dark eyes and then finally replied, "Maddison."

"What did you say to her?" I questioned.

"I told her that if she didn't want a painful death, she'd tell us her fucking name."

I beamed. "You really are perfect for me."

"I agree. Now, let's make this a night we'll never forget." Jack picked Maddison up, the chair and all.

"We're going back to my bedroom?"

"Or the living room. Make her watch me fuck you," he proposed.

"I've never had anyone watch me before. I've been the one to watch them. Or to watch *her*."

"Her?" He tilted his head toward Maddison as though to ask if I meant her.

I shook my head and smiled. "No, no one. Let's go."

"Please don't hurt me," Maddison pleaded.

I reached up and put the tape back over her lips. "When I watch, they can't hear me. It's better if she can't speak."

"I agree." Jack motioned with his head for me to start walking up the stairs. I knew he was strong, but now it was confirmed as I stared at him as he held Maddison awkwardly still strapped to the chair.

When I got to the top of the stairs, I turned to see that Jack was still at the bottom. "What are you doing?"

"I had to set her down and adjust. She's heavy."

I chuckled. "You're telling me. I had to get her from the car and down to the basement."

"And how did you do that?" He started to walk up the stairs with Maddison in his arms again.

"A wheelbarrow until I got here, and then I dragged her as I walked backward down the stairs."

Jack grinned. "Smart."

My heart swelled at his validation of me. I'd never had that before. We walked into my living room, and he set Maddison down near the couch. I briefly heard something outside my front door, my attention turning to the sound before I felt Jack come up behind me. He held a cloth to my face and then ...

*Ethan*

Guns were drawn, and we were moving in, going stealthily up the walkway toward the front door. We'd parked down the street, no lights flashing on our marked and unmarked cars because we didn't want to make our presence known.

I gave a nod to the officer with the battering ram, and a second later, the door flew open with a bang, the wood shattering. I didn't hesitate. I could feel it in my veins that this was the place, that this was the killer we were after. If it wasn't, I was going to lose my shit.

"Chicago PD, put your fucking hands up," I ordered as I entered and noticed a man standing near a couch. My gaze flicked to a chair where Maddison was tied down, and I momentarily sighed with relief. My attention turned back to the man, and I caught a glimpse of red hair fanned on the couch.

"I was helping," the man stated.

My gaze flicked back to his, and I realized it was Jack Clark. His hands were raised as I'd ordered and then Shawn started to cuff him and read him his rights. I moved toward Maddie and knelt in front of her.

"Are you okay?" I asked.

She nodded.

I removed the tape from her mouth. "Are you hurt?"

She shook her head.

After I got the rope off of her wrists and ankles, I pulled her into a hug. "Fuck. I'm so happy you're okay."

Maddie started to cry in my arms, her body shaking. "She was going to rape and kill me."

I looked over her shoulder at the woman on the couch. She was unconscious, multiple police officers surrounding with their guns aimed at her. This had to be our killer because of the red strand of hair we'd found at the most recent crime scene.

"They were going to rape and kill you?"

She shook her head. "Just the woman. She told him she was the Lakeshore Killer, and he was trying to help me."

"See!" Jack stated. "I wasn't going to let Katrina hurt her. She said she's killed three girls. I had nothing to do with that, and when we went downstairs to the basement, I had no idea Maddison was down there. Then I pretended to go along with it, and when we got upstairs, I knocked her out with the ether."

"We'll get your statement back at the station," Shawn replied.

"Were you knocked out with ether too?" Fucking ether. That was what the nut job used to knock out my sister when he tried to kidnap her.

"I think so. I woke up alone in the basement. I was tied up already."

"Fuck!" I groaned again. I turned my attention to Shawn, Maddie still in my arms. "I'm going to call a bus and get Maddie checked out. Cuff her"—I pointed to the redhead on the couch—"and when she wakes up, bring her in too."

"Will do. Are you going to call Reagan to come get Maddie?"

"Not yet," I stated. "I'm going to make sure Maddie's okay first, and then I'll take her home. Can you make sure everything's taken care of here, and I'll meet you at the station?"

"Of course."

I grabbed my phone out of my pocket and led Maddison out of the house. I kept her in my arms as I called for an ambulance. Her tears eased up, but I wanted her to get checked out before I took her home. When Ashtyn was drugged, she just needed fresh air and rest, so while we waited for the bus to arrive, we stayed out in the cold, fresh air.

"I'm sorry, Maddie, but you know I need you to tell me exactly what happened, right?"

We took a seat on the top step of the porch, and I wrapped my arm around her shoulders, bringing her against my side.

"I don't really know much."

"Tell me what you do know."

She sighed. "I had dinner with Mom and was walking back to your place when someone grabbed me from behind. Then I woke up in a cold basement, tied to a chair. I tried screaming, but no one came for a long time."

"How long?"

She shrugged. "I don't know. Thirty minutes or so."

"And what happened when they finally came down?"

"What he said was true. They were arguing, and he seemed surprised when she told him what she wanted to do and that she was the killer you've been after."

"Are you sure he didn't know?" Jack was the director of the IT department, and Katrina was his employee. All the dots were connecting, but all along, I'd assumed we were looking for a man—we were still waiting for the DNA results for the red hair. Women did have strength, but was it possible for one to pull off all of these murders without any struggle or anything out of place? Dead weight—or that of an unconscious person—was heavy.

"He didn't seem like he knew, and the woman kept calling me Mini Reagan. She said that she was going after Mom but then saw me and changed her plan."

"So, she *was* a target." Even though it had been months since Reagan got her plaque, I still knew that she was in danger, which was why I'd maintained private security for her. And I should have known to have them for Maddison, too. I thought we'd be okay since Maddie wasn't a student at Lakeshore U and was only here for a few days and nights.

I was wrong.

"What else happened?" I asked.

"They asked me what my name was after talking about raping me."

"Fuck," I breathed.

"But at first I wouldn't tell them my name, and then the guy whispered into my ear that he was going to help me, and I just needed to cooperate."

"And what he said earlier was true?"

"Yeah, the woman started to walk up the stairs, and he grabbed the stuff that made her pass out. A few seconds later, you were barging in."

"I'm so sorry this happened to you."

"I'm glad it wasn't Mom."

I was too, but having it happen to Maddie wasn't any better. Before I could respond, the bus pulled up, and I walked Maddison to the ambulance and got her checked out. Like Ashtyn, Maddie just needed time for the ether to get out of her system. When she was cleared, she gave a statement to Shawn, told him everything she told me, and then I drove her home to get some rest.

She was safe, Reagan was safe, and the killer was, hopefully, finally in custody.

# CHAPTER THIRTY

I couldn't sit still. My stomach was knotted, and I anxiously paced back and forth in the living. I was tempted to call Ethan every ten minutes, but I knew he'd call me if he had found her.

"Can I get you anything?" Pablo asked.

"My daughter," I snapped and then sighed. "I'm sorry."

"I understand. I couldn't imagine if my daughter was missing."

"You have a daughter?" I asked as I stopped pacing.

He nodded. "She's four."

I had no idea. Even though he and Evan were my private security, I didn't talk to them much. It wasn't because I didn't care, but they were on the outside, not the inside like Officers Belt and Chase were when they were my details.

"It's a horrible feeling," I replied.

"Sergeant Valor will get her back."

"I hope so." Fuck, I hoped so. Ethan told me that my email idea had led to something, but I didn't know what. I paced for what seemed like hours, but finally sat on the couch. I didn't turn the TV on, and all I could do was stare at the wall, thinking.

Finally, the door opened. My gaze jerked to see Maddie and Ethan walk in, and I stood and rushed to my daughter. "Oh, my God!" I shouted as I engulfed her in my arms. "Are you okay?"

"Yeah," she replied against my shoulder.

My gaze met Ethan's, and he smiled tightly. He kissed the side of my head as he passed. I pulled back, keeping my hands on Maddie's arms. "What happened?"

"You know … kidnapped," she said with a small shrug.

My gaze met Ethan's again, and he nodded. I turned back to Maddison. "You were kidnapped?"

"Yeah …"

I pulled her in for another hug. "I'm never letting you out of my sight again."

"Until I go back to Michigan on Sunday."

My heart dropped, and I pulled back again to look into her green eyes. "Are you sure?"

"Can we talk about this after I get some sleep?"

"Right." I finally stepped away. "It's been a long night. We should all get some sleep."

"I actually need to head back to the station," Ethan advised.

"Really?"

He walked the few steps to me and kissed me softly. "Thanks to you, we caught the woman, Buttercup."

"You did?"

"I'll fill you in after I get home, but both of you should get some sleep. The two of you had a long night."

"Wait," I said when I realized what Ethan had actually said. "You were taken by a woman? A woman who was the killer?"

Maddie nodded. "Yeah."

"No," I breathed and closed my eyes as a tear slid down my cheek. It was all my fault. *Everything* was my fault. And now Maddie had been put in danger because of me.

Ethan wrapped his arms around me. "Everything's over now. Maddison's safe. You're safe. The killer's behind bars. It's over."

"It's really over?" I asked, making sure I'd heard him correctly.

"It's really over. Now, get some sleep, and in the morning we can talk it all out."

"It is morning," I stated. The sun would be up in a few hours.

Ethan smiled slightly. "I know. We've all had a long night, but I need a few more hours to process everything that went down tonight."

"Okay." I looked at Pablo. "I guess we don't need your services anymore."

"Actually," Ethan cut in, "I'd like to keep your security until we're sure we caught the only killer."

"There could be more than one?" Maddie asked.

"You just said it was over," I retorted.

"While I'm almost certain we were only dealing with one killer, and it *is* over, I just want to make sure before I let Pablo and Evan go."

Ethan was right. I didn't know all the details about the case, but until this person—this woman—was convicted, it was probably a good idea to keep my security. With my luck, there was another person, and he or she would be out for revenge.

"Do you know why I was a target?" I asked.

"Not yet, but I'm going to find out."

Maddie yawned. "I'm going to head to bed."

I pulled her in for another hug. "Go ahead, honey. I'm here if you need me. I love you."

"Love you too." She turned to Ethan and wrapped her arms around him. "Thank you."

He hugged her back. "You don't need to thank me. I'm just happy you're okay." Maddie turned and went to her room.

"I'm sorry about tonight," Pablo stated.

"Don't do that," Ethan said. "Maddie wasn't your responsibility."

"No, but I could have at least walked her back while Reagan was working."

"There's no way we could have known. Everything worked out. Go get some sleep too."

"I'm going to kiss my daughter when I get home."

Ethan clapped him on the shoulder. "Do that. And please, don't blame yourself."

Pablo nodded. "All right. I'll see you tomorrow."

"Good night." I waved goodbye. Pablo left, and Ethan pulled me in for another hug. "I was so scared."

"I know, Buttercup, but it was you who helped solve this case."

"How?"

"The email led us to confirm it was an employee of the school. We were able to get CCTV and cross-reference the car we saw with the employee records."

"I can't believe it was an employee. Though, I guess it makes sense since the victims were students."

"And a woman."

"Yeah, that's crazy too." I heard the shower in the hall bathroom turn on. "Is Maddie really okay?"

Ethan kept his arms around me. "Physically? Yes. Emotionally? It may take her some time. She seemed headstrong through it all, and all that happened was she was taken and tied up."

"What *exactly* happened?" I pulled my head back and looked into his eyes. Ethan told me all he knew. The IT director at the college was involved, but he had plans to help Maddie when he learned of the killer's plan. "I can't believe this happened."

"I know." He kissed me softly. "It really did all happen because of you."

My stomach dropped, and a tear slid down my cheek again. "I know."

"I don't mean it like that. I mean the killer was caught because of your email tracing idea. If we didn't have that info, I don't think we would have caught her. Though, if Jack Clark was really going to save Maddie—which it appears he was—then all of it would have come to a head, and nothing would have happened to Maddison."

"Well, I'm glad she's safe."

"Me too, Buttercup. Go to bed, and I'll be home soon."

"Okay. Thank you for saving my daughter."

"Always."

We kissed again and then he left. I went to take a quick shower before I crawled into bed with Maddie. I held her tight until she was asleep.

# CHAPTER THIRTY-ONE

I was exhausted.

I had been awake for almost twenty-four hours, but Shawn and I needed to interview Katrina Carpenter. Before going into the interrogation room, I grabbed a cup of coffee.

"How's Maddison?" Shawn asked and then took a sip of his coffee.

"I think she's doing okay. Tired."

He sighed. "I'm exhausted."

I took a sip of my coffee. "I think I can sleep for a week after this."

"Me too. How's Reagan?"

"Thankful. Grateful. Relieved like all of us."

"I bet." He took another sip. "Let's get this interview over with so we can get some sleep."

I took another sip of my own coffee, and then Shawn and I walked down the hall to the room where the redhead was being held for questioning. Just before we entered, he stopped me with a grab of his hand. "Are you sure you're okay doing this?"

I stared into his eyes, and without missing a beat, I said, "I've been waiting months for this."

"Okay, because you know I can get Shay or someone to go in with me."

I clapped him on the shoulder. "I'm good."

And I was. I was pissed, but like Reagan, I was thankful, grateful, and relieved. If some harm had come to Maddison, I'd be throwing this bitch against the wall. She was a monster in my eyes. But I'd had over twenty years on the force, and I knew what we needed to do to make sure this bitch never saw the light of day again.

"Do you want me to take point?" Shawn asked.

I shook my head. "I got it."

I went in first and started to open my mouth when Katrina spoke. "Sergeant Valor, it's good to see you again."

My gaze flicked to Shawn's as he shut the door, and then I moved my stare back at Katrina and sat across from her. "Again?"

She smirked and adjusted, clasping her cuffed hands onto the table that separated us in the tiny room. I figured she meant because she was watching Reagan through her laptop, and I was always with Reagan, but I let her answer. "Yes, but I'm not sure if I like you better in your suit or out of it."

"Oh yeah? And when did you see me out of it?"

"Sergeant Valor"—she batted her green eyes—"a lady doesn't divulge her secrets."

"All right." I took a sip of my coffee and peered at her over the lip. She yawned. "Oh, did you want a cup of coffee?"

She laughed. "So you can have my DNA?"

"Why do you think we'd want your DNA?" I questioned. "You're being charged with kidnapping. We have you on that." We would charge her with more, but first we'd get her for what we could prove beyond a shadow of a doubt, and that was the kidnapping of Maddison. "So let's start there."

"I don't know what you're talking about."

I snorted. "The young woman we rescued from your house. You don't know who we're talking about?"

"What young woman?"

I glanced at Shawn, who was taking notes, and then continued. "What are you saying?"

"I don't know what woman you're talking about. I woke up from a nap with my hands in cuffs and surrounded by police officers with their guns drawn at me."

"And why do you think the police officers were there?"

Katrina shrugged. "I don't know. Why don't you tell me?"

Shawn leaned forward and placed a picture in front of her. "Isn't that your car?"

"A lot of people have that car, Detective."

I got the impression that Katrina thought she was smarter than us. Of course, she wasn't. "So, tell us how that girl got into your house after she was taken by someone in the same type of car you drive," I ordered.

She shrugged. "I don't know. I wasn't the only one there."

She wanted to play a game? Then we would play. "Who else was there?" I asked. Jack had been taken out of the house before Katrina regained consciousness.

Katrina tilted her head slightly. "No one else was there?" she asked.

I looked at Shawn. "There wasn't anyone else there, was there?"

"I didn't see anyone else."

"So, Katrina," I said. "I'm going to ask you again. How did the young woman get to your house in a car that looks like yours?"

She opened her mouth to speak but paused for a few beats as her gaze moved from me to Shawn and then back to me. Her shit-eating grin was gone, and she finally said, "I want a lawyer."

"Great." I stood. "An officer will come to get you to make that call. They'll also get a DNA sample from you."

"I thought you didn't need my DNA?"

I grinned as I peered down at her. "Don't you know, Katrina? A hair was found at a murder scene on Thanksgiving. When it matches yours, you're in hot water for more than just kidnapping. After all, what was it that you called yourself? The Lakeshore Killer?"

Without another word, Shawn and I left the interrogation room. She may have thought that she was smarter than me, but I had been doing interrogations for most of my life. Once Katrina knew I had her backed into a corner, she lawyered up. I usually hated when perps did that because I wanted to get more answers from them, but not this time. I was tired and on the verge of passing out. Plus, I heard they found wood plaques in her basement, and that was as good as any evidence for me at the moment. Shawn and I would gather more, and we'd send her up the creek for the rest of her life. She was lucky we were in Illinois because if we were in a state that had the death penalty, I would make sure the DA asked for it.

"You want to talk about it?" Shawn asked as we walked toward our desks.

"Talk about what?"

He smirked. "That she watched you and Reagan fuck."

I grinned. "Fuck off. We're never speaking of that with Reagan either."

"All right, but she might find out at the trial."

"I'll deal with it then. She and Maddie have been through too much already."

"So have you," Shawn argued.

"You mean my kids?" He nodded. "Nah. That was Jess being a bitch."

"True. Now you can rest."

"*We* can rest," I countered. "We got this bitch off the street."

"Yeah, we did!" We shook hands and shared a brief manly hug. It definitely wasn't the first case we'd solved, but it was the first that literally felt as though my life depended on it.

By the time I got home, the sun was starting to rise. Walking into my bedroom, I noticed Reagan wasn't in our bed. The sheets weren't disturbed, and it looked as though no one had slept in it. When I turned, I ran into her.

"Did I wake you?" I asked.

"No. I didn't fall asleep. I was just watching my baby sleep."

I pulled Reagan to me and wrapped my arms around her. "It's over."

She drew her head back and looked up at me with her emerald eyes. "Is it, officially?"

"Techs found the malware program on the woman's computer, the strand of hair is most likely a match, we're testing all of her knives, and we found a wood carving station in the basement of the house. I'd say it's over."

Reagan sighed. "Thank god."

"I'm going to shower and then sleep for a week."

"I'll wait for you."

I kissed her lips, and then I went to take a hot shower. When I got out, Reagan was curled up on her side of the bed, her back to me. I scooted in, pulled her against me, and kissed the top of her head.

"I think I'm going to go to Michigan with Maddie tomorrow. Make sure she gets there okay," Reagan stated.

I thought for a moment and then replied, "I think that sounds like a great idea. She may need to see a therapist."

"Yeah, I was thinking that too. I'm going to stay as long as she needs me."

"Want me to come with you?"

Reagan turned over and faced me. "Can you?"

"I can go for a few days if you need me too. I can use your laptop to type up my report for the case. Cap knows I need a break—Shawn too. I haven't had a vacation in a few years. But we have the boys on Wednesday, so I'll need to be back by then."

"Okay, I'd love for you to be there too. I think it will make her feel safer."

I kissed Reagan's forehead. "Then I'll make it work."

# CHAPTER THIRTY-TWO

*Reagan*

Ethan drove Maddie's car to the University of Michigan. We had no hotel room, or any plans other than to get her there safely. I'd gotten one of the other bartenders to cover my shifts, but I didn't think I could work at Judy's any longer. It was never part of my long-term plan, and I knew that whenever I'd walk out the door (front or back), I'd always fear someone was waiting for me. I needed to talk to Judy. Ethan was certain he'd caught the killer, but what if she wasn't the only one?

He parked in a campus parking spot for Maddison's dorm, and we all exited the car. He grabbed Maddie's bag from the trunk, and I grabbed her hand.

"Are you sure you're going to be okay?" I asked as we walked toward the door of the building.

"I'm not planning on going anywhere alone ever again."

I sighed. I hated this. There were so many reasons why I wished it had been me who had been taken. Maddie would be looking over her shoulder for a long time, I was certain of it. But she was also strong, and I knew she'd get through it. She didn't want to quit school, and I didn't blame her. Life deals out shit to overcome, and we all have to stay strong to get through it, and I'd raised a tough woman.

"You can always come live with us," I suggested and looked at Ethan. I hadn't mentioned it to him, but if Maddie needed to, we'd figure it out. We already needed a bigger place because the week after

Christmas we were going to have a houseful of kids—my one and his two.

"I'll be okay." She smiled.

We got to her dorm room, and Maddison put her key in the lock. Before she could turn it to unlock it, the door flew open and Maddie was engulfed in arms.

"Finally," the girl said.

"Ethan drives the speed limit since he's a cop and all." The girls broke apart, and we all chuckled.

"Mom, this is Sophie."

I stuck out my hand. "It's nice to meet you. Maddie has told me so much about you."

"You too, Mrs. McCormick." We shook hands.

"Please call me Reagan. And this is my boyfriend, Ethan."

I expected Sophie to shake his hand too. Instead, she engulfed him in a giant hug. "Thank you for saving my girl."

"Always," Ethan replied and looked at me over Sophie's shoulder. I smiled warmly back at him.

My gaze moved to Maddison. "Why don't the two of you catch up while Ethan and I find a hotel room? We'll meet you back here and take you both to dinner."

"Sure," Maddie replied.

"Maybe we can find a car rental place too?" Ethan suggested.

"Use my car," Maddie suggested. "I won't need it while you're here."

"Are you sure?" Ethan asked.

She nodded. "I can walk to all of my classes."

"Okay," Ethan replied.

"I'll text you when we're on our way," I said.

Maddison wrapped her arms around my neck. "I love you."

"I love you more."

Ethan and I left and walked back toward the parking lot. "So, Sophie?" he asked.

I smiled. "That's Maddie's girlfriend. I was going to tell you, but she didn't tell me she was dating a girl until she showed up on Wednesday, and then a lot happened."

"Understandable." He wrapped his arm around my shoulder. "What do you say about going somewhere at the start of next year, just you and me?"

"I'd say that I can't wait."

"Good. As long as there's no trial scheduled, I'll put in for time off."

"Do you think I'll be working by then?"

"You mean in the crime scene unit?"

"Yeah." I nodded.

"Maybe. I haven't heard anything."

"It's okay. The right job will come along at some point."

"That it will."

We got to Maddie's car, and Ethan started it up while I looked for the nearest hotel. Thankfully, we didn't have to drive far because there was a hotel within a four-minute drive. We got a room for three nights, and while I freshened up for dinner, Ethan worked. When he was done, I texted Maddison that we were on our way.

We went to a burger place not far from campus for dinner. Maddie was smiling and laughing, and it put me at ease to know that she *would* be fine. Even though her relationship with Sophie was new, I could tell they were in love. The way they touched, the way they looked at each other, it was the same way I looked at Ethan. Even if they weren't meant to last forever, I knew that it was what Maddison needed to get through this rough time.

Since the girls had class in the morning, we made it an early night. "Want to meet for coffee after your first class?" I asked Maddie.

"I'd like that. We can finally have coffee together instead of over the phone," she replied.

"You're more than welcome to come too, Sophie."

"I have classes until 11:45. Then Maddie has class."

"Yeah," Maddison agreed. "We usually don't see each other until dinner."

"Then we'll do dinner again," Ethan cut in.

"Perfect," Maddison replied.

We said our goodbyes, and as we started to walk away, a thought occurred to me. "Hey, Mads," I called.

"Yeah, Mom?"

"Are you going to tell your father?" I didn't need to elaborate.

"I haven't decided."

"You should," I replied.

She looked at her phone in her hands. "It's still early in Denver."

"Yeah," I agreed. "You can call me to come back if you need me. We're just down the street."

She sighed. "I'll be fine."

"Okay." I gave her one last hug before Ethan and I left.

When we got back to the room, I showered while Ethan worked. I wasn't sure if this was a new Ethan or if it was because of me, but I knew that Jessica had wanted a divorce because Ethan had chosen work over her. I wanted to believe it was because of me as a person—the love of his life—and not because he thought that I would leave him too.

"Almost done?" I asked as I came out of the bathroom, a white towel wrapped around me.

"Almost." He hit a few keys, and I came up behind him and ran my hand down his chest. "Are you trying to get in my pants, Buttercup?"

I smirked. "Maybe."

In one quick move, he spun around in the desk chair and pulled the end of the towel, causing it to fall to the carpeted floor. "Looks like I got in yours first."

I chuckled. "Yeah, and what are you going to do about it?"

Ethan stood and picked me up, my legs wrapping around his hips. "Do you remember the only other time we've been in a hotel room together?"

"How could I forget?" I leaned down and placed my lips onto his.

The time he was referring to was the May before I graduated high school. We told my parents that I was going to stay at my friend Rebekah's house, but we really drove to Indianapolis to watch the Indy

500 all day. Literally all day long. We stayed in a hotel the night before the race and drove home after it. The night in the hotel was the one night when we didn't have to worry about parents catching us, being fast, or being quiet. It was a night I'd never forget because, not only did we spend the whole night *connected*, it was the night I knew for sure that I wanted to spend every night for the rest of my life with him.

Before Ethan placed me onto the bed, he stopped and turned back around.

"What are you doing?" I asked.

He closed the laptop. "Just in case."

"Just in case what?" And then it hit me. "I thought you caught the person."

"We did. But you never know who could be watching."

I shivered at the thought. "That's creepy."

"Yeah, it is." He captured my lips again, and all thoughts of someone watching turned off just like the closed laptop.

My back hit the mattress as our mouths worked together. We were starved for each other. What if the killer had killed me, and I would have no longer been able to kiss his lips, feel his breath on my skin, love him? "Thank you." I broke our lips apart because I needed to tell him. I wasn't sure if I had thanked him for saving my daughter or not. Everything was still a blur.

He pulled his head. "For what?"

"With Maddie."

"Baby"—he rose onto his heels—"you never need to thank me for saving or protecting either one of you."

"I know. It's just all …"

"Shh, it's okay. Everyone's okay." He brushed my dark hair behind my ear.

"I know." I wanted to tell him that *this* time everyone was okay, but I also wanted to forget for the time being. So instead of saying anything further, I started to push his boxers off of his hips, but Ethan stopped me. He got off the bed and rummaged in his bag. He pulled out a condom, stepped out of his boxers, and sheathed himself.

"On your belly, baby."

I didn't hesitate to flip over.

"Your ass, mmmm," he moaned his approval of my backside. I turned my head to look over my shoulder at him and saw him stroking his cock as he stared at my butt. Only once in my life had someone claimed my ass, and that man was staring at it. I wanted everything with Ethan Valor.

I wanted forever.

The sight of Ethan stroking himself as he admired my body was turning me on. My belly clenched, my pussy became wet, and I moaned. His eyes flicked up to meet mine. "You ready for me?"

I nodded, still looking over my shoulder. He stepped forward as I lifted my hips to give him a better angle. Spreading my knees, I'd expected him to line up and enter me. Instead, he ran his fingers through my opening.

"Yeah, you're ready for me." I grinned and moaned as his fingers touched just the right spot. The bed dipped, and within seconds, Ethan entered me. He pumped a few times. "Raise up and hold on to the headboard."

Doing so caused my body to tilt and his shaft to hit the spot that drove me insane with pleasure. He picked up his speed, my tits bouncing with each drive, and Ethan grunted.

"You feel amazing at this angle."

"Oh, God," I moaned. I couldn't say anything else as he kept driving and hitting *the* spot. He groaned again. I moaned again. The hotel bed squeaked, and the headboard started to bounce off the wall over and over and over.

Without warning, I came. My body pulsed around Ethan's cock as he continued thrusting. The sensation returned and the pleasure built again. He kept hitting the spot, and my body loved it. Sweat coated my body while he still didn't stop and brought me closer to coming again at a rapid speed.

"Fuck," I hissed as my body moved in sync with his. And then I came again, my body trembling as I held onto the headboard. He didn't stop. "Ethan," I panted.

"Hang on. I know you can give me three."

Could I? Two was my max—or limit—and I wasn't sure if I could get to three. But Ethan kept going and I held on, the bed still rocking and banging. It may have even moved across the thinly carpeted floor. The pleasure started to build again, and I wasn't sure if it was because we kept going or because Ethan was still hitting *the* spot at the perfect angle.

"Ethan," I moaned again.

"You can do it, baby."

And I did.

I didn't moan my release, I screamed it. My body shook, and I couldn't hold on to the headboard any longer. Luckily, I didn't haven't to.

"Ah fuck," he hissed, and drove in a few more times and then groaned his release. Ethan pulled me back until my back was against his front, and we both rode out our orgasms until our breathing slowed. "Told you that you could do three."

We had breakfast before Maddie needed to be in class. Ethan and I rented a car and were driving back, so we said our goodbyes in Maddison's small dorm room that was only big enough for two twin beds and two small desks.

"Call me if you need me. I will be here in less than two hours." I didn't care that the drive from Chicago to her college was over three hours. If my baby needed me, I would drive as fast as I could.

"I'll be okay. Sophie is ..." Maddie looked at her girlfriend and smiled. "Well, she's going to be staying with me every night."

"Yeah," Sophie agreed. "Emily is never here."

"Where is she?" I asked.

The girls shared a look, and Maddie spoke, "She's a little boy crazy."

"Ah." I nodded my understanding and looked at Ethan. I wasn't boy crazy in college except for one boy who was a million miles away from me, but I did understand how college and boys and parties worked.

"Can I actually speak with you for a moment?" Ethan asked, looking at Maddison. My brows furrowed. He wanted to speak with Maddie? "Not about boys—*or girls*—but something to do with … that night."

"Sure," she replied, and the two of them walked out into the hall. I wasn't sure why he had to do it privately, but it was still an ongoing investigation, and maybe he needed to ask her something Sophie couldn't be privy to.

"I really will keep an eye on Mads," Sophie said to break the awkward silence.

"I know sweetie. I'm happy she has you."

"We just click, you know?"

My gaze moved to look out the door. Ethan was standing with his back to us. "I know." Ethan and I just clicked. We always had. "You can call me if you think Maddie needs me, and if you need anything, I'll be there for you too."

"I will." She smiled.

Maddison and Ethan walked back in, both of them smiling. "Everything good?" I asked.

Ethan draped an arm across my shoulders and kissed the side of my head. "Of course, Buttercup."

We said our final goodbyes, and Ethan and I took an Uber to a car rental place then we drove back to Chicago. It snowed while we were driving, and all I wanted to do was curl up on the couch with him and watch a movie.

"What's the plan for tonight?" I asked as we parked at the rental car return.

"I'm not sure. I need to go into the station for a few hours and then go and get the boys."

Oh, right, the boys. I hadn't forgotten that it was Wednesday, but I was tired from everything that had happened during the last week. Hell, the last several months had been exhausting, but I also knew that kids had a ton of energy and needed to do something other than sitting around. "Want to go ice skating?"

"Really?"

I lifted a shoulder. "Yeah, I haven't been in years."

Ethan nodded slightly. "Yeah, the boys will like that."

"Good." We got out of the car, and I half expected Pablo or Evan to come out of the shadows since Ethan was going to work. "Who will be with me tonight? Evan?"

"Oh." He came around the back of the car and took our bags out of the trunk. "I guess Evan. We should call and tell them we're back."

"*Do* I still need security?" I questioned as we waited for the worker to inspect and check in the car.

He thought for a moment. "No, I don't think you do anymore."

I nodded slightly. "All right."

Ethan draped an arm across my shoulders. "But if you want one, I don't mind calling the guys to help."

"No." I looked up into his blue eyes. "I'll be okay." It was going to be weird, but I couldn't have security following me for no reason.

We took an Uber home, and after having a quick sandwich, Ethan went to work. I sat on the couch, not sure what to do with myself. The condo was quiet after having Maddie here for a few days, and just like the past several days, I thought about that night. I thought about what could have happened. So, with nothing to do and being able to go wherever I wanted to go again, I drove to Lakeshore University.

I was nervous as I pulled up. Getting out of my car, I hurried across the parking lot toward the admin building. It was still snowing lightly, and the moment I walked into the building, warmth washed over my body. I was used to the snow since I lived in Denver and Chicago for most of my life, but I still wouldn't mind being in Florida where my parents had retired.

I was directed to the IT department and took the elevator down to the basement level. When I stepped out, I hesitated for a beat, took a deep breath, and continued. I stepped up to the front desk where a woman was sitting.

She looked up from her computer. "May I ... May I help you?" she stuttered.

"I'm here to see the IT Director."

"And you are?"

"Reagan McCormick."

"Is he … is he expecting you?" she stuttered.

"No." I shook my head. "But this will only take a minute."

"Let me … let me see if he's available." The woman stood and walked down a large hallway, turned a corner, and was out of sight.

I looked around the basement level. Even though it was an office of sorts, there were no decorations around. Though I supposed when all of your attention was in the cyber world and not the real world, it wouldn't matter if there was a motivational picture hanging on the wall.

The woman returned, walking next to a man, and I drew my head back slightly as I realized who it was: Whiskey Neat. My heart began to race thinking about all the times I'd run into him: Judy's, and then campus coffee shop on several occasions. How was he *not* involved?

He smiled. "Reagan."

"Jack?" I greeted back, but it came out as a question because I was confused. And scared. But, if he was involved, wouldn't he have been arrested too?

"Is everything okay? Sergeant Valor—"

"You helped my daughter?"

"Let's talk in my office?" He motioned behind him where he had come from.

"Sure." I followed him down the hall and then around the corner. His office was the first door on the left. We entered, and I took a seat in a chair in front of his desk. "Ethan told me what happened. I wanted to thank you."

He sighed and leaned back in his chair. "I have to admit, I never thought I'd have to save a hostage from being raped and murdered."

"How were you even there?" What I understood was that the killer was his employee. Everything happened late at night, so, *why* and *how* was he there?

"My staff doesn't know yet—and I'm not going to divulge it until I have to—but Katrina and I were sleeping together."

"Okay?" That still didn't necessarily tell me how he was involved.

"Just like I told your boyfriend and his partner, I went over to Katrina's for our nightly …" he paused. "For our nightly rendezvous."

"And my daughter was there to …"

"No." He shook his head. "Katrina and I did our thing, and then she took me down to the basement. That was when I saw your daughter tied up."

My stomach dropped. Even though I knew what had happened, it still got to me. That was my baby, and I'd put her in danger. "Why us?" I whispered.

Jack took a deep breath. "I wasn't able to ask Katrina much, but from what I gathered she didn't like that you were my bartender. She almost slipped and told me that she loved me. I didn't entertain it because I didn't love her, and that would have turned awkward, though walking down and seeing a woman tied up was fucking crazy."

My eyebrows furrowed. "So you think she did it because she loved you? That doesn't make a lot of sense."

"I think she fucked up because she loved me. She thought I would go along with her plan."

"And you obviously didn't," I stated.

He leaned forward. "You have to know I would have never let anything happen to Maddison. Once I saw a woman tied up, and Katrina told me that she took her because she looked like you, I knew Katrina was sick. I was going to do whatever it took to protect Maddison."

"Thank you," I finally said.

"You really don't need to thank me."

"Yes, I do." That was the reason I had come.

"I would have done it even if it wasn't your daughter."

"I know." I didn't technically know, but that seemed like the right response. Jack appeared to be a decent man, even if he had once told me that he wanted to tie *me* up. "Do you remember you told me that you wouldn't mind tying me up that time we ran into each other at the campus coffee shop?"

"I do, and now I regret it. I won't be tying anyone up in the future—even for pleasure."

I flushed. "Well, I better go. Thank you again. I truly appreciate it." I stood.

"You're welcome." He stood. "I'll walk you out."

"Thank you."

Jack and I rode the elevator to the ground floor, and then he walked me all the way to the doors of the admin building. "I'll probably see you at Judy's Friday night."

"Sounds good."

I waved an awkward goodbye and walked to my car.

Talking to Jack seemed to be exactly what I needed. My heart and gut felt as though it was all over with. I just hoped Ethan had enough evidence to keep this Katrina woman behind bars.

Forever.

# CHAPTER THIRTY-THREE

*Ethan*

Life hadn't slowed down over the past few weeks.

Shawn and I continued working on the Lakeshore Killer case, and we got all the evidence needed to keep Katrina Carpenter behind bars. Her home computer was analyzed, and the hacking program was found. Her hair was a match to the one found at Fiona's murder, and the wood found in her basement was a match to all of the wood plaques. We found the knife she used for her stabbings, and a 3D printer that had files to print keys was discovered. What put her nail in her coffin was we found her list.

Her watch list.

Reagan gave her two-week notice at Judy's. I didn't blame her. While it was the key that started our relationship again, I understood that being a bartender was only temporary for her. She still hadn't heard from any precincts, but I knew, in time, she'd find a position.

Given that Christmas was less than a month away from when Reagan and I had returned to Chicago after Michigan, we had little time to find a place big enough for our family.

*Our family.*

In the back of my mind, I had never given up hope that one day we'd get back together. Then Judy's made it happen, and my family had since dubbed it the bar that brings true loves together. I wasn't going to argue with that. Reagan had always been the one I wanted to build a life with. We might not have experienced everything in the past together, but we would in the future.

Since we needed a bigger place as soon as possible, we decided to look for houses to rent instead of purchase, at least for now. We found a place not far from my parents and my boys. To get our house ready, my family helped us move in and unpack. We really were a family, and Reagan and I had the house we always wanted—even if it wasn't one we owned.

And I had plans to make it *legal*.

Before we left Michigan, I'd pulled Maddison aside to ask for her permission to marry her mother. *"I don't really need to speak with you about the other night,"* I'd said as we walked out into the hall.

*"Oh?"* She'd drawn her head back.

I'd rubbed the back of my neck nervously. *"I actually wanted to ask you if you'd be okay with me asking your mom to marry me."*

Maddison's eyes had widened, and it looked as though she was trying to suppress a squeal. *"Are you serious?"*

*"Yeah,"* I'd stated. *"I've wanted to ask her since—well, since forever."*

*"She told me what happened when the two of you broke up when she was in college."*

*"Yeah,"* I'd sighed. *"But now we're back together, and I want to spend forever with her as my wife."*

Maddison had smiled. *"You, for sure, have my approval."*

*"Okay, don't say anything. I still need to get a ring and all that."*

*"My lips are sealed, Dad."*

I'd chuckled. *"I guess I will be, huh?"*

*"Yeah, but I'm excited."*

*"Me too."*

Since I had Maddie's blessing, it was time to make it official, and therefore, I needed to call the most romantic dude I knew.

"And to what do I owe the pleasure of this call?" Rhys asked the moment he answered.

"I need your help." It was silent on the other end of the line. "Rhys?"

"Did I just hear that you need *my* help?"

"Yes."

"Sergeant Valor, who saved *my* life, needs *my* help?"

"Yes, you idiot." I rolled my eyes even though he couldn't see me. I loved the guy, but he was wacko. A wacko who would take a bullet for my sister, which made him all right in my book.

"How can I be of service?"

I took a deep breath. "I need you to help me come up with the best proposal."

Rhys gasped on the other end of the line. "I knew it. I knew it. I knew it!"

"Everyone knew this day would come." I knew it the moment she fell asleep on my couch that first night we reconnected.

"Well, yeah."

"Are you going to help me or not?"

"Of course I am!"

"Okay, so, do you have any ideas?"

"Yeah, man. I have several."

We spent the next hour planning out the way I was going to ask my first and only true love to marry me. And I had to admit, I was fucking excited.

The house was decorated inside and out for Christmas. I had my woman, and all I needed were my two boys to make this the perfect Christmas. Of course, we needed Maddison here too, but she was in Denver and wasn't flying in until the day after Christmas.

I wanted to make Christmas special for my boys since I didn't see them for two long weeks, but they wouldn't care about going somewhere. I could buy them every toy they wanted, but that wasn't the way to go about it either. But what a child *would* think was the best thing in the world would be Santa showing up at their house. And I knew the perfect guy to play Kris Kringle.

"Get your PJs on and get ready for bed," I ordered the boys as we walked in from the garage. We'd had Christmas Eve dinner at my parents, and the boys were getting excited for Santa. Little did they know that once they were ready for bed, Mr. Claus was going to bring them an early gift.

"I'm bursting at the seams," Reagan stated, wrapping her arms around me as we stopped in the kitchen.

"Me too," I admitted, and it was more than just because Rhys was coming to surprise the boys. The night wouldn't end there.

"When Maddie was maybe four or five, I took her to the mall to take a picture with Santa. It wasn't the first time, but it was the first time she finally understood who the guy in the red suit was. She went nuts. I can't even imagine Santa knocking at the door and coming in."

"*Does* Santa knock?" I questioned as the thought occurred to me. It wasn't like Rhys was going to come down the chimney.

Reagan shrugged. "I don't know."

"I guess we'll find out." I smiled.

"That we will." She grinned back.

"Want a glass of wine?" I asked.

"You read my mind."

There was a reason I was trying to keep her busy, and it wasn't because Rhys was coming at any second. Reagan couldn't go into the bedroom. There would be a chance she'd see my plan, and I couldn't risk it. Rhys and Ashtyn had stopped by the house before arriving at my parents to carry out my plan. It was the only way to make it happen, given Reagan was home all day before we left to pick up the boys for dinner.

I poured us each a glass, and as I handed Reagan hers, Cohen and Tyson came running into the kitchen where we were.

"We're ready for bed," Cohen announced.

"Santa's coming!" Tyson shouted excitedly.

"Did you brush your teeth?"

The boys shared a look, and I knew they hadn't. I was going to tell them to do it, but then there was a knock on the front door. Apparently, Santa did knock.

"Who could that be?" I wondered out loud and started walking toward the front door.

"I heard Santa was in the area," Reagan responded. "Maybe it's him?"

Cohen sucked in a breath as he started walking behind me. "Why would Santa be at our house?" I questioned and reached for the doorknob. I opened it and almost started to laugh when I saw Rhys Cole dressed in a red and white suit, black boots, a black belt, a Santa hat, and a *giant* belly. He even, of course, had the white beard and a red sack over his shoulder.

"Ho, ho, ho," he said in a deep voice.

"Santa!" the boys shouted at the same time.

"Cohen! Tyson! I knew I'd find you here," Rhys replied, his voice still deep. He stepped inside.

"You did?" Cohen asked.

I closed the door and draped an arm around Reagan's shoulders as we followed behind the three, watching the show and sipping our wine.

"I had to come find you because I have something special for both of you."

"What is it?" Tyson asked.

"Come into the living room, and I'll show you."

The three of them did just that. Rhys sat on the couch, the boys on the floor in front of him. I looked at Reagan, and she was grinning ear to ear. I kissed the side of her head as so many emotions raced through me. In less than an hour, I was going to get down on one knee—something I'd wanted to do for as long as I could remember—and ask her to be my wife.

"Let me get a picture real quick," Reagan said and grabbed her phone from the back pocket of her jeans.

Rhys patted his legs, and the boys climbed onto each leg. After Reagan got her picture, she returned to my side, and the boys resumed their position of sitting on the floor in front of Rhys.

"I brought a book to read to you," Rhys opened his red bag.

"You did?" Cohen asked.

Rhys pulled the thin classic hardcover book from the bag. This version had Santa's face on the cover.

"That's you!" Tyson stated as he pointed at the book.

Rhys mock-gasped. "That is me!"

"There's a book about you?" Cohen asked.

"Many, but this one is about the night before Christmas, which is tonight."

"What does it say?" Cohen continued to question.

Rhys opened the book, and Reagan and I watched as he read the short poem, showing them each picture after he read the page.

"That was an old story," Cohen stated.

Rhys gave a big belly laugh while Reagan and I stifled our own chuckles. "It's because I'm old," Rhys replied in his deep Santa voice.

"How old?" Tyson probed.

"Very," Rhys replied.

"Older than my grandpa?" Cohen asked. We all laughed again.

"Yeah, Cohen. I'm older than all the grandpas."

"That's old," Tyson said matter-of-factly. We all chuckled again.

"Can we have our presents now?" Cohen questioned.

"Yes. I need to get going so I can deliver all the presents." Rhys dug into his red bag again. "I have a busy night, but I wanted to stop by while I was in the neighborhood because of how good you two were this year." He handed the boys each a pair of slippers. Cohen got The Incredible Hulk ones, and Tyson got Batman ones. They, of course, weren't wrapped because Santa and his elves didn't wrap presents. "Now, make sure you wear those tomorrow morning when you wake up and see what I left for you while you're sleeping."

"You can't give us our presents now?" Cohen wondered.

Rhys stood and slung his bag over his shoulder. "No. I don't have them. My reindeer have them in the sleigh."

Cohen's eyes widened. "Where's your sleigh? I wanna see it!"

"No can do." Rhys started for the door. "Mrs. Claus is making sure everything is packed inside for the night, and they only have a moment to swing by to get me."

"Mrs. Claus goes with you?" Tyson asked.

"Of course. She's the boss and makes sure I stay on time."

Reagan and I snorted. My sister *was* the boss, but Mrs. Claus stayed home in all the folklore I'd heard.

"Plus, she loves milk and cookies."

"We're going to leave you some before we go to bed," Cohen stated.

"Chocolate chip?"

Cohen looked over at me, and I nodded. "Yep!"

"Good deal. Now, I better go." Rhys opened the door and stood a few feet inside.

"Will we see you again?" Tyson asked.

Rhys patted the top of his brown head. "Maybe next year if you're still a good boy."

"We will be!" Cohen exclaimed.

"All right, good. Now go to sleep, and when you wake up, put your slippers on before going to see what I've left you."

"Bye!" the boys said in unison, and Rhys closed the door. The boys rushed to it, and when they opened it, he was gone. Rhys, of course, was probably hiding on the side of the house, but the boys didn't know that.

"That was so cool!" Cohen yelled.

"Yeah, it was," I affirmed. "You better go brush your teeth and get into bed, so when Santa comes back, he can leave your presents." The boys took off toward their bathroom without another word. "I'm going to tuck them in. Meet you in the shower?" I asked, looking at Reagan.

She smirked. "Yep."

The steam billowed out around me when I opened the bathroom door and I entered the bedroom, a towel wrapped around my waist. Reagan and I *showered* until the water started to turn cold. I walked to the light switch and flicked it on, which turned on both lamps on either side of the bed.

Reagan stepped out behind me with a towel wrapped around herself. "Why are you turning all of the lights on?"

"No reason," I lied. Reagan cocked a brow. "Get dressed, Buttercup. We have presents to put under the tree and cookies to eat."

We slid our pajamas on and then quietly slipped out of the bedroom, leaving the lights on as we made our way to the living room. I grabbed a cookie and stuck it into my mouth. "Putting gifts from Santa under the tree never gets old," I stated around the sweet chocolatey goodness.

Reagan grabbed a cookie. "I never thought I'd do this again since Maddie is almost nineteen. It's fun."

We went into the garage and grabbed all of the presents we'd bought for the boys. Cohen got a big boy bike and Tyson a Batmobile go-kart that he would have to peddle himself. We placed all the gifts under the tree and stuffed the stockings with candy and such before turning off the lights and heading back into our bedroom. My heart started to race as I felt the ring burning in the pocket of my flannel pajama pants.

"Can we turn off the lights, or are you now afraid of monsters?"

I grinned. "Get in bed. I'll get the lights."

Reagan climbed onto her side of the bed, and shut off her light. I glanced up as I flicked the overhead light switch off, revealing the glow of plastic stars. The first time we'd had sex was under their neon glow, and when I planned everything with Rhys, I knew the plastic stars would be romantic, given our past. I turned my light off, but didn't get in bed. It felt like hours as I waited for Reagan to slip onto her back and look up. When she did, she gasped.

"Ethan ..."

I walked to her side of the bed, the glow of the stars just bright enough for me to see where I was going. When I got to her side, I turned her light on and got down on one knee as I pulled the emerald-cut diamond solitaire on a platinum band out of my pocket. She gasped again as she sat up, covering her mouth with her hands.

"Reagan Hunter"—I swallowed down my emotions—"I can make this whole long speech like they do in movies, but I think you already know that I fucking love you. I've loved you my entire life, and I officially want to call you Mrs. Valor. So, Buttercup"—I turned off her light again and looked up at the stars to read the words shaped with stars out loud that Ashtyn and Rhys had stuck on our ceiling—"will you marry me?"

The neon glow was still bright enough for me to make out her features. She nodded and hurried out of bed to wrap her arms around my neck. The force of her embrace caused me to tumble back onto the carpeted floor. "Yes! A million times, yes!"

# CHAPTER THIRTY-FOUR

*Reagan*

When I'd imagined the day Ethan and I got married, I never thought I would have to wait until I was in my forties. I also didn't think that our engagement would last less than a week, or that we would get married at the Marriage and Civil Union Court.

But that's what happened.

And I didn't care. Because if Ethan had asked me to marry him the night he walked into Judy's for the first time, I would have said yes. It didn't matter that we hadn't seen each other in over twenty years. I had never stopped loving him. There was always that piece of my heart that was broken just waiting to be glued back to the other chambers so it could be whole again.

And finally, it was.

The day after Christmas, Maddie flew in from Denver. From the airport, we went to buy me a dress. It wasn't like the first wedding dress I'd worn. This one was just above the knee, white, sleeveless, with a lace overlay and scalloped hem. Honestly, it was perfect. I didn't need the big poofy gown that you needed help going to the bathroom in. I didn't need to have a wedding that lasted all day. I didn't even need the first dance as husband and wife because what I did need, I already had. I had the man I'd always wanted to marry, and the family that I loved with all of my heart.

"Ready?" Maddison asked as we freshened up my makeup in the courthouse bathroom.

Everyone had arrived at the same time to witness our nuptials, and while Ethan made sure all of our paperwork was in order, I took Maddie into the bathroom because I needed a minute. I needed time to absorb the fact that, in just a few short minutes, I was finally marrying my guy.

*The one* who gave me my first kiss.

*The one* who carried my books for me.

*The one* who made love to me under neon stars for the first time.

*The one* whose heart I broke because of a stupid drunk kiss.

*The one* who didn't bat an eye when fate gave us a chance to get back together after twenty-three years.

*The one* who hired security to keep me safe.

*The one who always loved me.*

We took the long, broken road to get here, but I wouldn't change how it all turned out because if I hadn't broken his heart, I wouldn't have Maddison, and he wouldn't have Cohen and Tyson.

I looked at my daughter and took a deep breath. "Ready." I smiled.

"Yay!" She handed me the bouquet of dark purple Persian buttercups. Since it was winter, they were in season, though any flower would have sufficed because I was marrying Ethan Valor.

Before we walked out the door, my phone rang in my clutch. Pulling out my phone, I saw that it was a local number. I answered it. "Hello?"

"Hi, yes. Is Regan McCormick available?"

"This is her. May I ask who's calling?"

"Yes, this is Heather Wentworth. I'm the lead investigator for the 15th District for CPD. I received your application, and I was calling to schedule an interview."

I sucked in a quiet breath. "Yes, of course. I'm available anytime."

"Since today is New Year's Eve, how about we schedule it for the third, ten o'clock?"

"That sounds perfect, thank you."

"Great. I'll email you the address just in case, and I look forward to meeting with you."

"Same here. Thank you again."

We hung up, and I turned to Maddie. "I have a job interview with the 15th District!"

"Yay!" She rushed into my arms and hugged me tightly. "I'm so happy for you."

"Thanks, honey."

With one final squeeze, she pulled back. "Let's go get you hitched, and then tonight we have more things to celebrate."

"Let's." We exited the restroom and walked to the waiting room just outside where the ceremony would be held.

"Ready?" Ethan asked, grabbing my hand.

My answer would never change, no matter who was asking me. "Yes."

Everyone went into the room, and Ethan and I walked in together, still holding hands. My parents had come up from Florida, and even though we had exceeded the fifteen person limit allowed in to witness our vows, the judge allowed it, since Sergeant Valor was a colleague of sorts, and he had put the Lakeshore Killer behind bars.

The seats filled up fast, and others lined the back wall as Ethan and I waited in front of the dark wood desk. The judge walked in and stood behind the desk. He read a script about promises and joining together as one family, but I wasn't listening. I was staring into Ethan's blue eyes and trying not to cry. I had never been so happy in my entire life. Maddie's birth and the day I married my soulmate were tied as the best days.

"Ethan, do you take Reagan to be your lawfully wedded wife, forsaking all others, to love, honor, and cherish her in sickness and in health and in good times and bad, whatever your future may bring?"

"I do," he responded with a huge smile directed at me.

"And Reagan, do you take Ethan to be your lawfully wedded husband, forsaking all others, to love, honor, and cherish him in sickness and in health and in good times and bad, whatever your future may bring?"

I grinned at Ethan. "I do."

In a blur, we exchanged rings that were a sign of faith and love, repeating after the judge and slipping the rings on each other's fingers. The judge declared us husband and wife and told Ethan he could kiss me. I'd expected a sweet kiss—especially since we were in front of our family—but Ethan surprised me by pulling my face to his and kissing me long and deep until we were breathless. Rhys was in the background whooping and hollering, then Carter yelled for us to get a room, and I wanted nothing more than to do that with my husband, but we had singing to do. At least Rhys did.

"Ready to go ring in the new year as husband and wife, Mrs. Valor?" Ethan asked.

I grinned wide. "Yes, I am, husband."

He kissed me again and then we shared hugs with our family before walking out of the courthouse to start our forever. Maddie rode with us to our after party.

"I have news," I announced as Ethan drove toward the bar.

He looked over at me briefly. "What's that?"

"While I was in the bathroom, I got a call for a job interview."

His blue eyes widened. "You did?"

"Yep!"

"Congrats. I know you'll get it."

"Well, we don't *know* that."

"No reason for you not to," he countered. This was true. The position was entry level, and I had to start somewhere. Granted it all depended on how many people wanted the same job too.

We were silent as we continued toward the bar until Maddie leaned between the two front seats of the truck and asked, "Are you going to sing?"

"Maybe," I replied.

"Are you, Ethan?" she questioned.

Ethan smiled at me. "I have a song in mind."

"You do?" I inquired. I thought he could only sing if he were drunk. Granted, he might end the night that way.

"It's a surprise, Buttercup." He squeezed my bare knee just below the hem of my coat.

"Is it a country song again?"

"You sang a country song?" Maddie cut in.

"Yes, he sang a country song when we sang karaoke before," I confirmed.

"Wow, I didn't peg you as a country singing type."

"There's nothing wrong with country music," Ethan stated.

"Of course not. I love country music," Maddie said.

"So, is it?" I prodded.

He chuckled. "I'm not telling you."

I grinned. "Well, I can't wait."

And I didn't have to wait long.

Getting married on New Year's Eve was perfect. Rhys had hooked us up with a few VIP tables at Otis's karaoke bar, and everyone came to celebrate our marriage and sing karaoke. We arrived at the bar and went to our sectioned off corner where everyone met us. We accepted more hugs and congratulations from our friends and family.

Rhys started our group off by singing first, then Maddie and I shared a knowing grin as I watched Ethan in his black tux get on stage. Ashtyn and Rachel sat at my table, watching Ethan. I had a momentary déjà vu feeling, remembering the night we went out to sing karaoke and Ethan was on stage. And what made this night even better was watching my *husband* get on stage and knowing that whatever song he chose to sing would be sung to me.

He nodded to the MC, and when the guitar strings started to strum in short beats, I knew exactly what song it was.

"It's a country song," I said to Maddie.

She smiled, and we returned our attention back to the stage. Ethan started to sing on time, staring at me as he did. He changed the first line of the lyrics to be about me taking care of Maddie. Then he sang about taking care of him, the way I light up any room, and how he wanted to be the man that I wanted him to be. I didn't need a song to tell me that because Ethan Valor was the man I'd always wanted.

Everything about him, from the teenage boy I fell in love with, to the man with specks of gray in his hair I'd just married, was just right. I started to sway in my seat as I listened to the lyrics about waking up next to each other every day and never leaving I love yous left unsaid.

Ashtyn leaned over to me and said the same words she'd said when Ethan had sung to me before. "My brother's in love with you."

I grinned and replied with the three words I had told her before because they were still the truth. "Yeah, he is."

Ethan hopped off the stage, and I grinned at him as I stood. He continued to sing as he brought me into his arms and we danced as man and wife.

After twenty-three years, we were finally Mr. and Mrs. Valor.

### The End.

# NOTE FROM THE AUTHOR

Dear Reader,

I hope you've enjoyed *Watch Me*. Please take a moment to spread the word so everyone can discover Ethan and Reagan. I'd also love to hear from you. You can email me directly at authorkknight@gmail.com.

Please also sign up for my newsletter so you can stay up to date on all the Knight news. You can find the link on my website at www.authorkimberlyknight.com. You can also follow me on Facebook at www.facebook.com/AuthorKKnight.

You can really help me out by leaving a review where you bought the book as well as on Goodreads and Bookbub. Your love and support mean everything to me, and I cherish you all!

Thank you again.

XOXO,
*Kimberly*

# ACKNOWLEDGMENTS

Mr. Knight, thank you for "arguing" with me about my plot and for giving me ideas about how my serial killer could watch people. Making everything click is stressful. Welcome to my daily state of mind. I love you, you know?

To my editor, Jennifer Roberts-Hall: Thank you for always working with me and for talking me off the ledge when I'm stressed about my deadlines and whatnot. We're really a well-oiled machine at this point, don't you think?

To Laura Hull, The Red Pen Princess: Thank you for your eyes and helping me make this beauty perfect.

To Candi Kane: You're amazing with your organizational skills and I'm truly happy I found you!

To Melissa Mendonza: I've said it once, and I'll say it again: Go Giants!

To my alphas: Leanne Tuley, Kerri Mirabella, Stacy Nickleson, Kristin Jones, and Carrie Waltenbaugh. Thank you for always being my sounding board and for helping me create story after story. Also, please thank your husband, sister, and cousin for answering my questions. I truly appreciate all of you and what you bring to my tribe.

To Jennifer King Ortiz: Thank you for letting me pick your brain about all things IT. I'm so happy you were stalking me when I needed help.

To Fiona Jones: Thank you for letting me kill you. Well, not really, but you know. Thanks for taking one for the team and agreeing to be killed in my story.

To Lisa Vitous, Ebonie Hill, Cherica Hasner, Sally Oey, Samantha Burch, Michelle Cable, Pat Wood, Samantha Pitman, Wendy Ballard, and Debbie Taylor: Thank you for offering to be on Katrina's watch list. I hope you enjoyed seeing your name in a book!

To my Steamy Knights: Thank you for your continued love and support. You all rock. I love how I can share my personal life with you as well as all things Knight News!

To all the bloggers and authors who participated in my cover reveal, release day blitz, review tour, and release day party: thank you! I can't tell you how much I appreciate each and every one of you who are willing to help me spread the word about my books. Without you, I wouldn't be living my dream.

And finally, to my readers: Thank you for believing in me and taking a chance on my books again and again. Without you guys, I wouldn't still be writing and bringing you all the stories that captivate my brain on a daily basis.

# BOOKS BY KIMBERLY KNIGHT

Club 24 Series – Romantic Suspense
Perfect Together – The Club 24 Series Box Set
Halo Series – Contemporary Romance
Saddles & Racks Series – Romantic Suspense
By Invitation Only – Erotic Romance Standalone
Sensation Fantasies – Erotic Romance Novellas
Dangerously Intertwined Series – Romantic Suspense
Burn Falls – Paranormal Romance Standalone
And more …

# ABOUT THE AUTHOR

Kimberly Knight is a USA Today Bestselling author who lives in the mountains near a lake in California with her loving husband, who is a great *research* assistant. Kimberly writes in a variety of genres including romantic suspense, contemporary romance, erotic romance, and paranormal romance. Her books will make you laugh, cry, swoon, and fall in love before she throws you curve balls you never see coming.

When Kimberly isn't writing, you can find her watching her favorite reality TV shows, binge-watching true crime documentaries, and going to San Francisco Giants games. She's also a two-time desmoid tumor/cancer fighter, which has made her stronger and an inspiration to her fans.

www.authorkimberlyknight.com
www.facebook.com/AuthorKKnight
Follow her on Instagram: authorkimberlyknight
pinterest.com/authorkknight
twitter.com/Author_KKnight

Made in the USA
Middletown, DE
10 January 2023

21265459R00156